HURT ROAD

BRUCE A. STEWART

www.cleanreads.com

Hurt Road
by Bruce A. Stewart
Published by Clean Reads
www.cleanreads.com

HURT ROAD
Copyright © 2017 BRUCE A. STEWART
ISBN 978-1-62135-749=0
Cover Art Designed by AM Designs Studio

To the brave Americans, men and women, who fought and gave their lives in a place called Vietnam.

ACKNOWLEDGMENTS

Many play a part in the writing and publishing of a book. I'd like to take this opportunity to recognize some of them.

My family, both near and far: Thank you all so much. I love you to the moon and back!

The team at Clean Reads Publishing: Thank you, Stephanie Taylor, for believing in my story and letting me share it with the world. Thank you editors Julie, Katie, and Leslie for shining it up. You guys are the best.

My agent, Cyle Young: Thank you for your continued efforts on my behalf. I am truly blessed to have you and Hartline in my corner.

Alan Clack: Thank you for your superior knowledge of all things automotive. And for being my friend and brother all these years.

Jean Chatman: Thank you for taking an early trip down *Hurt Road*.

Most of all, thank God from whom all blessings flow!

PART I

PROLOGUE

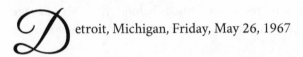etroit, Michigan, Friday, May 26, 1967

FOR SIXTEEN-YEAR-OLD HANK GOODMAN AND THE OTHER TENTH graders in first period algebra, it was another thrilling ride through Mr. Savage's funhouse. Barely halfway through the class and already bored out of his mind, Hank had resorted to doodling colorful limericks in the back of his favorite notebook. Just to stay awake. If he could hold out one more week, school mercifully would be over and summer break would begin. After an up and down year he couldn't wait to put behind him, three whole months of sweet relief lay just around the corner.

Hank had honestly started out trying to pay attention but soon developed a throbbing headache trying to keep up with all the mathematical hieroglyphics his high-strung instructor was busy scribbling on the blackboard. And let's face it—once you fell behind, you might as well hang it up anyway.

If anyone ever looked the part of a math teacher, John Henry Savage certainly did. With his neatly combed hair, black horn-rimmed glasses, starched white shirts, and dark, skinny ties, he was Dennis the Menace's dad made over. Sadly, the poor guy had chosen one of the toughest jobs on the planet. Trying to make algebra—the single most uninteresting subject known to man— seem the least bit interesting. A skill Hank's sharply dressed educator had yet to master and probably never would.

Mr. Savage dropped his slight piece of chalk, and all heads turned when the heavy wooden door creaked and Janice Woolsey walked in. Petite and still in her twenties, she was the principal's secretary and a regular topic of discussion among the hormonally charged boys of the sophomore class. When she cupped her hand around her mouth and whispered something in the teacher's ear, all chatter ceased, and the room became deathly quiet. The minute the door closed behind her, Mr. Savage pointed directly at Hank and summoned him to the front of the room.

An impending sense of dread swept over him, and he took his time climbing out from behind his desk. A lesson being interrupted, by Janice or anyone else, was completely unheard of. And messages from Mr. Rockford's office were never hand-delivered. They were relayed over the intercom. Not just occasionally or every now and then. Always.

"Report to the principal's office," Mr. Savage said, narrowing his eyes and motioning toward the door. "And be quick about it."

Hank's hands shot up, the tiny muscles in his face visibly tightening. "Why? What did I do?"

"I don't know, Goodman. She just said he needs to see you. Now hit the road before I have to take you there myself."

The short walk to the administration building would have taken the average person two, maybe three minutes. For a repeat offender like Hank, it took slightly more than ten. Having become one of the regulars, he was certainly in no hurry to rush over and face the music. During a recent and quite memorable counseling session, the principal made his position perfectly clear. "And I don't want to see your smiling face in this office again any time soon. Do you understand?" Regrettably, less than a week had passed since their last unforgettable encounter.

Never a real troublemaker, so to speak, simple, harmless stunts usually landed Hank in hot water as he tried to impress his friends or anyone else who happened to be looking on. Especially those of the female persuasion. Mr. Rockford, as it turned out, was quite a bit harder to impress than the free-spirited members of the student body.

Back at her desk, Janice greeted him with a somewhat forced smile and then pointed over her shoulder at the open door. "You can go on in," she said. "They're expecting you."

They? Hank swallowed hard. Things were worse than even he expected. Too far to turn back now, he hiked up his belt, gathered what little courage he could, and headed inside.

Leaning back in a brown leather chair more than twice his size, fingers interlocked, thumbs tapping together, was Nathaniel J. Rockford. His middle initial, most of the students speculated, stood for Jughead. Even the multitude of certificates plastered on the wall behind him failed to reveal the truth of the matter.

On either side of the room stood a policeman Hank had never seen before and Patrick Mulcahey, the school's official chaplain. Appearing before three men of authority, all with serious, gloomy expressions on their faces, caused his level of concern to rise tenfold.

Why had the police been called in? Now, visions of being led down the long, dreary hallway of a penitentiary in shackles with the preacher tagging along to perform last rites flashed before his eyes. If he'd done anything serious enough to merit jail time, he certainly didn't remember it. Maybe one of the other students committed the crime, and, having a prior record, they would simply cut through the red tape and pin it on him. Had someone erroneously picked his photograph out of the latest edition of the high school yearbook?

"Please have a seat," the principal said, pointing to the only empty chair in the room. "This is Trooper Hines with the state police. You already know Reverend Mulcahey."

Not an ounce of anger or hostility could be detected in the man's voice. Instead of his usual authoritarian delivery, his words were spoken calmly and evenly. Almost kindly.

Hank turned to the officer and extended a trembling hand. "Nice to met you, sir." He cleared his throat. "I mean, meet you."

Oh, brother. By saying "sir," he wanted to show the officer he had a healthy respect for members of law enforcement. Hopefully, his little slipup wouldn't infer additional suspicion. Or guilt.

"No need to be nervous, son." The trooper moved closer. "These gentlemen tell me you don't have any brothers or sisters. Is that right?"

"Yes, sir," Hank said, nodding. "It's just me. Oh, and my mom and dad."

When Mr. Rockford buried his face in his hands, the trooper nodded to the clergyman. Reverend Mulcahey knelt beside the uneasy teen, placed his arm around him, and exhaled the breath he'd been holding. "There's something I need to tell you, Hank." A long pause followed. "Your parents were involved in a terrible accident this morning. I'm sorry to say, they didn't make it."

CHAPTER ONE

*W*ith an aunt and uncle in Denver ill prepared to take on a teenage boy, Hank had been sentenced to life with his only surviving set of grandparents. Of all the other good and decent places in the world, why did it have to be some backwoods hole in the wall like Louisiana?

Hank had been to the tiny town of Crosscut only twice in his life. Once at age two and again just after he turned ten. Too young to remember the first trip, the second time, he couldn't get away from there fast enough. His mother's mom and dad, Jacob and Ada Taylor, may have been his grandparents, but he barely even knew them. What he did know was they were backward, uneducated rubes who, for the most part, didn't have two nickels to rub together. They were dirt farmers with chickens and cows and pigs. All the disgusting stuff a teenager from a big city wanted absolutely no part of.

Driven straight through, the grueling pickup ride from Michigan to Louisiana still took over twenty hours. The entire trip, answers to his grandparents' questions were limited to one-word responses. If he answered them at all. They'd stopped only a few times for gas and snacks and once for about an hour to allow his grandfather to take a nap in the truck at a near-capacity roadside park. Hank stretched out on a hard, concrete, picnic table bench just to get away from the boring old codgers for a while.

Lucky for them, Crosscut's only traffic light had been green when they rolled into town. Jake's blue 1962 Chevy pickup with the top painted white sped through at a breathtaking twenty miles per hour and never even slacked up. Passing the antebellum courthouse with the huge white columns, his grandparents waved to three old men sitting on a rusty wrought-iron bench next to a badly buckled sidewalk. The village idiots waved back, of course, one even tipping his greasy, sweat-stained hat and flashing a toothless grin. Embarrassed, Hank cast his eyes to the floorboard, pretending not to have witnessed the exchange. What was it with these hillbillies anyway?

Puttering slowly but steadily along, his grandpa pointed through the windshield and said, "All this is Lee Parish, son. You see, a parish is what folks in most other places call a county."

So the great state of Louisiana just had to be different. Imagine that.

To Hank, the south end of Lee Parish was a carbon copy of the north end. Everywhere there wasn't a tree, a gravel road, or some dilapidated old barn, long green rows of plants, straighter than arrows, stretched for miles in every direction. He'd landed in farming country, no doubt about it. The last place he ever wanted to be. In Detroit there were tall, magnificent buildings and people too numerous to count. Rock and roll and fun, exciting things to do. Here, there was absolutely nothing.

Hank stared aimlessly out the window next to his head with fingers wrapped around the chrome-plated door handle. If they didn't get somewhere soon, he'd jump from the moving truck and put himself out of his misery. Ten miles south of town, Jacob braked hard and made a sweeping right turn off the main highway.

For the next mile and a half, they drove directly into the sun. Loping along a narrow, gravel road and kicking up a sky high cloud of dust. When the pickup finally rolled to a stop and the dirt particles settled, there in front of him stood the tiny, white house with the black shutters and rusty tin roof he remembered from several years earlier. Hank felt a strong urge to scream. After throwing a major fit, he had told his mother he would never come back to this place. And now, a mere six years later, here he was again. Yippee.

In 1928, Linda Taylor had been born in the little two-bedroom house on Hurt Road. Hurt Road. Could there have been a more fitting name? She'd grown up during the Great Depression and told him numerous stories about how hard times were then. How her parents worked in the fields hoeing cotton for fifty cents a day while she earned only a meager twenty-five. Though Hank listened to her stories with some amount of interest, none of them quite hit home for him. Growing up an only child in a big city, he'd pretty much lived the good life. Now, for all intents and purposes, he could kiss that way of life goodbye.

Hank's parents met in early 1950 when Linda waitressed at a roadside café in the small Louisiana town of Leesville. A native of Michigan, Charles Goodman served in the army at the time and had been stationed at nearby Fort Polk. They'd married in August of the same year, and when Charles received his discharge in 1951, they packed up and moved to his home state. He'd landed a job in the automotive industry, and they eventually saved up enough to buy a home in Detroit.

On May 2, 1951, the couple was blessed with a healthy baby boy. Hank Greenberg Goodman. After the move, Linda wrote to her parents on a regular basis but only made it home on two separate occasions. Once in 1953 and again for a short visit in 1961. Prior to her death, the Taylors hadn't seen their daughter in six long years.

"Grab your things, sweetie, and I'll show you to your room," Ada said, her voice soft and kind, welcoming.

Things? His "things" consisted of one worn-out leather suitcase stuffed mostly with clothes and the couple of comic books he'd managed to squeeze in. The rest of his belongings he'd been forced to unceremoniously leave behind. "I have to use the bathroom first," Hank said.

"It's around back." Jake dropped the truck's tailgate with a loud, metallic thud. "You can't miss it."

"Wait," Hank said. "What?"

His grandfather quickly made the correction. "It's 'sir.'"

Hank sighed. "Yes, sir. I heard what you said. I just didn't get the *around back* part."

"It's behind the house," Ada confirmed.

"Your bathroom's behind the house?" Hank said, swallowing hard.

Jake hooked his thumbs behind the straps of his faded blue denim overalls and laughed out loud. "Nope, but the outhouse is. Just follow your nose."

The outhouse. Now Hank remembered what he'd hated most about the place. He hung his head and shook it slowly from side to side. Though there was running water in the kitchen, all business of a personal nature required a trip to an outdoor toilet, or what his grandfather had so lovingly referred to as an "outhouse." So this little adventure was going to be far worse than he ever imagined. Not only would he be forced to stay with people he hardly knew, these clodhoppers didn't even have a proper bathroom.

"You could go behind the tree over there," Jake said, pointing to the stately live oak towering in the corner of the yard. "Won't nobody see you."

Learning there were no neighbors in either direction for at least a mile, Hank slipped around behind the tree and let nature take its course. At some point, he'd have to deal with the stinky outhouse, but only when it became an absolute necessity.

～

THE CELL ASSIGNED TO HANK CAME EQUIPPED WITH A TWIN-SIZED bed, one tiny nightstand with a Big Ben wind-up alarm clock, and a tall, antique, wooden chest of drawers. The bed, with its thin, wrought iron head and footboards both painted white, appeared better suited for someone's daughter than a strapping sixteen-year-old boy. Though it never even crossed his mind, when he spotted the framed five-by-seven photograph of a familiar bright-eyed teenage girl staring back at him from atop the chest, it all began to make sense. This had been his mother's room.

Dropping the heavy suitcase to the floor, Hank sighed and shoved it under the bed with his foot. He wasn't about to unpack. To do it would make everything seem so—so permanent. With any luck, he wouldn't be here long at all. Once his aunt and uncle in Colorado had time to reconsider.

Sitting on the edge of the bed, Hank cradled his head in his hands. Prison might be tough, but he couldn't imagine it being much worse than this.

"Hank! Come here! Got something to show you!" Hank's moment of silent reflection had just been interrupted by his grandfather's ear-splitting shouts from somewhere out in the yard. Not wanting to risk upsetting the old man, he reluctantly got up and headed out to the porch.

The crudely constructed pen Jake stood in front of was made from old, weathered lumber and covered with wire somewhat resembling a honeycomb. Confined to the enclosure were around ten to twelve brightly colored chickens of various shapes and sizes. Jake had captured a rather healthy-looking, speckled specimen and was holding it upside down by its legs.

"Ada says we're having fried chicken for supper." Jake raised his catch even higher. "How's this old Dominicker suit you?"

Squawking frantically, the bird flapped its wings and pecked at its captor in a futile effort to escape. Jake exuded a certain confidence. Whatever he was about to do, he left little doubt that he'd done it many times before and quite successfully.

Hank craned his neck for a better look. "What are you doing to him?"

"First of all, it's a her," Jake said. "And if we're having chicken tonight, then we'll have to kill one first. Simple as that."

Hank's stomach did a double flip and his knees began to weaken. "Are you serious?"

Switching his grip from the bird's legs to its neck, Jake twirled the chicken in a circular motion several times then dropped it to the ground. There it flipped and flopped for a good, solid minute before finally giving up the ghost. Apparently taking note of his grandson's reaction, Jake said, "Can't cook a live one, now can we?"

Hank soon found himself behind the same big oak he'd visited a little earlier. If this wasn't the backside of nowhere, he didn't know what was.

∽

When Ada called out supper was ready, Hank's eyes flew open, and he glanced around the room to get his bearings. After watching his grandfather's grisly demonstration of the first step in the chicken frying process and throwing up most of his guts, he'd stretched out across the bed for a well-deserved and much needed nap. Slowly rising to a sitting position, he yawned and reached skyward to loosen the tight, weary muscles in his back. He had no idea he'd been out for the past two hours.

The door to Hank's bedroom opened directly into the Taylor's ample kitchen. Without a formal dining area, it served as both a space for cooking and for eating. He stumbled in and found his grandfather already seated at the head of the table.

"Come on in, sleepyhead," Jake said, beckoning Hank with his hand. "Your grandma's cooked us a fine supper."

Still wearing her grease-stained floral apron, Ada took the chair closest to her husband. The slight woman who'd traveled for hours on end had no doubt been slaving over a hot stove the entire time he'd been napping.

From what Hank could see, there was enough food in front of them to feed a small army. Fried chicken, of course, mashed potatoes and gravy, peas of some sort, corn on the cob, and a tall stack of golden brown, homemade biscuits. Living with two parents working full-time, ham and cheese sandwiches, greasy bags of potato chips, and sugar-loaded, carbonated soft drinks were more what he was accustomed to.

"Have a seat and join us," Jake said, pointing to an empty chair. "Would you like to say Grace?"

Hank's eyes narrowed, and he shook his head vigorously. He didn't even know what "grace" was, much less how to say it.

Jake nodded curtly. "All righty then. I'll do the honors."

Once the older man lowered his head and began to speak, Hank realized he'd been talking about a prayer. He knew what it meant to pray but always managed to stay away from such things. So had his friends. Other than the "now I lay me down to sleep" nonsense he'd recited as a child, Hank had never asked God for anything and didn't intend to start now. Not to mention, he'd heard enough praying at his mom and dad's funeral to last him a lifetime.

Jake concluded with a spirited "amen" then picked up the plate of crispy fried chicken and passed it to his grandson.

Hank pushed his chair back forcefully. "No way. I'm not eating that."

"Suit yourself," his grandfather said, "but you don't know what you're missing."

Ada said, "You have to be hungry, son. You haven't eaten a bite all day."

She was right, of course. Just because he'd passed on the chicken didn't mean he wasn't about to starve to death. He'd have to eat something just to keep his strength up. Strength he might need if the opportunity ever came to escape this wretched place.

Grudgingly scanning his options, Hank pointed to the mashed potatoes. "Guess I'll try some of those."

"How about a little gravy?" Ada said, smiling.

Hank followed up an exaggerated sigh with only a nod.

Ada spooned a generous helping of potatoes onto his plate then covered them a ladleful of rich, brown gravy. Hank took his time stirring the two together, and then took a slow, cautious bite.

The combination being one of the tastiest things Hank had ever wrapped his lips around, he had to catch himself when he realized he'd come dangerously close to smiling. He wasn't the least bit satisfied in his current condition, and, excellent food or not, he didn't want these yokels thinking otherwise.

Jake cleared his throat. "Son, I know you've had a tough go of it and all, losing your folks like you did, but someday I hope you'll be happy here with me and your grandma."

Happy? Here? There was nothing for him here. He missed his house. His own room and his friends. But more than all those things combined, he missed his mom and dad. Oh, he might be happy again—someday, somewhere—but it wouldn't be anywhere near this useless piece of real estate.

Hank jumped up, simultaneously kicking his chair out from under him. In an angry, cutting voice, he said, "Why did you even bring me to this place? I hate it here." He stormed back into his bedroom and slammed the door behind him. *Stupid idiots.*

CHAPTER TWO

The Taylors had slept together in the same bed for the past forty-two years. Only twice during that entire time had they not. Once, when Jake got caught in a terrible storm and had to spend the night in his truck, and the other, the night of their only daughter's birth. Afraid he might accidentally crush his newborn baby, Jake slept on a pallet on the floor beside the bed. The next night, following a spirited debate with Ada, and against his better judgment, he returned to his usual spot without incident.

Rolling onto his side, Jacob gently tapped his motionless wife on the shoulder. "You asleep yet?" he said, barely above a whisper.

Ada sighed. "I'm not now. What is it?"

"Got my mind on the boy."

"What about him?"

"Think he'll come around?" Jake lightly cleared his throat. "Eventually, I mean."

Ada took her time moving from her back to her side. Now facing her husband, she said, "I'm sure he will. We just have to give him time. He's lost his folks, and this place is strange to him."

Jake knew all too well what it meant to lose a parent at such a young age. He was barely fourteen when his own dad, Albert, tragically died in a logging accident. With only a handful in attendance, they'd buried him the following afternoon in the Walnut Grove Cemetery. Being the oldest of three boys, Jake had no choice but to step up and take his father's place. In one day's time, he became both the man of the house and the family's primary provider. Working each day from sunup to sundown, "can to can't" as the old folks used to say, left little time for such luxuries as mourning.

"It'll take some time for his heart to heal," Ada said softly in the dark. "Mine, too, I'm afraid."

Hearing his wife softly crying, Jake scooted closer and slipped his arm around her. Only a few things in this world genuinely upset him, and her tears were chief among them. His tired old ticker simply couldn't take it.

The couple's grandson wasn't the only one having a difficult time. Learning of the accident hit them both hard, but poor Ada had been devastated. Through it all, she'd kept up a brave face. But, in the end, she'd lost her precious, beautiful daughter. Ada had lived a lot of years and lost loved ones many times, but this had been, without a doubt, the toughest blow life had ever dealt her.

Jake offered tender words of encouragement until her tears ultimately subsided. He kissed her softly on the cheek, her fading words reverberating in his head until he finally fell asleep himself. "Don't be too hard on him, Jacob," Ada had said. "He's just a boy."

~

AROUND MIDNIGHT, HANK AWOKE TO UNFAMILIAR SURROUNDINGS and in somewhat of a panic. Just then, the moon slipped out from its hiding place behind a large, puffy cloud and lit up his mother's photograph atop the antique chest of drawers. As she had for the past sixteen years, Linda still watched over him. A knowing smile came over his face, and he rolled onto his side, content. For the time being.

Hank's contentment came to a screeching halt when, less than five minutes later, his stomach cried out long and loud. He needed food. The meager portion of mashed potatoes and gravy he'd eaten for supper had long since played out. If he could slip into the kitchen without waking the elders, maybe he could locate a little something to tide him over until morning.

Out of bed, Hank moved slowly across the hardwood floor on his tiptoes. The creaking of a loose board could easily compromise his mission. Once he reached his objective, anything even remotely resembling food would be considered fair game.

Fumbling around in the dark, Hank located the doorknob and gave it a turn. He'd have to be careful here, too. A noisy door could also spoil his plans. One good push and two steps later, he'd arrived safely in the kitchen.

Working his way to the noisy old refrigerator, Hank pulled down on the handle until he heard a distinctive click and the heavy door opened. The light inside popped on and pretty much lit up the entire room. Instead of the food he so desperately needed, Hank found himself looking at a one gallon, wide-mouth jar filled with milk, probably three dozen eggs, and a stoneware pitcher containing what appeared to be grape Kool-Aid. And nothing else. Disappointed, he sucked in his lips and shook his head slowly.

The refrigerator being a total bust, Hank left the door open slightly to benefit from its light and turned his attention to the table. There, near the center, sat a large oval platter covered with a red and white striped dish towel. Peeking underneath, he was overjoyed to find the remainder of the homemade biscuits and fried chicken he had passed on earlier in the evening. Along with a note from his grandmother.

I left this out in case you get hungry. Milk and Kool-Aid are in the ice box. Love, Grandma.

Hank picked up a cold chicken leg and studied it in the dim light. Hunger overriding uncertainty, he shrugged and took a convincing bite. Not too bad. Another quickly followed, then another and another. In no time flat, he'd devoured the whole thing. Right down to the bone.

By the time he finished, Hank had eaten both legs, one thigh, a breast, two biscuits, and washed it all down with a tall, cold glass of Kool-Aid. *At least the food here in maximum security is good.* With his belly filled to capacity, he headed back to the bedroom for round two. If it took a while for him to doze off, it wouldn't be a problem. With not a thing lined up for the following morning, there was no reason whatsoever Hank couldn't sleep until noon.

~

AT BARELY DAYLIGHT, THE PINT-SIZED RED ROOSTER OUTSIDE Hank's window began to crow as if his young life depended on it. And, with his crazy grandpa running around committing homicide on unsuspecting poultry, maybe it did.

Hank opened one eye just wide enough to check Big Ben for the time. Six-fifteen. The previous day, a chicken's neck being wrung had made him deathly ill. Today, he could've easily done the same thing himself. So much for sleeping in.

A few minutes later, the noisy little yard bird was completely drowned out by the loudest, most annoying popping sound Hank had ever heard. He sat straight up in bed. It was an engine of some sort, no doubt about it, but unlike anything he'd ever heard before. The source of this dreadful sound would require further investigation.

When the noise began to fade into the distance, Hank redirected his attention to the undeniable smell of bacon frying. Already starving, he hopped up and slipped on the same jeans and T-shirt he'd worn the previous day. Opening the door leading into the adjacent kitchen, he found his grandmother standing in front of the stove poking at a cast iron skillet with a long-handled, two-pronged fork.

"Morning, son," Ada said without looking up. "How'd you sleep?"

Hank didn't respond. Instead, he coughed twice and quickly moved to the nearest window. Peeking out, he said, "What's all that racket?"

"The popping? It's just your grandpa on his John Deere."

"What's a John Deere?"

Ada stopped her work and gave him a curious look. "Why, it's a tractor."

"Oh."

Hank took a seat at the kitchen table. Though certainly no expert in the field of agricultural implements, he knew a tractor when he saw one.

"Breakfast will be here on the stove," Ada said, leaning over and shutting off the gas. "I left some coffee in the pot, and you already know where the milk is. When you're done, if you'll put your dishes in the sink, I'll see to them later. If you need me, I'll be in the field out back."

Hank responded with an exaggerated, military style salute. *Whatever.*

Ada dried her hands on a threadbare towel, draped it over the dish rack on the counter, and headed out the back door. Hank took a deep breath and blew it out slowly. What a wonderful country bumpkin life she enjoyed. Get up before dawn to cook everyone's breakfast, then head out to the cotton patch to work in the hot summer sun. Oh, well. It wasn't like the old girl hadn't signed up for it.

After piling his plate high with scrambled eggs and several strips of bacon, Hank took a bite of the eggs and couldn't help wondering if the same chicken he'd scarfed down the previous night had contributed to the cause before so tragically losing her life. He picked up a slice of the bacon and studied it carefully. One of the Taylors' poor farm-raised pigs had most likely met the same fate as his next-door neighbor the chicken. But when you got right down to it, what difference did it make? Bacon had been a part of his diet ever since he could remember and never once had he stopped to question where it came from. No matter how you sliced it, some poor unfortunate swine had made the ultimate sacrifice. Hank grabbed another crunchy piece and popped it in his mouth. *Now this is good stuff.*

Hank's celebration of all things bacon ended when his thoughts shifted to his home back in Michigan. What would he be doing right now if he were still in Detroit? Easy. He'd be in bed asleep like all the other normal kids his age. From what he had seen so far, a good night's sleep was never going to happen here. From what he had seen so far, nothing of any consequence was ever going to happen here either.

~

HANK HAD DRAINED THE LAST DROP OF MILK FROM HIS GLASS WHEN a sharp, stabbing pain hit just below his belly button. Hurrying out the back door with determination in his step, he had a single destination in mind. The smelly outhouse. He'd told himself he would go only when it became absolutely necessary. Sadly, the time he'd dreaded with every fiber of his being had finally arrived. Holding his nose—and his breath—Hank jerked the door open and rushed inside.

If the ambient temperature was eighty-five degrees, then it was a good hundred and ten in the toilet. Outdoors, at least somewhat of a breeze could be felt. This poor excuse for a john had no ventilation whatsoever. Until then, Hank had never even considered how long a human being could go without breathing. Could he have just shattered the Guinness world record for breath-holding by a frustrated and angry sixteen-year-old? More than likely.

After his horrific, life-altering event, Hank headed back inside the house to wash up. Now he'd have to figure out some way occupy his time while the warden romped around on his tractor and his assistant toiled her life away out in the cotton field. Regardless of where they were or what they were doing, it felt great just to have them out of his hair for a while.

Hank could have probably pitched in and helped, but he knew absolutely nothing about farm work. And, he wasn't the least bit interested in learning. Being forced to stay here in Hooterville didn't mean he had to like it. And it certainly didn't mean he had to participate in any of its boring everyday activities.

Instead of sitting around in his room all day and staring at four dreary walls, Hank decided to go outside and do a little exploring. Check the old place out a bit. Already well acquainted with the chicken pen and the outhouse, he couldn't wait to see what other grand amenities were at his beck and call.

On the east side of the property, and only a short distance from the house, sat an aged, drooping barn with a rusty tin roof. In years gone by, it probably stood strong and red. Now it was stooped and badly faded, its better days undeniably lost to history.

To the rear of the barn lay a narrow strip of land surrounded by three strands of wire tightly stretched and stapled to equally spaced, skinny wooden posts. The wire was equipped with tiny, sharp barbs, apparently designed more for keeping things in rather than keeping things out. He estimated the entire area to be somewhere around ten to fifteen acres but honestly, didn't have a clue. With its wavy green grass and multitude of bright yellow flowers, the pasture was quite picturesque. Several cows of different shapes, sizes, and colors could be seen milling about. A few, just standing around, appeared to be chewing on their tongues.

Quickly tiring of his grandparents' 4-H exhibit, Hank redirected his attention to the field behind the house where Ada was working. According to her, the green plants with the pointy leaves were cotton. In all the pictures he'd seen, in books and magazines, cotton had been white and fluffy. If this stuff was cotton—well, he'd just have to take her word for it.

Off in the distance, Hank could see the tiny woman in the faded blue bonnet steadily chopping away with her long-handled hoe. Occasionally, she'd reach up and wipe her brow with the sleeve of her shirt then get right back to it. If he had worked up such a sweat just walking around the yard, how hot must she be laboring out in the field? Oh, well. That was her problem, not his.

By eleven, Hank had completely run out of things around the sprawling plantation to look at. Ada returned to the house to prepare the noon meal and her wrinkled, leathery face still glowed from overexposure to the heat. For a fleeting moment, Hank couldn't help wondering if she was okay. But he wasn't about to ask.

The house wasn't equipped with air conditioning, and in all probability, his grandparents had probably never even heard of such a thing. A huge attic fan mounted over a double window on the back of the house provided the only source of cooling. This powerful machine could suck air in from the outside with the force of a Category 5 hurricane. The downside would have to be the amount of humidity it drew in with it. Hank recalled his blanket being slightly damp and tacky when he woke up.

Hank had no intention of striking up a conversation with someone he had nothing whatsoever in common with. There was one question, however, he'd been dying to ask his multi-tasking, red-faced grandmother. "Don't you ever get tired of this?"

"Tired of what?"

"Having to work all the time."

"I don't work all the time," she said, turning to face him. "Just during the week. And little on Saturday."

Crossing his arms, Hank stuck out his chin and said, "Yeah, well what about Sunday?"

"Oh, no," Ada said with narrowed eyes. "We never work on Sunday."

"Why not?"

Ada dropped the metal spoon she'd been holding and it bounced off the edge of the sink. "Cause it's the Lord's Day, Hank."

CHAPTER THREE

*T*he next three mornings started out exactly the same. The rooster Hank wanted to strangle crowing to beat the band. Jacob's loud, psychotic tractor angrily popping. Ada cooking breakfast then heading out to work in the hot, dusty cotton patch. Him left alone with absolutely nothing to do. By Friday, Hank had had about all the fun one out-of-place teenager could stand. Something had to give.

Hank finished his breakfast without saying a word. With Jake long gone and his grandmother on her way to the field, he headed back to his room to prepare for the long trip to Colorado. To pull it off, he'd have to do something he'd never done before in his life. He'd have to hitchhike.

How hard could just sticking out your thumb be? With a little luck, he'd be strolling into Denver in only a couple of days. Once his aunt and uncle got to know him, they'd ask him to stay on and become a valued member of their family. It had to work. There was no Plan B.

Hitchhiking meant he wouldn't need money for gas and such. He would, however, need it for food. The previous day, when Ada sent her husband to the store to pick up a ten-pound bag of sugar and a loaf of bread, Hank had seen her reach into the faded coffee can on the window sill over the kitchen sink and pull out a crisp five-dollar bill. He'd never stolen a thing in his life, and technically, this wouldn't be stealing. Once he got settled in Colorado, he'd send every bit of the money back. Along with interest, of course.

Hank picked up the metal can, briefly scanned the label, and then shook it up and down. Hearing the sound of coins jingling inside, he pursed his lips and blew out a mouthful of disappointed air. Hopefully, when he peeled off the plastic lid with the crude slot carved out of the center, he'd find more than just a meager collection of nickels, pennies, and dimes.

Hooking a fingernail under the edge of the lid, Hank pried upward and gently popped it off. When he peeked inside and saw actual paper money amid the handful of change, he could barely contain himself. Hank unfolded the bill and his jubilation skyrocketed when he found himself eye-to-eye with the seventh president of the United States. Old Hickory never looked so good. By eating nothing but snacks and staying away from costly restaurant food, he could make twenty bucks go quite a long way. Hopefully it would be enough to tide him over for the entire trip.

With his suitcase ready to go, Hank cracked the back door open for a peek outside and a quick listen. He spotted Ada in her usual place, quite some distance from the house and headed in the opposite direction. Jake's tractor was nowhere to be seen. The faintness of its popping, however, told him the old farmer had traveled far enough away to allow his escape to go unnoticed. Sound the all clear. Time to hit the road and put *Green Acres* solidly in the rearview mirror.

~

IT TOOK HANK WELL OVER AN HOUR TO COVER THE MILE AND A half from his grandparents' house to the main paved highway leading back into Crosscut. With each weary step down the rutted gravel road, his suitcase grew heavier and heavier. More than once, he'd been tempted to toss it in the ditch and keep on going without it. Civil War soldiers—one of Hank's history teachers had explained—would start out marching with a full pack. Then, after struggling several miles to keep up, they would begin to discard items they deemed not absolutely necessary. A couple of times, he'd been forced to set the bag down just to catch his breath and wipe away the sweat. Once again, Hurt Road was certainly living up to its name.

Making it to the big oak at the intersection had been quite a milestone, and Hank couldn't have been prouder. He'd spotted the massive tree from a considerable distance away, and just the sight of it served to put a little pep in his step. Now in the comfort of its shade, he set the heavy suitcase on the ground and plopped down on top of it. With the first leg of his journey solidly behind him, the reality of the situation had finally started to sink in. Hank had left thinking the trip would be easy. Now he knew it would be anything but.

The distance from Crosscut to Denver had to be at least a thousand miles. Maybe more. From paying at least some attention in geography class, Hank knew Colorado lay to the north and west of Louisiana. Staring at a north/south highway, his only option would be to hang a left and strike out for town. Once there, he'd stop and ask directions. Maybe he'd luck out and find one of the locals who was a little smarter than he actually looked. If such a person even existed.

~

HANK SOON FOUND OUT WALKING ON HOT, BUBBLY ASPHALT WASN'T going to be an option. Instead, he'd have stay on the narrow, grassy shoulder complete with its angry red fire ants and, most likely, venomous snakes. He hadn't spotted any of the slimy reptiles yet but, based on the terrain, pretty much expected to at any time.

After plodding along for nearly a mile and not seeing the first car or truck, Hank was beginning to lose heart. Still far from Crosscut, his bag wasn't getting any lighter, each step more difficult than the last. Hank needed some relief. The sooner, the better.

Another grueling mile went by, and Hank sincerely began to second-guess his decision. Back on the farm, he could at least be sitting by an open window under the powerful breeze of the attic fan. Or relaxing in the shade of one of the leafy oak trees. Anything at all had to be better than this.

Hank thought he heard a low rumble in the distance and stopped to listen closer. Hearing it again, a sense of relief swept over him. This time, there was no mistaking it. It was the sweet sound of a motor vehicle coming up from behind. The challenge now would be getting it to stop.

With his hitchhiking skills about to be put to the test, Hank wasn't taking any chances. He'd seen others keep their backs to the flow of traffic, stick out their thumbs and keep walking. Not him. Desperate times called for desperate measures. With potential rides being so far non-existent, he'd do his best to flag this baby down.

Hank dropped his bag then stepped onto the edge of the pavement and started waving both hands in a frantic downward motion. By all indications, the older-model, black Ford pickup had no intention of even slowing down, much less stopping. Hank was about to jump back and give way, when at the last possible second, the driver laid on the brakes. Pungent smoke from the tires filled the air, and Hank held his breath. Was he about to be picked on or picked up? Hopefully, it would be the latter.

The truck screeched to a grinding halt right beside him. With the passenger window already down, Hank stooped to address the driver and plead his case. When he saw a girl about his own age sitting behind the wheel, his mouth dropped open, and he found himself speechless. With long, blond, wind-blown hair and transparent blue eyes—and not wearing a stick of makeup, best he could tell—she was undoubtedly the most gorgeous young woman he had ever laid eyes on.

"Where are you headed?" she said, bouncing slightly, her eyes lighting up.

"Into t-town, I guess." At this point, Hank could barely think. Much less speak.

Miss Beautiful frowned at first but then broke into a laugh. "What do you mean, you guess?"

"Honestly," Hank said. "I'm on my way to Colorado. Just trying to get to the right road."

"Hop in and maybe I can help you find it."

"You sure it's okay?"

"Sure, I'm sure. Let's go."

Hank happily tossed his suitcase over the side and into the bed of the pickup. For some reason, it no longer seemed quite so heavy.

As he settled into his seat, the young lady said, "You got a name or should I just call you Stranger?"

"Hank," he said, reaching across the seat to shake hands.

She clung to the steering wheel with her left hand while reaching for his with her right.

"Becky Rayburn," she said, throwing in a curt nod. "You got a last name to go with the other one?"

For the first time in a quite long time, Hank couldn't contain his excitement. "Yeah," he said. "It's Goodman."

"Goodman. Is that what you are, Hank? A good man?"

"I don't think so." Hank could feel his face turning ten shades of red. "It's just a name."

Becky found first gear, gave the truck some gas, and eased her foot off the clutch. To say Hank was impressed would have been quite an understatement. A girl driving a standard shift? He couldn't drive one if someone held a gun to his head.

"So where are you from?" Becky said. "You sure don't sound like one of us."

"I'm not," Hank said. "I'm from Michigan."

"Michigan," Becky narrowed her eyes. "So, you're a Yankee, huh?"

Hank chuckled. "No way," he said. "Actually, I'm a Tiger."

Becky shot him a strange look. "A tiger? Well, aren't you the confident one?"

"Detroit Tiger," Hank said, blushing again. "A fan, I mean. You know. The baseball team."

"I see."

After an extended moment of quiet passed, Becky finally said, "I'm no brain surgeon, but if you're from Michigan, wouldn't it be easier to get back the same way you came? Unless you hitchhiked down here."

"I didn't hitchhike," Hank said, shaking his head. "My grandparents brought me. I've been staying with them ever since my mom and dad were killed in a car wreck."

Becky's face softened. "Aww. Bless your heart."

Pointing back over his shoulder, Hank said, "They live on Hurt Road. Ever heard of it?"

"Everybody's heard of Hurt Road." Becky giggled but tried to stifle it. "It's where all the teenagers go to park."

"To park?"

"You know—to park." Becky cleared her throat. "The boy and girl thing."

"Oh," Hank said, chuckling under his breath. Though unfamiliar with the terminology, he understood exactly what she meant.

"So, who are your grandparents? I bet I know them."

Hank sighed, hesitant to admit kinship, but what other choice did he have? "Jake and Ada Taylor," he said.

With the words barely out of his mouth, Becky jerked the pickup to the side of the road, jammed on the brake, and skidded to an unexpected stop.

"What's the matter?" Hank said. "Did I say something wrong?"

Becky gripped the steering wheel with white knuckles. "No, you didn't. I just need you to get out of the truck."

Hank had just gotten in and already she was putting him out? Surely he'd said something to upset her.

"You heard me," Becky said. Her tone had undeniably shifted from pleasant to stiff and cold. "And be quick about it, too."

"Couldn't you at least tell me why?"

"It's a long story."

"I've got nothing but time," Hank said. "Trust me."

Becky nodded, blowing air from her nose, her lips a thin line. "Okay," she finally said, grinding the truck back into gear, "but I could get in a lot of trouble for this."

After a hard right on the next gravel road and another rough, dusty mile, Becky pulled the truck in beside a narrow white church with peeling black shutters. The sign in front read *Mt Zion AME Church, Services Every Third Sunday.*

Becky killed the engine then adjusted herself in the seat. "My daddy'd kill me if he ever found out about this."

"Found out about what? What are you even talking about?" Hank was confused and understandably so.

For the past forty-some odd years, Becky went on to tell him, friction had existed between her grandfather, Lester Rayburn, and Jacob. And over the years, the bad blood had been passed on to her father, Bill. When Hank asked what started the feud, she couldn't say for sure. Only that it had something to do with Mr. Taylor and her grandfather's sister. None of her family had ever filled her in on the details, and she'd never had any good reason to ask. Her standing orders were to stay away from the Taylors and anyone even remotely associated with them. Relatives or otherwise.

Hank listened intently the entire time but couldn't stop staring. There were beautiful women in Detroit, no doubt about it, but none more stunning than Becky. Her hair was the exact same color as the honey his grandmother served with breakfast each morning. And when she smiled, it made him feel giddy and lightheaded. Could this be what love at first sight felt like? Hank had another question for the future Miss America. The most important one of all.

"Do you have a boyfriend?" he blurted out.

"No," Becky said, her hand to her chest. "Why do you ask?"

Good answer. "Just curious, I guess."

Becky chuckled then glanced at her watch. "We have to go so I can get on home. I'll drop you back off at the highway."

"Could you take me to my grandparents' house? It sure is hot out there."

"I thought you were going to Colorado," Becky said, eyeing him suspiciously.

Hank shrugged. "We'll see. Maybe I'll get around to that later."

~

BECKY DROPPED HANK OFF ABOUT A HALF-MILE FROM HIS grandparents' house and made a U-turn in the narrow gravel road. By then, it was almost ten a.m. They had talked a little more along the way and—taboo or no taboo—he couldn't wait to see this Louisiana cutie-pie again.

Just knowing pretty girls existed in this part of the world had lightened Hank's load considerably. In less than twenty minutes time, he had made it back to the Taylors' house. In the distance, he could hear Jake's tractor popping to beat the band. Out in the field, good, old, faithful Ada still chopped away at the unforgiving grass and weeds. Perfect. They would never even know he'd left.

Hank made a beeline for the house, headed straight for his room, and shoved the suitcase back underneath the bed. Next, he hurried to the coffee can on the windowsill and returned the twenty-dollar bill he had *borrowed*. Hank had just put the money back in its rightful place when he caught a glimpse of his grand-mother heading to the house with her hoe thrown over one shoulder. From his seat at the kitchen table, and with the windows all open, he could hear her singing but couldn't quite make out the words. "Yes, we'll grab her by the liver." No, that couldn't be right. As she neared the house, the lyrics became clear. "Yes, we'll gather at the river. The beautiful, the beautiful river. Gather with the saints at the river. That flows by the throne of God." How could anyone who worked so hard be so happy and cheerful?

Opening the door and seeing her grandson, Ada took a step back with her hand on her chest. "Oh, Hank. You nearly gave me a heart attack."

"Sorry," he said with a shrug.

Ada hung her sweat-soaked bonnet on a nail by the door. "So, what have you been up to this morning?"

"Not much," Hank said, grinning like the proverbial opossum. "Just hanging out."

CHAPTER FOUR

*H*ank had walked home thinking Becky Rayburn would be his only reason for staying on the farm. He couldn't have been more wrong. When Hank noticed Ada's face, glowing even redder than ever before, a pang of guilt shot through him unlike anything he'd ever experienced. This sweet woman—probably in her mid to late sixties—toiled out in the field every day then came in and cooked over a hot stove. And while she was hard at work, he'd been sitting around on his lazy rear end doing absolutely nothing. Anyway you sliced it, it simply wasn't right. Becky or no Becky, there had always been a reason for Hank to stay where he was. It had just taken him some time to figure that out.

After the heartbreaking loss of his parents, Hank had adopted a "me against the world" attitude. And he'd been selfish, as if the recent tragedy only affected him and none of the other members of the family. His uncle, Tony, had been forced to deal with the death of his baby brother. Jake and Ada had lost their only child. Now, the old couple, who barely made ends meet, were doing everything they could to take care of him while at the same time sacrificing many of their own needs. He'd been a jerk right from the start. Not once had he even offered so much as a "thank you" to the ones who'd come to his rescue at the absolute lowest point of his life. The time for a change was at hand. Now, for the first time in his young life, Hank Goodman was about to step up and do the right thing.

Hank joined Ada at the kitchen sink. Realizing what he was about to ask might send her into cardiac arrest, he opted to approach the subject rather cautiously. He tapped on her upper arm and said, "Anything I can do to help, Grandma?"

Ada looked around, surprised, then gave him a loving pat on the shoulder. "I don't need any help, sweetie."

Maybe she didn't, but he wasn't about to give up so easily. "There has to be something I can do," Hank insisted. "Anything at all. You just name it."

Ada thought for a moment, tapping her chin with a crooked forefinger. "Have you ever peeled potatoes?"

"No ma'am," Hank said with a shake of his head, "but I'd be willing to give it a try."

"Then let's see what you can do."

The potatoes were kept in a tall wooden bin next to the stove. Ada said Jake had built it for her himself. Hank lifted the heavy lid while she reached inside and plucked out six medium-sized potatoes. Ada placed the potatoes in a speckled bowl then dug a short, wooden-handled paring knife from a drawer full of other assorted kitchen utensils.

Hank stood there with his mouth slightly open, watching with great interest as his grandmother carefully demonstrated the process. Best he could tell, there wasn't all that much to it. He couldn't wait to get his hands on one and give it a try. When Ada finished, she said, "Think you got it now?"

"I think so," Hank said. *I hope so.*

Ada handed the knife over to her grandson then stepped back

and watched with amazement—and amusement—as he peeled his first potato in record time. While speed hadn't been an issue, his accuracy needed a good bit of work. The poor potato had been whittled down to less than half its original size.

"Pretty good," Ada said, "but what we're trying to do is take off just the peel and leave most of the potato."

Hank tried a second and then a third. And the more he worked at it, the better he got. By the time he made it to the last one, he was pretty much a wizard with the paring knife.

Ada continued the lesson by rinsing the peeled potatoes and cutting them up into small cubes. She put the cubes in a metal pot, filled it with cold water, and then slowly brought the water to a boil. Once they were tender, she drained the water off and then added lots of butter and just a splash of cold, fresh milk.

Pointing back to the utensil drawer, his grandmother cleared her throat. "Reach in there and get me the potato masher."

The potato masher? Hank shrugged. "I've never seen one of those," he said. "What does it look like?"

"It's the thing with a squiggly wire on one end and a green, wooden handle on the other."

Being the only item in the drawer even remotely resembling her colorful description, Hank found it rather quickly. And, in no time, Ada was mashing the unsuspecting potatoes into submission.

"Mind if I try?" Hank said. "Looks like fun."

So, this was the recipe for the delicious mashed potatoes he had eaten during his first meal on the farm. Now, he would get to enjoy them again. Hank felt good knowing he had contributed to their preparation. Regardless of how insignificant his contribution had been.

∾

By the time Jake's old tractor popped its way back to the house, Ada had already finished cooking and had the food sitting on the table. She was proud of her grandson and couldn't wait to tell her husband that Hank had pitched in and helped.

Hank's eyes held a sort of gleam she hadn't seen in them before. And, for the first time since he'd come home with them, she honestly thought maybe, just maybe, things were going to be okay. She'd prayed for it every day and knew her husband had as well.

Jake took his place at the head of the table and surveyed the food before him. "Now this is a meal fit for a king, Ma."

When the old man chuckled at his own comment, Ada said, "I can't take all the credit. Hank helped me peel the potatoes."

"Did he now?" Jake said, cocking his head just a bit. "Good job, son."

Jake asked the Blessing and during the prayer thanked the Good Lord for sending Hank to them. Before he finished, Jake prayed they would always be good role models for their one and only grandson.

Though Hank didn't bow his head, he listened to what Jake said very carefully. "Grandpa," he said, after swallowing a spoonful of potatoes and gravy. "I sure wish you'd teach me how to hoe cotton."

Putting his fork down with a clink, Jake wiped his mouth with the back of his hand. "Are you sure, son? Gets mighty hot out there."

"I'm positive," Hank said. "Grandma needs the help, and I'm certainly not doing anything else."

Jake gave Ada a questioning look. Though her eyes were now red and a little moist, she managed a slight nod. "In that case," he said. "I'd be happy to."

The rest of the meal was mostly small talk and lively chat. Ada, realizing Hank had said more to her and Jake during one meal than he had the entire time he'd been with them, knew they'd finally reached a turning point. The effectual, fervent prayers of her and her husband had gratefully been answered.

~

OVER THE PAST FEW DAYS, HANK HAD BECOME ALL TOO FAMILIAR with Jake and Ada's daily ritual. Every afternoon, as soon as they'd finished their meal, the old couple would stretch out for a short thirty-minute nap. Ada would take the couch in the living room while Jake snoozed beneath the large pin oak tree between the house and the barn. He decided both must have internal alarm clocks because almost exactly one half hour later, they were up, revived and ready to go.

After his thirty-minute siesta, instead of firing up the tractor, Jake grabbed a hoe and joined Ada and Hank on cotton field turn row. The turn row, he'd told Hank, was the little stretch of uncultivated ground at the end of the rows set aside specifically for the farm equipment to turn around.

Jake gave his grandson a playful pat on the back and held up a long-handled hoe. "You ever used one of these before?"

Hank shook his head, now covered with the large, round, straw hat his grandmother had given him to ward off the relentless rays of the sun.

"There's only one thing we're trying to do out here, son," Jake explained. "Cut down the weeds and not the cotton."

"This here's the cotton," Ada said, pointing to the short stalks with the green, pointy leaves.

Jake nodded. "Watch me just a bit, and I'll show you how it's done."

His grandfather's ability to handle a hoe was quite impressive. He could hoe forwards and he could hoe backwards. And, he was a switch-hitter. He could hoe right-hand dominant then switch over to left-hand dominant. But then again, so could his grandmother.

Jake handed the hoe off to his grandson. "I've found the best way to learn something is to take a deep breath and jump right on in."

Starting off slowly, Hank did his best not to chop down any of the cotton. Ada told him if he did cut down a stalk or two every now and then, not to worry about it. Still, he thought it best to proceed with caution. He soon realized his amateur status was only holding his grandmother back.

"You go on ahead, Grandma, and I'll try to catch up."

"You're doing fine, son," she said. "Just fine."

Hank had been extra quiet, trying his best to concentrate on the job at hand. After almost an entire hour without incident, he finally felt confident enough to chat with his grandmother while swinging his hoe at the same time.

"You know," he said, stopping just long enough to remove his hat and wipe the sweat from his brow. "This wouldn't be so bad if it wasn't for the heat."

"It's a hot one, all right," Ada agreed.

Hank resumed hoeing and almost immediately chopped down two stalks of cotton. He winced and shook his head but kept right on going. "I was just wondering, Grandma. What do kids my age do around here for fun?"

Ada stopped and dabbed her forehead with a blue and white paisley handkerchief. "Well," she said, dragging the little word out. "Most of them live on farms like we do and have to work during the week. But on Friday and Saturday nights, they go up town and make circles around the square.

"Make circles?"

"They ride around and around the courthouse."

Hank stopped hoeing again. "So, they go cruising."

"I'm not sure they call it cruising," she said, "but I guess you could. All the kids know each other, so they ride around the square hollering and yelling. Waving. Just cutting up and having fun."

Hank knew exactly what it was like to be with those your own age, especially your friends. "It would be fun if I knew some of the others."

"You'll get to know them," she said. "In time."

"So, what else do they do?"

"They like to hang out around the eating places. Like the Tasty Cream."

"What's the Tasty Cream?"

"It's a little ice cream joint on the square, but I'm here to tell you, they make some of the best hamburgers you'll ever put in your mouth. We don't go there much because you have to eat in the truck, and Jake would rather eat inside. Then there's the Twelve Point."

Hank snickered. "The Twelve Point?"

"Little café just north of town. We passed right by it coming home the other day."

"How did it get such a name?"

"There's lots of deer in these parts. Story goes, the owner killed a big twelve-point buck and named the place after it."

Hank tossed it around a bit and thought it sounded pretty reasonable.

"I hear the food's pretty good," she said, "but me and Papa don't eat out a whole lot. Costs too much."

They continued working and a few minutes later, Ada stopped again. "I slam forgot to mention the Magnolia."

His grandmother went on to tell him that the Magnolia was not only a movie theatre but, with a full-sized stage, it hosted a monthly variety show featuring mostly local talent. The owners, Bob and Nancy Sutton, had been long-time friends of the Taylors, and their daughter, Nancy, had been Linda's best friend all through high school. The girls both graduated at the top of their class. Nancy had been the valedictorian with a 4.0, while Linda came in second with a whopping 3.95.

When Hank asked about the different types of music, Ada told him it was mostly country and bluegrass. Every now and then, the kids would slip a little of that "long-haired rock and roll" in.

So, Lee Parish had rock and roll. Who would have ever guessed it? And beautiful girls to boot. Something told Hank small-town life might not be so bad after all. Despite the agonizing heat and the sky-high humidity, he suddenly felt a strong urge to whistle while he worked.

CHAPTER FIVE

*I*n just one week's time, Hank not only learned to hoe cotton with speed and precision, but he'd also become fairly proficient in the operation of a John Deere tractor. Though his grandfather hadn't thought him quite skilled enough to turn him loose in the field with a set of plows, he had let him pull a hay trailer all the way over to Buck Jones's place. And all the way back. For both legs of the trip, however, Jake followed along behind in his old pickup truck. Just in case.

Hauling hay ended up being the hottest, most grueling work young Hank had ever encountered. The entire hay hauling crew was Jake, Buck, Buck's son Allen—some five years older than Hank—and Hank. Being the senior member of the bunch, Jake had naturally taken over the tractor-driving duties. Buck's job was to stand on the moving flatbed trailer and neatly stack the rectangular bales while Allen and Hank jogged alongside picking them up and tossing them onboard. Hoisting seventy-pound bales of hay from the ground and onto a moving trailer was challenging enough, but back at the farm he discovered the difficulty of transferring each heavy, scratchy bale from the trailer into his grandfather's barn in near one-hundred-degree heat.

With each passing day, Hank not only grew fonder of his grandparents' farm, but of Jake and Ada themselves. These were good, down to earth, hard-working people. Not a day went by he didn't think about his mom and dad, Detroit, and his friends back home, but as much as he loved them all, the more he stayed occupied, the less time he had to dwell on the unfortunate hand life had dealt him. Crosscut was home now, and he was bound and determined to make the most of it.

～

AFTER A SIGNIFICANT FRIDAY EVENING RAIN SHOWER, ADA TOLD Hank there would be no work the following day and he could sleep just as long as he wanted. Walking into the kitchen the next morning around nine, he found his grandparents both sitting at the table sipping cups of hot, steaming coffee.

"Welp," Jake said, leaning back in his chair. "Get enough rest last night?"

"Yes, sir." Hank scratched at his head. "More than enough, actually."

Jake stood and walked over to the sink. "I have to make a little run into town this morning. Thought you might like to tag along. What do you say?"

"Uh—I don't know," Hank said, raising one eyebrow. "Maybe. How long will you be gone?"

"Just long enough to run by Craft's and pick up some chicken feed. Be a good chance for you to get away from the farm here for a bit."

When Hank didn't answer right away, Jake added, "Might need a little help loading the stuff. It's pretty heavy, you know."

So, his grandpa needed his help. Nothing more to talk about. "Sure," Hank said with a convincing nod. "I'd love to."

This would be the first time Hank had ventured out since arriving on the farm. Not counting the day he'd decided to hitchhike to Colorado and ran into the lovely Becky Rayburn. This trip into town would strictly be to help his grandfather. If he happened to run into Becky somewhere along the way, then so be it. He knew the chances of hooking up with her were pretty much slim to none. Especially after what she had told him. But a slim chance was still a chance nonetheless. After all, she'd told him with her own luscious lips that she didn't have a boyfriend. Stranger things had happened, he supposed.

On the way into Crosscut, Jake told Hank that Craft's Feed and Hardware Store was a third-generation business now being run by the original owner's grandson, Homer. Homer had a son about Hank's age, but Jake couldn't remember the kid's name to save his life. "Not being able to remember nothing," his grandfather had said, "is a sure sign you're getting old."

Instead of pulling into one of the parking spots located in front of the store, Jake drove around to the side and backed up to the wide, open door of the loading dock. Near the center of the large opening stood a tall, muscular teen wearing Buddy Holly glasses, a white muscle shirt, blue jeans, and a dark blue baseball cap sporting the unmistakable Detroit Tiger *D*. Hank didn't know the guy from Adam, but if he was fan of the Tigers, he liked him already.

Hank followed his grandfather up the steep ramp leading into the warehouse. The big guy met them at the top and shook hands with Jacob. "Morning, Mr. Taylor," he said cheerfully.

"Morning, uh...son." Apparently, Jake still couldn't remember the kid's name to save his life.

"Who's this you got with you?" Tiger cap said, acknowledging Hank with a quick jerk of his head.

"This is my grandson," Jake said proudly. "Hank Goodman."

"Nice to meet you, Hank. I'm Ernie." Ernie extended his hand. "Folks around here call me Big Ernie."

Based on his size, the name seemed to be a good fit. But since

Hank had just met the guy, he'd better play it safe and stick with his given name. "Nice to meet you, Ernie."

"You can call me Big Ernie. Everybody else does." The younger Craft turned his attention back to Jake. "Papa's up front, Mr. Taylor. If you know what you need, I can go ahead and get it loaded up for you."

"A hundred-pound sack of chops." Jake clamped down on his grandson's shoulder. "Hank here can help you load it in the truck."

Jake headed for the front of the store, and Ernie motioned for Hank to follow him. Hank said, "He told me we were picking up chicken feed. First time he's ever mentioned chops."

Ernie tossed his head back. "We'll get to the chicken feed soon enough. Come with me."

The two young men sat down on the edge of the dock, their feet dangling lazily over the side, Ernie's nearly touching the ground. "So where are you from, Hank Goodman? You sure don't sound like one of us."

Hank chuckled when he remembered Becky Rayburn saying the exact same thing. Pointing to Ernie's head covering, he said, "I like your cap. It reminds me of home."

"Detroit?" Ernie said with genuine surprise. "You're from Detroit? Man, I can't believe it."

Hank chuckled under his breath. Ernie had said Dee-troit. Not once, but twice. Though he did find it somewhat humorous, it certainly wasn't the first time he'd heard it pronounced like that. And not just in Louisiana.

"I am," Hank said, throwing both hands up. "Born and raised."

"You lucky dog. Mama gave birth to me right here in the big city of Crosscut." Ernie pointed over his shoulder. "Meyer's Clinic over on the other side of town."

Hank repositioned his rear end on the hard, unforgiving concrete. "So, what's the deal with Tigers' cap? You a fan or just trying to make a fashion statement?"

"You better believe I'm a fan," Ernie said. "Looks like they might have a good shot at the pennant this year, too.

Hank pursed his lips and nodded.

"If you're from there, I bet you're a big fan, too."

"I am, and so was my dad," Hank said. "I got my name from Hall of Famer Hank Greenberg."

"Ain't you the lucky one? I wish I'd been named after some big-time baseball player. The best my folks could come up with was Ernie. A lot of thought went into mine, huh?"

The Tigers' famed play-by-play announcer suddenly popped into Hank's head. "You have a great name. I bet they named you after Ernie Harwell."

The big guy shook his head. "Nice to think so," he said, "but I sort of doubt it."

"Maybe you can ask your dad sometime."

"When you mentioned your daddy a minute ago, you said was. What happened to him? If you don't mind me asking."

"My parents were…" Hank took a deep breath and then blew it back out slowly. "They were killed in a traffic accident a while back."

"Tough deal, man," Ernie said, giving Hank an understanding but firm pat on the shoulder.

"Thanks. So now you know why I'm down here. I'm living with my grandparents."

"Mr. Taylor's a good man. Daddy says he's been doing business with us since way before I came along."

"How old are you anyway?"

"Seventeen," Ernie said. "Be a senior next school year. How about you?"

"Sixteen this past May."

As much as Hank enjoyed a conversation with someone near his own age—and talking about himself—a certain question had been eating away at him. "You wouldn't happen to know Becky Rayburn, would you?"

Ernie drew back, narrowing his eyes a bit, but then laughed out loud. "You've got to be kidding. How could I not know the best-looking girl in this part of the country? Why do you ask?"

Hank didn't want to sound overly interested. "Oh—just curious."

"How do you even know about her?"

"She picked me up the other day."

Ernie shot him another puzzled look. "She picked you up? Wow."

Hank sighed and ran his fingers through his hair. "It's a long story."

"Well, let me tell you about Becky. She's the sweetest girl you'd ever want to meet. Not to mention extremely easy on the eyes."

"Does she have any brothers or sisters?"

"No brothers or sisters, but her mama's nuttier than a fruit-cake. And her daddy..." Ernie scoffed. "That man watches over her like a hawk."

From what Becky told him, Hank wasn't surprised to hear it. One of the other things she'd said was she didn't have a boyfriend. This would be a good time to confirm the information with someone who might actually know.

"Do you know if she has a boyfriend?"

Ernie shook his head vigorously. "I don't think so. She dated Carl Walker for a while but when she caught him in the back seat with one of her best friends that pretty much ended whatever they had. Somebody told me he was pretty rough on her, too. Wouldn't surprise me none. He's one of the biggest jerks on the planet. One of the spoiled little rich kids who thinks he's a tough guy. And not to mention a gift to women. You know the type."

"I bet he doesn't mess with you, does he?" If he did, Hank knew it would probably be a monumental mistake."

They both stood, Ernie's six-six frame towering a good half a foot above Hank.

"Nobody messes with Big Ernie," he said confidently. "Now let's get your grandpa's chops loaded up before we both get in trouble."

Hank brushed off the seat of his jeans then caught Ernie's elbow. "Wait a minute," he said. "You never told me what chops are."

Ernie slapped him on the back and laughed out loud. "Corn, my new friend from Detroit, Michigan. Plain old chopped up corn."

~

HANK STOOD BACK AND WATCHED IN AMAZEMENT AS ERNIE JERKED up the hundred-pound sack of feed and easily tossed it into the back of the pickup. As he and his grandfather were getting in the truck to leave, Ernie shouted after them, "Holler at me when you get a chance. We'll hang out or something."

Sticking his head out the window and waving enthusiastically, Hank yelled back, "For sure."

Jake went through the series of gears and the old truck gradually began to pick up speed. So far, Hank hadn't said a word but had a good mind to ask his grandfather what caused the rift between his family and the Rayburns. But if things were as bad as Becky had led him to believe, there was no telling how Jake might react.

After a mile or more of aimlessly staring out the window, Hank finally mustered up a bit of courage. Still, he opted to take an indirect approach. Hank readjusted himself in the seat so he could face his grandfather. "Ernie says there are lots of pretty girls around Crosscut."

"He ought to know I guess," Jake said with a nod.

Hank began to squirm, mulling over what to say next. "He said the prettiest of them all is Becky Rayburn."

Jake didn't respond immediately, but Hank couldn't help

noticing how red the old man's face was beginning to turn. It also hadn't escaped his attention how his grandfather's tight grip on the steering wheel had caused his knuckles to turn white. At the next driveway—one leading into an old, abandoned service station—Jake slammed on the brakes and wheeled the truck in. Hank swallowed hard. Whatever was coming next wasn't going to be good.

The pickup came to an abrupt stop, and Jake immediately shut off the engine. Still looking straight ahead, and in a tone Hank was unfamiliar with, Jake said, "You stay away from the Rayburn girl."

His grandfather's words were even more severe than Hank had expected. Quite clearly, this wasn't a suggestion.

"And why should I?" Hank said defiantly.

Jake turned to Hank with a look the boy would never forget, angry words spewing from his mouth like venom. "Because I said so."

CHAPTER SIX

*B*efore telling her daughter she was going to the store to pick up a few necessities, Susan Rayburn gave Becky specific instructions on how many eggs to boil and how long to boil them. Now, with her mother long gone, Becky couldn't remember those instructions to save her life. The numbers five and ten had been mentioned. No doubt about that. But was it five eggs for ten minutes or had her mother said ten eggs for five minutes?

Ever since Becky picked up her hitchhiker a few days earlier, she'd had difficulty concentrating on just about everything. Good-looking wouldn't even begin to describe the guy. Handsome—maybe. Gorgeous—a much, much better choice. Every bit of six feet tall with deep, mysterious green eyes and dark, wavy hair worn slightly over his ears and shirt collar, he was simply a dreamboat. Becky had always heard that for every girl, there was a boy out there somewhere who could make her heart flutter with just a smile. She, of course, had never believed such nonsense. Until she ran into the likes of Hank Goodman.

Even if he didn't go on to Colorado and stayed on with his

grandparents, and even if he did have a thing for her like she had for him, Becky knew there was zero chance of the two of them ever getting together. With a last name different from his grandparents, they might be able to pull it off for a while. But once her daddy found out, and he would find out, it'd all be over but the crying. A fair and reasonable man—most of the time—when it came to anything even remotely associated with the Taylors, Bill Rayburn had no flexibility whatsoever.

When Becky told Hank she didn't know much about what had started the long-standing feud, she'd been telling the truth. Up until now, she'd never had a reason to worry about it one way or the other. When her mother got back from her errand running, she'd ask her about it, and hopefully she would be forthcoming. She wasn't about to ask her daddy.

Becky put five eggs in a boiler, filled it three-fourths full of water, and checked the time on the wall clock over the stove shaped somewhat like an exploding star. Was this what her mother had asked her to do? Oh, well. Better too few than too many.

When her mother returned and told her she'd done an excellent job with the eggs, Becky breathed a huge sigh of relief. Susan also said they needed to hurry it up if they were going to have the food on the table by the time her father came in. Bill Rayburn expected to be fed at straight-up twelve o'clock each and every day. No exceptions and no excuses.

While the eggs were boiling, Becky had been considering the best way to approach the subject of the feud with her mother. After much deliberation, she believed she had come up with a pretty decent plan.

She would start a conversation about something completely different and then at some point, try to work the Taylors in. It would be a bit tricky, but with a little luck, she might just be able to pull it off.

"The roads around here sure have some strange names," Becky said casually. "Don't you think so, Mama?"

"Oh, I don't know," her mother replied, stirring the large glob of mayonnaise she'd just dropped into her bowl of chopped-up hard boiled eggs. "I've never thought too much about it."

Becky sighed rather loudly. "Well, you've got Hickory Stump Road and Buck Snort Lane." She paused for a second. "And then there's Hurt Road. Got to be the goofiest name of all time. Don't you think?"

Susan stopped stirring just long enough to cut a glance in her daughter's direction. "Hurt Road does strike me as being a little odd. The other two make pretty good sense though."

Showtime. "Don't the Taylors live on Hurt Road?"

Her mother nodded and continued folding in the ingredients for her world-class deviled eggs.

"You know what I've always wondered?" Becky said.

Susan shook her head. "No, what?"

"Why Daddy and Grandpa don't get along with the Taylors."

Susan shrugged.

Inching closer to her mother, Becky added, "Why do you think they don't?"

"I don't know," Susan said impatiently. "They just don't."

By now, Becky was beginning to squirm. This wasn't going at all like she'd hoped it would. "Come on, Mama. There has to be more to it. I'd like to know what it is."

"You shouldn't even be worrying about such things. You're just a girl, for goodness sakes."

"I'm not worried about it." Becky scratched at the top of her head. "I'm just curious."

Susan tapped the excess egg off her spoon and laid it on the counter. Narrowing her eyes, she pointed directly at her daughter. "Curiosity is what killed the cat, Becky. Now just drop it and help me get your daddy's dinner on the table. We're running out of time."

"But, Mama."

"I said drop it."

"But, Mama I..."

"Becky Marie!"

This lively conversation had just come to a screeching halt. The matter was apparently not open for discussion, and Becky knew better than to push any further. Though she didn't get the information she needed from her mother, she wouldn't sweat it. When it was all said and done, she'd know everything there was to know about it. Grandma Rosalie lived only about a half mile down the road. Becky may have lost the battle, but if she played her cards right, a little visit to her granny's and she'd most likely win the war.

~

BECKY FINISHED UP THE NOON DISHES AND THEN STRUCK OUT ON foot for the hot, fifteen-minute walk to her grandmother's house. Crossing the old wooden bridge over Hog Branch, a creek running right through the middle of the Rayburn property, she spotted a large, dark cottonmouth and a couple of turtles sunning themselves on a log next to the bank. She made a mental note to remember the reptile being about as big around as her arm and probably longer than her leg.

Though there were many things in the world she was afraid of, only one thing scared her half to death. Snakes. She'd told a friend once there were actually two things. Snakes and sticks that looked like snakes. Becky had never been bitten, and her long-term goal was to keep that streak intact. She'd do everything in her power to steer clear of any sort of snake. Living, dead, or otherwise.

Like the Taylors, Lester and Rosalie Rayburn had lived in the same house for many long years. Lester still farmed the original three hundred acres his great-grandfather acquired nearly a century earlier. The land had been passed down from generation to generation with the stipulation it would always remain in the hands of the family. Even during the Great Depression, when times were much harder than they'd ever been before, Lester had managed to hang on to the old place and somehow eke out a living.

For as long as Becky could remember, her grandmother had looked exactly the same. She'd seen old photographs of Rosalie when she was just a tiny little thing, her figure all slim and trim. But the years had stolen all that and replaced it with the plump, round physique her granddaughter had grown to love.

Rosalie wore simple, button-up-the-front, printed cotton dresses and kept her hair wound tightly on her head in a bun. Becky recalled the first night she ever spent with the older couple and how she'd marveled when her grandmother let her blond hair down and it nearly fell to the floor. Becky could never put her finger on it, but something about simply being in the presence of the older woman had a relaxing, calming effect on her. The way things were meant to be, she supposed.

When her grandmother's house came into view, Becky could see the little lady on the front porch working away at a butter churn tucked firmly between her knees. Not wanting to startle her, Becky called out her greeting from a distance. "Hey, Grandma!"

Steadily pumping the long-handled wooden dasher up and down, Rosalie stopped just long enough to look up and give her granddaughter an enthusiastic wave. Making butter was one of the oldest and time-honored processes known to man and not an uncommon sight in such rural locations as Crosscut. The old, once white, Stoneware churn with the bright, blue stripes encircling it had been given to Rosalie as a wedding gift. Only sixteen at the time, she'd managed to keep it intact all those years. And just like her, it was still going strong.

A dip of snuff tucked between her bottom lip and gum,

Rosalie spit a long stream of juice off the edge of the porch and into the dry, loose dirt. The impact kicked up a tiny cloud of dust, which quickly dissipated. "Come on around, sweetie," the old woman said kindly. "Pull yourself up a chair."

Like many women her age in the area, Rosalie dipped snuff. Sweet snuff to be exact. And so did Lester. Growing up around such a thing, Becky was thankful her father never picked up the habit. Bill told Becky that when he was just a boy, he'd begged and pleaded with his father for a dip. Lester relented with the stipulation Bill not spit the dry powder out under any circumstances. Ten short minutes later, after gagging and throwing up all over the place, Lester finally let him wash his mouth out. After that, he never asked his father, or his mother, for a dip of snuff again. Like most of life's lessons, Bill's had been hard-bought.

Rosalie remained seated, and Becky planted a firm, convincing kiss on her soft, wrinkled cheek. Of all the people she knew, her grandmother had to be the sweetest and kindest of them all. She'd never heard her speak an unkind word about anybody or anything.

"Looks like you could use a break," Becky said. "Mind if I give it a try?"

"Be my guest," her grandmother said with a groan. "My arms are starting to get a little tired."

Rosalie moved to the empty chair next to hers while her granddaughter got in position behind the churn. Becky grabbed onto the long handle and resumed the steady up and down motion. At her own house, she didn't like doing this sort of thing. But this was different. Becky would do anything to help her sweetheart of a grandmother.

"Grandma," Becky said softly.

"What dear?"

"How come our family and the Taylors don't get along?"

Rosalie shot her granddaughter a curious look. "I figured you'd know all about it by now."

Becky stopped churning. "Nobody will tell me anything. Other than it has something to do with Mr. Taylor and Grandpa's sister. Can you fill me in on the details?"

"Just keep churning, sweetie, and I'll tell you all about it."

Back in 1920, Rosalie told Becky, Lester's younger sister, Clara, had gone on a picnic to Simmons Lake with Jacob Taylor. After the two of them finished eating, they paddled a small wooden boat out into the middle of the lake and a thunderstorm came up. Before they could row back to shore, the wind got to kicking up, and the boat overturned. Clara couldn't swim a lick, and Jacob wasn't able to save her. They didn't recover her body until late the following day.

"Sad," Becky said, shaking her head. "So sad."

Rosalie sighed and nodded.

"So, Grandpa can't stand Mr. Taylor because of a terrible accident."

"I'm afraid so. Lester says Jake knew Clara couldn't swim, and his daddy told Jake in no uncertain terms not to take her out on the lake."

Becky stopped churning again. "You think there's a chance they might ever make up?"

Rosalie shook her head slowly. "After all these years—no, sweetie, I don't. You know, sometimes, it's just best to let things lie. Maybe you should, too."

Becky helped finish up the churning before striking out for home. It was getting late, and she still needed to get ready for the annual summer carnival being held at the high school gymnasium. The big event didn't kick off until six p.m. but she wanted to be there at least an hour early to help set up the kissing booth. Just as she had for the past couple of years, she'd be manning it along with a couple of her closest friends.

Becky now knew what had brought about the Rayburn/Taylor feud. But it didn't help her situation any. Hank being Jacob Taylor's grandson meant he was strictly off limits.

And sadly—for everyone involved—things were never going to change.

CHAPTER SEVEN

$\mathcal{T}$he remainder of the trip home from Craft's had been awkward to say the least, the tension suffocating and thicker than molasses. Just the mention of Becky Rayburn's name had been enough to elicit an angry, heated reprimand from his grandfather. Hank had thought about trying to dig a little deeper but decided it best not to agitate Jake any further. According to Becky, something happened between him and her grandfather's sister. She'd never mentioned the sister's name. If the opportunity presented itself, he would ask Ada instead. Maybe she would tell him what he wanted to know.

The hundred-pound sack of feed Ernie Craft had single-handedly tossed into the back of the pickup ended up being almost too much for Jake and Hank together. Maneuvering the oversized burlap bag from the truck bed and onto the open tailgate had been the first test of their combined efforts. The second, and most difficult, was carrying it the thirty-some odd feet over to the barn and then wrestling it inside.

With Jake on one end and Hank on the other walking backwards, the going had been slow but steady. The most glaring mistake was neither of them thinking to open the wide, cumbersome barn door ahead of time. Hank learned the difficulty of balancing a heavy, bulky object on his knee while at the same time reaching over his shoulder to pry a rusty cotton-picker spindle out of a closed door latch. With some amount of skill and dexterity—and an even larger portion of luck—they finally delivered the enormous sack to its proper place. Hank sincerely hoped the hungry chickens would appreciate his and Jake's hard-fought efforts to insure they had something to eat. Though many of them would eventually wind up becoming food themselves.

The entire time they'd been fighting with the bag of chops, no words had passed between Hank and his grandfather. Other than Jake barking a couple of one- and two-word commands during the procedure, quiet pretty much ruled the day.

By the time they were finished, a light drizzle had started to fall. Before they could move the truck and get inside the house, the bottom had dropped out. Being cooped up together in the tiny farmhouse would no doubt make for a long and tense rest of the day.

To lessen any chances of further conflict, Hank opted to eat his meal of golden brown Spam, French fries, and a couple slices of bread in his own room. He would spend the remainder of the afternoon lying across the bed with his grandfather's copy of Jack London's *The Call of the Wild*. He'd read the book twice before, but for some reason it never seemed to lose its appeal. At four p.m., Hank was startled by the ringing of the light blue telephone hanging on the wall in the kitchen. Phone calls, he had come to realize, were few and far between in his grandparents' quiet home.

On a party line system, each of the four families had its own distinctive ring. For the Taylors, it was one long followed by another, much shorter one. Ada answered after the second short ring but with her speaking in her usual soft voice, Hank couldn't make out exactly what was being said. Momentarily, she called out, "Hank! It's for you!"

Closing the book, Hank immediately hopped to his feet, his teenage mind racing with all sorts of possibilities. Most likely, Becky Rayburn was calling to find out what time she should pick him up for their first of many dates. The masculine voice on the other end quickly dashed any hopes for a rendezvous with a beautiful maiden.

"Hey Hank, it's Ernie." A short pause. "You know, Big Ernie from up at Craft's."

Did he honestly think Hank had forgotten him so quickly? "Hey, man. What's up?"

Hank had only met Ernie just a few short hours ago. And though his first impression of the gentle giant had been a good one, he couldn't quite figure out why he would be calling. Especially so soon. Maybe he just wanted to talk Tigers' baseball.

"I smooth forgot about the carnival tonight. It's at the high school, and anybody and everybody will be there. I thought you might like to go. I can show you around a little and introduce you to some of the other kids. It'll be fun, trust me."

Unconvinced, Hank cleared his throat while Ernie continued.

"Rumor has it Becky Rayburn's heading up the kissing booth again this year. Be a good chance to 'talk' to her, if you know what I mean. How about it?"

Though Hank found the opportunity to see Becky again quite tempting, he was tentative. To go, he'd have to ask his grandfather's permission. The two of them hadn't said a word to each other since they'd left Crosscut earlier in the day. Oh, well. If he had to do it then he had to do it. Tough as it may be.

"Sounds good to me," Hank said, "but I'll have to run it by my grandpa first. Can I call you back?"

"You bet. Let me give you my number?"

"Hang on while I find something to write with."

Hank turned to find Ada holding a small, spiral flip pad in one hand and a long, yellow pencil in the other. He jotted Ernie's number down and told him he'd call back just as soon as he found out something.

Ada had taken a seat at the kitchen table. When Hank hung up the phone, he pulled out a chair and joined her. Obviously, she wanted to talk. "Jake said you mentioned the little Rayburn girl," she said softly.

Hank nodded in the affirmative. "Yeah, and he got a pretty mad about it, too."

Ada reached over and placed a soft hand on his arm. "Don't hold it against him, son. Something bad happened a long time ago. And to this day, it's still pretty painful."

"I understand," Hank said dryly, "but that was years ago. What could it possibly have to do with Becky?"

His grandmother sighed. "She's a Rayburn."

Hank threw both hands in the air. "And her only crime is having a last name she never asked for in the first place?"

"If you get involved with her, Jake knows the time will come when he'll have to deal with the rest of her family. It's nothing against the girl herself."

"But I've never even met her," Hank lied with narrowed eyes. "Ernie said she was cute, and when I mentioned it to Grandpa, he went nuts."

Ada clicked her tongue. "Jacob don't mean no harm, son. He's just trying to head something off before it ever gets started."

The explanation, so far, didn't hold water. And even if something terrible had happened years ago, it certainly wasn't fair to penalize Becky for it. And penalizing her was penalizing him.

Hank crossed his arms. "So, what happened then?" he said. "I think I have a right to know."

"You do," she agreed. "You sure do."

Ada sat up straight and then took a deep breath. "June of 1920, two years before I met your grandpa, Jacob took Lester Rayburn's little sister, Clara, out for a boat ride on Simmons

Lake. While they were out on the water, a bad storm came up, and the boat flipped over."

Hank swallowed hard. "And Clara drowned?"

"Jake said he did everything he possibly could to save her."

"Pretty terrible," Hank said, shaking his head.

"Lester Rayburn thinks Jacob didn't try hard enough."

"I can see such a thing being tough on both families."

"It was," Ada said with a sigh. "Especially since Jake and Lester had been so close all those years."

Hank leaned back. "You mean they were friends?"

"They were closer than friends," she said, nodding. "More like brothers."

Hank mulled over what his grandmother had just shared with him and wondered how he would have reacted in a similar situation. He honestly didn't know. At least now he knew why both men felt the way they did. Knowing, and even feeling bad for his grandfather, still didn't mean he would commit to staying away from Becky.

"Thanks, Grandma," Hank said. "You've shed a lot of light on things."

Ada simply nodded.

With the explanation in his pocket, there was something he still needed to ask his grandfather. He would run it by Ada first and see what she thought.

"Ernie Craft wants to know if I can go to the carnival with him tonight. You think Grandpa will mind?"

"Why don't you go ask him?" she said, motioning with her chin. "He's out on the front porch just watching it rain."

Hank shrugged, unable to disguise the apprehension in his face.

Ada reached over and put her hand on top of his. "Go on out and talk to him, son. He feels pretty bad about what happened this morning."

~

Hank pushed the screen door open and walked out onto the porch. Jake, sitting in one of two matching straight-back chairs with seats covered in tightly stretched and well-worn cowhide, glanced up when he heard the rusty hinges creak. He didn't speak but simply reached over and patted the seat of the identical chair next to his.

Hank plopped down and ran both hands down the front of his jeans. For the first time since he'd been on the farm, he noticed the many wrinkles on his grandfather's tanned and leathery face. Every line, he surmised, had been well earned over the years as the old man struggled to scratch a meager living out of the dirt. Before Hank could muster up enough courage to voice his request, Jake spoke up.

"I've never been good at this sort of thing, son, but I've been thinking on it quite a bit. I just want to say I'm sorry about the way I acted this morning. You didn't know anything about the Rayburns, and the way I treated you wasn't right. I should have taken the time to explain."

Silence hung heavily in the air for several seconds. "Grandma told me about it," Hank finally managed.

"She did?" Jake said. "Well, good." He put his hand on his grandson's knee and gave it a firm squeeze. "Now you know why we can't have nothing to do with the Rayburns."

Hank swallowed hard and nodded. "Yes, sir."

What Hank had said implied agreement with the ban on Becky Rayburn. And for that, he felt pretty bad. He'd simply said what he had to say to keep the peace. In reality, he would never pass up any opportunity to spend time with Becky. If such an opportunity ever presented itself. As far as asking permission to attend the carnival with Ernie, Hank knew it was now or never.

"Ernie Craft called, Grandpa," Hank said just as fast as he could. "He wants to know if I can go to the carnival tonight."

Jake leaned back in his chair and chuckled. "Well, of course you can. And have a good time, too. Just make sure he gets you back here by ten o'clock."

Hank hadn't anticipated a curfew but wasn't about to argue the point. In the grand scheme of things, ten would work just fine. "Don't worry, Grandpa. I'll make sure.

CHAPTER EIGHT

*I*n Hank's humble opinion, fifty miles per hour down a narrow gravel road seemed a bit much. But then again, what did he know about driving down gravel roads? There was a bigger picture here, and at the moment, nothing else seemed to matter. The faster Ernie drove, the faster they'd get to the school. The faster they got to the school, the faster he could spend the five dollars that had been burning a hole in his pocket ever since Jake had given it to him. If she was in the kissing booth, like Ernie said she would be, then Hank was prepared to spend every penny on an extended lip lock with the lovely—and no doubt equally talented kisser—Becky Rayburn.

"I forgot to tell you," Hank said, shouting to Ernie across the wide bench seat of the pickup. "I have to be home by ten."

Ernie looked over at him and frowned. "No, you don't. I do."

"No, seriously, man. Grandpa said..."

"You don't understand," Ernie said, shaking his head side to side. "If I have to be home by ten then you have to be home by nine-forty-five. Then I'll have fifteen minutes to get my tail to the house before Daddy locks me out and I have to spend the night in the truck."

"Got it," Hank said, giving his new friend a big thumbs up.

By the time they made it to the lone parking lot on the north side of the gym they found it already packed to the gills. Ernie had no choice but to pull to the other side of the highway and leave his truck in the knee-high grass. Crossing traffic wouldn't be a problem. Judging by the number of vehicles present, pretty much all of Lee Parish was in attendance for the annual summertime event.

Walking toward the gym, Hank grew more nervous with every step. Being the new guy on the block he would no doubt stick out like a giant sore thumb. On the plus side, his new super-sized buddy was there to accompany him. If the going got too rough.

The long rows of seats in the gym had been folded to make room for the many colorful booths that had been set up. Those for the children were made mostly from large pieces of cardboard taped together and painstakingly painted with colorful logos and other interesting shapes that appealed to the younger crowd. The organizers, whoever they were, had put a great deal of time and effort into setting up the event.

Though most of the games were designed specifically with kids in mind, a few were for teenagers like Hank and the surprising number of grown-ups in attendance. Most of the adults, however, seemed to gravitate toward the cake walk taking place in the middle of the gym floor. Though he loved a good piece of cake as much as the next guy, tonight Hank would only be spending his allotment of cash on sweet kisses from Becky.

Out of all the booths lined up side by side, the one designated for kissing had been decorated to stand out. Made from two-by-fours and plywood, it was painted from top to bottom with long, vertical red and white stripes. The sturdy construction meant it could be used year after year and had probably seen action many times before. Across the top, and above where the girls were standing, the words KISSING BOOTH had been written in shiny black paint. Below them, in even larger letters, the plywood was inscribed FIFTY CENTS. Hank had never been too good at arithmetic, but even a C student knew five dollars equated to ten long and passionate kisses. If he didn't chicken out first.

From Hank's vantage point, he could see three girls manning the booth. One a short, slender redhead, one a taller, full-figured brunette, and last but certainly not least, the one and only Miss Becky Rayburn. Hank swallowed hard. Even with her facing the opposite direction, he recognized her immediately. Based on her lively hand gestures, she appeared to be engaged in quite a colorful conversation with the other two girls.

Becky's long, blond hair hung loosely down the back of her red and white checkered blouse and stopped just above her narrow, perfect waist. Being the red-blooded, All-American boy he was, Hank couldn't help noticing her jeans fit rather nicely as well. This was the first time he had seen the new love of his life since the day of his foolhardy attempt at cross-country hitchhiking. Not sitting behind the wheel of a pickup truck, she was even more beautiful than he remembered.

Ernie gave him a slight nudge then motioned with his chin. "You see who I see?"

Hank frowned and answered with a series of quick nods.

Crossing his arms, Ernie laid down the challenge. "Well," he said. "You going over there or not?"

"I am, man," Hank said, followed by a stern look. "Just give me a minute."

Pointing to the handful of guys who had just shuffled up in the front of the booth, Ernie said, "I wouldn't wait too long if I were you, Romeo. The line's getting pretty long already. At this rate, she'll be all kissed out by the time you get up there."

Ernie slapped Hank on the back and announced he'd be headed to the other end of the gym to try his luck at shooting free throws. Sometime later, they would catch back up with each other.

Hank swallowed hard then took a swipe at the tiny beads of sweat rapidly forming on his forehead. On the way to the carnival, he'd been cool, calm, and collected. Now that he was there, he was beginning to have second thoughts. What if she wouldn't even speak to him, much less give him a kiss? This was nothing like the day in the truck when she had been so scared about being seen with him. This was in full view of everyone attending the carnival. In retrospect, maybe this hadn't been such a good idea after all.

A feeling of relief swept over Hank when he suddenly realized no one in the place knew him from Adam. Worst case scenario, he'd be mistaken for one of Ernie Craft's long lost cousins. Hank sucked a lungful of air in through his mouth and exhaled it out his nose. No more putting it off. Time to man up.

By the time Hank made his way across the gym, six other would-be kissers had already lined up ahead of him. But that was all right. He fell in behind one a good head taller and just a tiny bit wider. If he stayed close to the guy and kept his head down, Becky would never even see him coming. Until it was too late. By then, she wouldn't be able to run away and hide, even if she wanted to.

Hank timed the other guys on his watch. Once an eager participant made his way to the front of the line, the entire process took approximately three minutes. The highly-anticipated one-second kiss would be preceded by two minutes and fifty-nine seconds of talking and laughing it up with the hospitable, fun-loving girls.

The big guy in front of Hank—the one the girls laughingly referred to as Jimbo—finally got his turn and then lumbered off to the side. As soon as he moved out of the way, Hank stepped forward and slowly raised his head. There on the other side of the plywood counter—looking at him eye to eye—was the beautiful girl he'd lain awake every night thinking about. On the day they'd met, she'd been gorgeous without any makeup. Now, with just a little strategically applied, she was absolutely stunning.

Becky took a step back but then quickly recovered. Leaning forward, she motioned Hank closer. Then after looking both ways, she said in a loud whisper, "What in the world are you doing here?"

Not exactly the response Hank wanted to hear, but what could he do? He came back with, "Glad to see you, too."

"I didn't mean for it to come out like it did," she said with a frown, again looking both ways. "I'm just surprised to see you here."

Hank threw his hands up. What could he say?

"I'm sorry," Becky said, "but Mama and Daddy are both here tonight." She scanned the gym trying to locate them. "Thank goodness they're busy trying to find an empty chair over at the cake walk."

"So, you're saying a kiss is out of the question."

Becky shook her head and sighed. "Across the gym—right over there—is a set of double doors beneath the exit sign. Meet me outside, and we can talk in private."

Hank wasted no time heading for the exit. Becky asked the other two giggling girls if they would cover for her while she was gone. The brunette said, "Don't do anything we wouldn't do."

Becky rolled her eyes and took off.

IN THE DIM LIGHT OF THE PARKING LOT, HANK CAREFULLY MADE his way to the edge of the old red-brick building and peeked around the corner. From what little he could see in the dim light, there didn't appear to be anyone else around. A short time later, Becky showed up and, taking him by the hand, led him further into the shadows.

"I'm a Christian girl," Becky said. "So, don't go getting any ideas. We're out here to talk and nothing more."

A teenage boy with raging hormones, of course Hank had ideas. For the time being, however, just being this close to her would have to do.

"So, what have you been up to?" she said, nervously digging her toe into the loose pea gravel beneath her feet. "I see you never left for Colorado."

"I'm not going anywhere. I've decided to stay here and help my grandparents out at the farm." Hank cleared his throat. "How about you? What have you been up to?"

"Oh, you know. Girl stuff, mostly."

Actually, Hank didn't know much at all about "girl stuff." He said, "Not a day's gone by I haven't thought about you. I sure am glad I stuck around."

Becky took a deep breath and then blew it out slowly, her frown mostly hidden in the dim light. "I hope you didn't do it just for me."

"So what if I did?" he said, tossing his head back.

"If you did, then—well, you shouldn't have."

Becky's response felt like a dagger through his heart. Hank took a short, determined step closer. "Are you saying you don't like me?"

"I'm not saying I don't like you," she said. "There's nothing I would love more than spending time with you. It's just, Daddy would..."

"He won't ever have to know."

"You don't know him like I do," she said. "Sooner or later, he'll find out."

Hank moved even closer, grabbing onto both of Becky's arms. "Can't we at least give it a try?"

Becky immediately pulled away. "Look, Hank, I need to get back inside before they start to miss me."

"But..."

"It'll be better this way," she said, softening her tone as she walked away. "Trust me."

Hank felt his chest tighten. He'd hoped against hope they could somehow work around this ridiculous family feud. That—he had just learned in no uncertain terms—was never going to happen.

Becky stopped suddenly and planted a convincing kiss on his cheek. "This one's on the house."

Before Hank even had a chance to respond, an unfamiliar voice rang out through the darkness. "Well, well, well. And what do we have here?"

Hank could make out a figure of a guy about his own height but thinner moving through the shadows toward him. He had no idea who he was or what his intentions might be.

"What do you think you're doing back here with my girl, hot shot?"

"We were just talking," Hank said. "If it's any of your business."

"Oh, I'm about to make it my business. And I didn't hear no talking either. Looked to me like y'all were kissing."

"Shut up, Carl," Becky said firmly. "I'm not your girl, and you know it. Now leave us alone."

So this was Carl Walker, the self-proclaimed tough guy and Becky's former boyfriend Ernie had told him about.

Carl moved even closer. "I've got a good mind to clean your plow."

Hank countered with, "Well come on then. Nothing between us but air and opportunity."

Carl lunged forward, shoving Hank to the ground and knocking the wind out of him. He managed one good punch to Hank's cheek just before Ernie Craft's welcome voice called out, "Get off of him, you idiot!"

Ernie grabbed Carl by the waistband of his jeans and tossed him about ten feet through the air. "Hit the road, Walker, before I beat your sorry rear end into next week."

Hank stood slowly and brushed himself off, the cheekbone beneath his left eye throbbing painfully.

"You okay, man?" Ernie said, putting his arm around Hank's shoulder.

"I'm fine," he lied. "Just fine."

Hank would never forget the last thing Becky said before she quickly disappeared into the night. "I'm sorry, Hank. So sorry."

The pain in the young woman's voice had been unmistakable. Hank knew full well she wasn't talking about the brief altercation between him and Carl Walker. The relationship he'd stayed up nights thinking about was now officially over. Over before it even started.

CHAPTER NINE

Hank awoke the next morning to the combined smells of coffee brewing and bacon frying. And a cheek too sore to touch. By the time he crawled out of bed and stumbled into the kitchen, Ada and Jake had already poured themselves a cup and were sitting next to each other at the table. Thankfully, both of them had already been sleeping when Ernie dropped him off the night before. The evidence of what had happened, however, was no doubt prominently etched on his face.

Jake blew across his cup and took a slow, cautious sip. When he glanced up at his grandson, coffee spewed from his mouth. "What in the world happened to you?" he managed, his face stretching into a frown.

"Ran into a door knob," Hank said glumly.

His grandfather laughed out loud. "I've done the same thing myself." Jake looked to his wife for confirmation. "Haven't I, sweetie?"

Ada rolled her eyes. "How about a cup of coffee, Hank?" she said. "Bacon's ready and the biscuits will be any minute now."

Hank refused the offer with a wave of his hand, pulled out a chair, and plopped down in it. If his grandparents noticed he wasn't his usual self, the fist-sized bruise on his cheek should more than speak for itself. But no more was said about it, and he offered up no further explanation.

~

OVER THE NEXT TWO MONTHS, HANK KEPT PRETTY MUCH TO himself. The situation with Becky still eating away at him; he spent the majority of his time working and simply hanging out around the farm. Occasionally, he would venture into town with Jake but never any further than Craft's store. He confided to Ernie everything Becky had said to him that night at the gym. His new friend told him not to worry, there were plenty more girls in Crosscut to choose from. Maybe so, but there was only one Becky Rayburn.

Hank hadn't seen Becky since the fateful night at the carnival, and as far as he knew, she hadn't seen him either. Before long, he would have to enroll in the public school system, and once it started, there would be no way to avoid her. Being in the same grade, they were bound to have at least a few classes together. Maybe all of them. Hank knew he needed to do something. He just didn't know what.

Early one Sunday morning, Hank had just sat down with his grandparents for breakfast when an approaching car's horn shattered the peaceful quiet. Jake and Ada turned to each other and shrugged. Hank threw both hands up. Company of any kind was indeed a rare commodity at the Taylor farm. Before church on a Sunday morning—completely unheard of.

"Who in the world?" Jake said, setting his cup down and scooting his chair back.

The curious trio headed for the front door, still baffled as to the identity of the enthusiastic horn-blower. Even after getting a look at the vehicle, they were still no closer to identifying their mysterious guests.

The shiny new Venetian Blue Cadillac looked terribly out of place when it pulled off the gravel road and came to a stop near the Taylors' front porch. Hank stared curiously at the man in the gray felt hat and the diminutive lady seated next to him wearing a bright red sundress with matching head scarf and dark glasses. He elbowed Jake's arm and said dryly. "You know these people?"

Jake rubbed his chin between thumb and his fingers. "I don't rightly…" Ada gave him a stern look and then a nudge. He quickly changed it to, "Well, maybe."

Hank strained for a better look at the tall, broad-shouldered man now stepping out of the car, and a strange sensation ran the entire length of his body. Had it not been for the much larger frame, he would have sworn the man was his own father, Charles. Then it hit him. He had met this fellow before.

At his parents' funeral, and for the first time in his life, Hank had been introduced to his father's older brother, Tony. The resemblance was uncanny. Spooky, even. Seeing his uncle was almost like seeing a ghost.

"It's Uncle Tony and Aunt Alice," Hank said, diving off the porch to greet them.

"Y'all get out and come in," Jacob called out. His voice held little enthusiasm.

The five of them greeted one another with handshakes and hugs. After exchanging pleasantries, Ada said, "Let's go inside where it's cooler. Y'all are just in time for breakfast."

Tony and Alice looked at each other and shrugged. Then Alice nodded her approval, and they followed Jake, Hank, and Ada into the house. Making it as far as the living room, Jake stopped in front of his easy chair and plopped down in it. Tony and Hank took a seat next to each other on the couch while Alice and Ada continued on into the kitchen.

To the best of Hank's knowledge, these four people were his only living relatives. After the funeral, they'd sat down together to discuss who would take care of him. For two nights in a row after his parents died, he stayed with Roger and Carol Johnson. The Johnsons had been long-time, close friends with Charles and Linda. The Johnsons' only son, Kevin, had been like a brother to Hank growing up.

With no children of their own, Tony had told Jake he and Alice would love to take Hank in, but at the moment, they simply couldn't. When he mentioned the possibility of him going to live with the Taylors, Jake had pointed out they didn't have a whole lot and nothing whatsoever to offer a growing teenager. They'd also discussed the inevitability of Charles and Linda's house being put on the market at some point. Since there was no place to put it, the couple's furniture and appliances would have to be sold right along with the house. Their only car had been completely destroyed in the accident. Once everything was finalized, the money would be put into a trust fund Hank could access at some point in the future. Tony would take on the sale of the home and its contents while Jake had agreed to let Hank come and live with him and Ada. For as long as he wanted or at least until he reached his eighteenth birthday.

Jake kicked back in his recliner and locked his fingers behind his head. "So, Tony. What brings you folks all the way down here?"

"Just passing through," Tony said. "We've been visiting Alice's folks in Birmingham, and now we're headed back home. While we were down this way, we thought we'd stop by and check on old Hank here." Tony grabbed his nephew's knee and gave it a little shake. "See how he's getting along."

"Oh," Jake said, nodding.

"So, how's Louisiana been treating you?" Tony said to Hank. "Everything going your way?"

"Can't complain," Hank replied.

"I bet you have two or three girlfriends by now." Tony said, followed by a loud chuckle. "Maybe even more, huh?"

Of all the things Hank didn't want to talk about, girlfriends sat at the top of the list. He shook his head slightly. "Not really."

A few minutes later, Ada saved the day when she announced from the kitchen that breakfast was on the table.

~

THE SMALL TALK CONTINUED UNTIL NEARLY TEN A.M., AND BY THAT time, Hank had heard just about all he could stand. He politely excused himself, leaving the grownups at the kitchen table to discuss whatever grownups discussed when there were no young people around. He headed into his room and closed the door behind him.

Hank picked up the book he'd been working on, stretched out across his bed, and began to read. He'd finished only two pages when, through the closed door, he overheard his uncle mention his name. He closed the book then got up and put his ear against the door. Hank didn't like to eavesdrop, but the ongoing conversation definitely had something to do with him.

"Sure, it'll be tough," Jake said. "We know it will. But we'll manage somehow."

"What about school supplies?" Hank heard Tony ask. "What about clothes and shoes? Those things cost money, too, you know."

Jake cleared his throat. "We'll deal with it when we get to it."

"But you're almost there now," Tony said emphatically. "Let's face it. You folks are barely making ends meet as it is."

Ada, who'd been quiet, finally spoke up. "We'll find a way, Mr. Goodman. We always have, and we will this time."

Hank heard a loud, screeching sound. Like a chair sliding across the floor. A moment or two of silence followed then he heard Jake say, "Y'all haven't even been to Birmingham, have you? You came all the way down here just to take the boy back with you."

"It's what's best for him, Mr. Taylor," Tony said. "You know, and I know."

Jake said, "I know no such thing."

Another awkward silence then Tony spoke again. "Look, Mr. Taylor, I appreciate everything you've done for Hank, I honestly do, but Alice and I have talked this over and…"

"You could have picked up the phone, you know," Jake said firmly.

"I know, and I'm sorry now I didn't."

Feeling his chest tighten, Hank slowly backed away from the door. For some strange reason, Tony and Alice had had a change of heart. Now they wanted him to come live with them in Denver. He'd always known that though his grandparents were barely getting by; they had taken him in anyway. But the last thing he wanted to be was a burden to these kind and generous people. And then there was the thing with Becky Rayburn.

Jacob cleared his throat just before he called out his grandson's name. "Hank. Can you come in here a minute?"

Hank took a deep breath. He already knew what he had to do and dreaded it more than he'd ever dreaded anything. His grandparents clearly didn't want him to leave, but doing so would be best for everyone involved.

"Son," Jake said. "Tony and Alice want you to go back to Denver with them."

Hank glanced over at Jake and Ada then his aunt and uncle. Tony said, "What do you say, Hank? Sound good to you?"

As much as Hank wanted to give the appearance he was thinking things over—for Jake and Ada's sake—his mind was made up. He said, "I bet Colorado's nice this time of year."

Jake and Ada stared at each other with sad, blank expressions. Turning back to Hank, Jake said, "You know you don't have to go, son. You're more than welcome to stay here with us."

"I'm sure I'll love it there," Hank said, forcing a smile.

Hank gave his grandparents each a long, loving, goodbye hug.

Ada kissed him tenderly on the cheek and ran her fingers through his thick, dark hair. With his meager belongings stuffed in the trunk, he climbed into the back seat of the Cadillac and settled in for the long ride to Denver. He loved the Taylors with all his heart and would miss them terribly. Other than the death of his parents, this had to be the saddest moment of his young life. Through the thick cloud of dust, he could barely make out the two old people with the broken hearts still standing on the front porch, frantically waving their goodbyes. Though Tony had told him he could always come back for a visit, Hank knew he would never see his grandparents—or Becky Rayburn—again.

PART II

CHAPTER TEN

$\mathcal{M}$ onday, July 10, 1972

WITH NO OFFICIAL BUS STOP IN CROSSCUT, AND BEING AN OLD military man himself, the bus driver had no problem dropping his new friend off in the middle of nowhere. To Hank Goodman, however, it was anything but.

Hank retrieved his green canvas duffle bag from the seat behind him, shook hands with the driver, and stepped off in a place he hadn't seen in quite a long time. The old, stately oak once standing guard over the intersection—and whose shade he'd once unashamedly taken advantage of—now lay crumpled and broken. Most likely the victim of one of Mother Nature's violent outbursts.

As the bus picked up speed, Hank watched it slowly fade into the distance. He filled his lungs with hot, humid air then headed out down the narrow gravel road he once despised but eventually learned to love. Mostly because of the people who lived on it. Hank had always had second thoughts about leaving this place, and now—even on a scorching July day with the temperature firmly in the nineties—it honestly felt good to be back.

Hank hadn't seen his grandparents once since leaving Louisiana. They'd stayed in touch with an occasional phone call but for the most part through lengthy, hand-written letters. It was during the last of his two grueling tours in Vietnam that Hank learned of his grandfather's death from a massive heart attack. Clear on the other side of the world, Hank hadn't been able pull enough strings to attend Jake's funeral. He had, however, managed to get a call through to his grandmother. Over the phone, he told Ada how much he loved her. And he made her a promise. As soon as he made it back to the States and got his affairs in order, he'd be on the first bus headed south.

Fresh out of high school, while thumbing through his uncle's June 27, 1969 copy of *Life* magazine, Hank unexpectedly announced his plans to join the army. For him, the issue probably had a completely different effect than the publishers intended. He hoped that by enlisting he could do his part to ensure those 242 brave young Americans had not lost their lives in vain. His uncle tried his best to talk him out of it, but at eighteen, Hank knew it all and he'd already made up his mind. Seeing his resolve, Tony reminded him Charles's time in the army was how Hank's father ended up in Louisiana and met his mother. Though he knew the story well, Hank wasn't about to steal his uncle's thunder. Tony and Alice had been nothing but good to him, and he would be eternally grateful.

War has a way of changing people, and Hank was certainly no exception. The same could be said about Debra Sue Mills, the young woman who promised she would wait for him, no matter how long it took. Two months after his deployment, apparently, she could wait no longer. But Hank wasn't the only one to receive a "Dear John" letter from the company mailbag. And though he felt bad for a couple of his buddies, it was kind of nice to know he wasn't the only one who'd been dealt a cruel hand.

In Vietnam, Hank had done things he never even knew he was capable of. In kill-or-be-killed situations, soldiers are taught to do whatever is necessary to survive. He'd found himself in such positions many times. In all likelihood, he would carry the gruesome images of war with him all the days of his life.

Hank stopped a couple of times just to catch his breath, but long, difficult marches under challenging conditions subsequently had him in the best shape of his life. He'd left Louisiana five years ago, a scrawny, six-foot-tall sixteen-year-old who might have weighed a hundred and fifty pounds soaking wet. Now, at twenty-one and six-two, Hank carried two hundred pounds of nothing but solid muscle.

When the little white house with the peeling black shutters finally came into view, Hank couldn't help picking up his pace. He couldn't wait to wrap his arms around his grandmother and tell her in person just how much he loved and missed her. He had called from a pay phone just before leaving Denver but couldn't tell her with any certainty how long the trip would take. The coach line had said at least a couple of days. Depending on weather and how well the tires held up. After an extended layover in Wichita and spending the night in a most uncomfortable bus seat, the entire trip had taken just under two days.

Hank spotted Ada in her faded blue cotton dress, standing just outside the chicken coop. A round metal pan tucked loosely under her arm, she busily tossed handfuls of chopped corn to the squawking birds inside. Hank heard her tell them, "Easy girls. There's plenty to go around." He couldn't help wondering if Ada still got the big hundred-pound bags of chops from Craft's store. And if so, what Good Samaritan dragged the heavy sacks out of the back of their truck and wrestled them into the barn? Something he would have to ask her about.

Seeing Ada busy with the chickens and with her back to the road, Hank knew he couldn't have planned it any better. He had hoped to surprise his grandmother and now, he'd been given the perfect opportunity to do so. At the edge of the yard, he announced his arrival.

"Ada Taylor!" Hank shouted just as loud as he could. "Look alive! You've got company!"

Ada spun around, and her pan hit the ground with a loud, metallic thud, spilling all its contents. To the delight of the hungry fowl, most of the corn bounced through the wire, and a cackling "free for all" ensued.

"Hank!" Ada called out, covering her heart with her hand. "Oh, Hank!"

Hank tossed the heavy duffle aside and ran to meet her. He picked Ada up, spun her around, and she squealed like an excited schoolgirl. He realized he probably shouldn't have—given her age and all—but he simply couldn't help himself. After five long years, Hank had finally made it back to the place where he belonged.

Back on her feet, Ada reached up with rough, trembling hands and lovingly cradled Hank's face. Through warm, salty tears, she said, "I've asked the Good Lord every day just to let me live long enough to see this sweet face again."

During the long walk down Hurt Road, Hank kept telling himself he wouldn't get all emotional when he saw his grandmother for the first time in years. He should have known better. In Vietnam, he'd been told crying was good for you, that it had healing power and could cleanse the soul. As a teen, he hadn't shed the first tear when he found out about his parents. But when he watched his best friend take his last, long, labored breath, Hank had broken down and wept uncontrollably. And for those tears, he felt embarrassed and ashamed. Later the same day, the unit's chaplain stopped by to check on him and asked if he'd ever heard the song "Turn, Turn, Turn" by The Byrds. He told Hank the song's lyrics were taken straight from the Bible's book of Ecclesiastes. "Even the Good Book tells us there's a time to cry, Hank." Hank, however, was skeptical. He had cried, all right, but after what happened to Steve, a devout follower of Christ, he had little room in his heart for anything to do with the scriptures.

Swiping at his damp eyes with the bottom of his T-shirt, Hank was finally able to speak. "I've missed you so much, Grandma."

Ada wrapped her arms around his mid-section and squeezed with all her might. "Let's get you in the house and get some food in your belly. You must be starving."

Following her up the front porch steps, at the top Hank suddenly stopped and snapped his fingers. "Forgot my bag," he said.

Hank retrieved his duffle, and by the time he made it into the kitchen, his grandmother had already fired up the stove and a cast-iron skillet was sitting on one of the burners. Over her shoulder, she said, "You already know where your room is. I'll have something for you to eat here in just a jiffy."

As far as Hank could tell, the room had not been altered or rearranged since the day he left. *The Call of the Wild* still lay there on top of the chest of drawers, right next to his mother's picture. Big Ben still ticked away over on the nightstand. He could only assume the little red rooster that had awakened him every morning had long since joined his ancestors in the great chicken coop in the sky.

∽

HANK STORED HIS GEAR AND THEN HEADED BACK INTO THE kitchen. "Sure smells good in here," he said, sidling up next to his grandmother and giving her a quick smack on the cheek. "I'm so hungry I could eat a horse."

Ada hummed a happy tune as she poked at the slices of country ham with a long, two-pronged fork. "Be nice to have a man around the house to cook for again. I haven't done a lot since Jake passed away."

Hank couldn't help noticing how much his grandmother had aged during the time he'd been gone. While it was most likely part of the natural process, he couldn't help thinking the passing of her long-time companion had contributed as well. Thinner and pale, she appeared much more stooped through the shoulders and, quite possibly, even an inch or two shorter.

Walking over to the window above the sink, Hank gazed out across the long, straight rows of cotton waving in the warm breeze. "You're still renting the place out, I see."

Ada nodded. "Only way I can make ends meet. Since I lost Jake."

Turning back to his grandmother, Hank said, "I bet you miss the sound of Grandpa's old tractor, too."

"I'll still hear one every once in a while. But it's not the same. You know I had to sell his to help pay for the funeral."

Hank just stood there slowly shaking his head. Next to burying her devoted husband, having to part with his tractor must have been one of the hardest things she'd ever had to do. Hank would never mention it, but if he could find out who she sold the tractor to, one day he would buy it back and bring it home where it belonged.

Ada walked over and took Hank by the arm. "Come with me," she said. "I want to show you something." She led him to the back door. "Open it up. I've got a surprise for you."

Hank's eyes widened when he opened the door and saw not only a lavatory and a porcelain bathtub, but a shiny, white commode. After all these years, Ada had herself a bathroom. Though getting to the back door meant passing through the bathroom, he didn't have a problem with it. Anything beat high-stepping it through the dark of night with a flashlight in order to answer the call of nature. Ada beamed with obvious pride.

"So, when did all this come about?" Hank said.

"About two years ago. Jake said we were the only ones he knew of who didn't have an indoor toilet, and he was tired of it.

So instead of adding a new room onto the house, we just took in the back porch."

"Do you like it?"

"Like it?" she said, hurrying back over to the stove. "I absolutely love it."

Hank sat down at the table next to Ada and sat quietly as she blessed the food. Soon he had devoured two ham sandwiches and a tall, cold glass of fresh milk. She apologized at least three times for having to serve "light bread" and not biscuits. Hank assured her anything she fed him would be much better than the army food he'd grown so accustomed to.

Hank had seen times, and not too long ago, when he'd been thankful just to get his hands on a box of cold C-Rations. The hungrier you are, he'd found out the hard way, the better things taste. Even things you might not ordinarily eat.

After draining the last drop of milk from his glass, Hank pushed the empty plate back. "You sure know the way to my heart."

Ada reached out and touched him lightly on the arm. "I'll make us a cake later," she said. "Sound good?"

"You'll get no argument from me."

Hank stood and stretched then excused himself to the bathroom. When he returned, Ada had already finished putting the dishes away. "I was thinking about running by the church for a few minutes. Would you like to go?"

"The church?" Hank said with a frown.

Ada brushed her previous comment off with a wave of her hand. "I said church, didn't I? I meant to say cemetery. It's at the church."

CHAPTER ELEVEN

*H*aving never been there, Hank had no idea Shiloh Baptist Church had a cemetery. Any time his grandparents had asked him about attending Sunday services, he'd been stricken with a massive, throbbing headache or some other unexplained medical malady. The minute the old couple left, he would miraculously begin to feel better. By the time they made it home, he would have experienced a complete recovery and be ready to chow down on the scrumptious Sunday dinner Ada never failed to prepare.

The church turned out to be only about five miles from the farm. Hank had never ridden in a vehicle with Ada behind the wheel and was quite impressed at her alert and careful driving. That observation, however, had been made before she came to a sliding sideways stop in the gravel-covered parking lot and nearly took out the formidable set of white concrete steps in front of the church.

"Pretty close, huh?" Ada said, looking to Hank for confirmation.

Hank—who'd grabbed onto the dashboard and held on for dear life—could only nod. It had been close. Too close.

"Jake used to say close only counts in horseshoes and hand grenades. Have you ever heard that, Hank?"

"Not only have I heard it," he finally managed. "I know it to be a fact."

Jake and Ada had been members of the little Shiloh church for the past fifty years. Both had joined prior to their marriage in 1925. Though they were both affiliated with the same church, the young couple had elected to elope in order to save Ada's parents the unnecessary expense of an all-out wedding. In their young minds, they were in love and wanted to get married. Nothing else mattered. A Justice of the Peace would work just fine for them.

Once Ada's mother found out what had happened, she was fit to be tied. Not because Ada married Jacob Taylor, but because she had always dreamed of her daughter having a big church wedding with all the trimmings. Mary had even planned to announce it in the local paper so the entire parish could be there for the grand event. It had taken the birth of Linda for Ada to finally receive her mother's forgiveness. Her frugal father, Thomas, on the other hand, had been quite thankful for his daughter's thoughtfulness, though he never voiced his gratitude in the presence of his disgruntled wife.

Ada climbed out of the truck then reached over on the seat and picked up the fresh-cut flowers she had brought. She motioned to Hank, who still had a firm grip on the dashboard, and said, "You ready, sweetie? Cemetery's just around back."

Hank couldn't help chuckling, recalling his first day on his grandparents' farm when Jake had used the same idiom. He cringed when he remembered the necessary facility had indeed been located "around back."

A four-foot tall, once-white picket fence—badly in need of repair and a fresh coat of paint— enclosed the cemetery. The only access was through a narrow opening in the fence where a heavy, metal gate once swung. At some point, the gate had fallen off its hinges, and some concerned individual had been thoughtful enough to prop it up against one of the large, shady oak trees located nearby.

Hank followed his grandmother into the cemetery and over to a mound of dirt with only a few sprigs of grass growing out of it. Though rain over the past year had settled it significantly, Jake's plot still stuck out like a sore thumb. With a stiff rake and a hoe, Hank knew he could take care of it in no time. What bothered him more than anything was the fact his grandfather didn't have a headstone, only a small aluminum marker inscribed with his full name and date of death: Jacob Albert Taylor, April 2, 1971.

Ada held onto Hank's hand. Slowly and carefully, she took a knee and laid the flowers at the head of her late husband's grave. Listening closely to the one-sided conversation, Hank felt his eyes began to moisten and sting. Having been unable to attend the funeral had been bad enough. Not being there for his grandmother would probably be something he would never live down.

Hank helped Ada back to her feet. Unlike his, her eyes were bright and clear. And dry. Earlier in the day when they embraced, she hadn't held back her tears. Maybe when it came to Jake, she had cried all she possibly could.

For a couple of weeks after her husband's death, Ada cried every day and often for long periods at a time. The outbreaks became so severe and unpredictable she almost never got her chores done and couldn't go anywhere. Including church.

One day, after her pastor stopped by for a brief visit, her battle with tears came to a screeching halt. A strong woman of faith, she already knew what Brother Calvin would say before he even said it. Life is a journey and death only a small part of it. Ada had been so overcome with grief, she'd completely lost sight of the bigger picture. And though she missed her husband terribly and often struggled to make ends meet, she knew that someday they would be reunited.

"Jake used to talk about you all the time," Ada said, pulling her grandson closer. "He loved you so much."

Hank cleared his throat. "I just hate I couldn't be here for you."

"You were on the other side of the world, son. Now, I don't want to hear another word about it."

Hank took a deep breath then took his time blowing it back out again. Scanning the cemetery, he couldn't help noticing that —just like Jake's—many of the graves had no permanent marker.

Turning back to his grandmother, Hank said, "Why are there so many plots without headstones?"

"Most folks around here don't have money for such things," she said, her shoulders drooping slightly. "I know because I'm one of them."

"Didn't Grandpa have life insurance?"

Ada sighed. "He had a little. I paid on his policy for years. And when I needed it, it was barely enough to pay for Jake's casket." She shook her head slowly. "Shameful."

Hank silently nodded. As soon as he could access the money, Jacob Taylor would have the grandest headstone in the cemetery.

~

HANK DROVE BACK FROM THE CEMETERY WITH ADA HAPPILY RIDING shotgun. Once they made it home, she told him she'd fix them a bite to eat, and he told her he was going to stretch out on the couch and rest his tired eyes. The little sleep he'd managed during the long bus ride had been in the seat and all in an upright position. Hank nodded off quickly and didn't awaken until two hours later when Ada announced supper was ready and on the table.

After a good stretch and a yawn, Hank headed into the kitchen and took a seat behind the plate and utensils Ada had already laid out for him. "It ain't much, sweetie," she said, "but I hope it'll do. Next time, I'll fix the mashed potatoes and gravy you used to love so much."

"You may think I'm lying, Grandma," Hank said, adjusting in his chair, "but I haven't had mashed potatoes even once since I left."

She chuckled out loud. "You remember the first time you peeled a potato?"

Hank's face tightened into a frown.

"Wasn't that something?" Ada sang out.

"It sure was," Hank said, laughing as well. "My first one started out big as my fist and ended up about the size of a golf ball."

Ada prayed over the food, and the rest of the meal ended up being pretty much a stroll down memory lane. Most of it revisiting Hank's short stay on the farm five years earlier. He'd only managed to make one friend during his brief time there and had every intention of staying in touch with Ernie Craft. Sadly, he had not. Now that he was back, Hank would make it one of his top priorities. He'd love nothing more than to sit down and visit with the big guy. Maybe Ernie had been in the service as well. Maybe Ernie had done time himself trying to stay alive in the rice patties and jungles of an Asian country most Americans had never even heard of prior to the current "conflict."

Hank's fork rang like a bell when he dropped it onto his empty plate a little harder than he'd intended. He cringed then pushed it away slowly. "Some mighty fine eatin', ma'am," he said playfully. "Give my compliments to the chef."

Ada waved him off with a swipe of her hand.

Chugging the last of his tea, the ice cubes jingled when Hank set his glass back down on the table. "You ever hear anything out of Ernie Craft, Grandma?" he said. "I was wondering if he still works up at his folks' store."

She turned away for a moment then glanced up at the ceiling

and cleared her throat. "For some reason, I thought you already knew about it."

Hank scooted his chair closer to the table. "Knew about what?"

"The Craft boy," Ada said softly. "He got killed last year."

As he sat there in stunned silence, Hank wondered how such a thing could even be possible. Big Ernie couldn't be dead.

"Happened not long after Jake passed away," she added.

"Was he in Vietnam?"

"Oh, no, honey," Ada said, shaking her head slowly. "It didn't happen overseas."

She told him that one evening, a little more than a year earlier, Ernie had gone walking in the woods with one of his dogs. Deathly afraid of snakes, he'd taken a shotgun along just in case he ran across one. What she had heard was Ernie propped his gun up against a barbed-wire fence to climb through and somehow, it fell over and went off. Popular opinion was the dog had somehow managed to knock it over.

"His poor daddy, bless his heart, was the one who found him."

The news was devastating. Hank had hoped to hear about Ernie finishing school. About him getting married and taking over his father's business. Not of his friend dying in some sort of freak accident. Though the circumstances were completely different, too many of Hank's friends had been killed already.

Ada took a deep breath and blew it out slowly. "The worst thing was his little wife being about four months pregnant at the time."

Hank could only sit there and shake his head. A tragic story if he'd ever heard one. He'd always had difficulty putting things like this into perspective. How bad things happened to good people. How life could be kind one minute and then the next, slap you squarely in the face. His mom and dad were prime examples. And so was Steve McMillan.

Few words were exchanged while Hank helped Ada with the

dishes. Afterwards, she kissed him on the cheek and told him she was headed on to bed. After his two-hour nap, Hank wasn't ready to turn in just yet.

Walking out onto the front porch, Hank reached up and stretched with a loud, exaggerated sigh. What struck him most about the country was just how many stars you could see on such a clear night. In Denver, the bright lights of the city eclipsed the distant glow of the stars. But here from the Taylors' front porch —in complete and total darkness—you could see for an eternity.

During his short stay in the South, Hank had learned something about front porches. They were special. They were places where families gathered for fun-filled visits. Where friends met up just to sit around and talk. Where problems could be sorted out and controversial topics such as sports or politics could be safely approached. Where large, green watermelons bursting at the seams were sliced open while excitable children laughed and clapped their hands for joy. Where one hearty soul turned the wooden ice cream maker crank while another added ice and handfuls of rock salt. What he wouldn't give to sit on the front porch with Jacob Taylor again. Just one more time.

Hank's thoughts soon drifted back to Ernie Craft and the disturbing information Ada had shared. He'd have to find out where the big fellow was buried, go there, and pay his final respects. Besides being his only friend in Crosscut, Big Ernie had rescued him from Becky Rayburn's crazy ex-boyfriend that fateful night at the summer carnival. Becky Rayburn. What a beautiful and vivacious young woman she had been. Hank couldn't help wondering what ever became of her. Maybe he'd ask around a bit and see what he could find out.

CHAPTER TWELVE

His first week on the farm, Hank stayed close to home and helped Ada with her chores. It wasn't quite the same without Jake around, but he hoped the relative peace and quiet of the place would be just what the doctor ordered. The dream visited him almost every night, but only twice had Ada hurried into his room after hearing him cry out. At some point, something had to give.

The brilliant rays of sunlight streaming through the solitary window were a pretty good indicator Hank had overslept. Shielding his eyes with his hand, he turned his head slightly to confirm the time with Big Ben. All he could do was shake his head when he saw the big hand pointing directly at the three and the little hand resting firmly on the nine.

Hank threw the covers back then grabbed the same jeans he'd worn the day before from the foot of the bed. One thing needed to be taken care of right away. He had to find Ada and apologize for sleeping half the day. His expanded bladder quickly reminded him there were at least two things needing his immediate attention. Like Ada, he was also thankful taking care of one's personal business no longer involved venturing outdoors.

Locating his grandmother hadn't been difficult at all. Standing at the kitchen sink, Ada was cutting up a chicken she'd no doubt harvested and plucked that very morning.

"Morning, Grandma," Hank said, hurriedly passing through the kitchen on his way to the bathroom. "What's left of it anyway."

Ada glanced over her right shoulder and her face lit right up. "Morning." Her follow-up question had a painfully obvious answer. "You sleep good?"

"Too good," he said, feeling his face flush. He opened the door to the bathroom and quickly disappeared inside.

Back from his duties, Hank poured himself a cup of strong, black coffee, pulled a chair out from the table, and plopped down in it. Ada took a seat next to him.

"Sorry I slept so late, Grandma," he said, shaking his head from side to side.

Ada lightly touched his arm. "It's fine, sweetie."

"To me it's not," Hank insisted. "It's embarrassing."

"I said it's fine, and I don't want to hear another word about it."

Blowing across his coffee, Hank took a long, cautious sip. "So, what's on the agenda for today?"

"I need to run up to Craft's," Ada said, frowning slightly. "Having a devil of a time talking myself into it."

Hank set his cup down with a heavy thud. "I could go for you, you know. Be more than happy to."

Ada chuckled. "I didn't bring it up so you would go, son. I can do it myself. I'm just being lazy this morning."

"No, seriously," Hank said, sitting up straighter in his chair. "I wouldn't mind it at all."

Ada squinted then cocked her head. "You sure?"

"Sure, I'm sure," he said. "Just tell me what you need."

"All I need is a salt block."

Hank's eyes widened. A salt block. Now there was something he'd never heard of before. "What in the world is a salt block?"

"It's a little something for the cows to lick on. If I don't get one pretty quick, they're gonna chew up everything on the place."

"Oh?" Hank said, laughing out loud. "And what makes them want to do that?"

"Jacob used to say cows need salt and other minerals. And they'll get them any way they can. I've even seen the rascals eat dirt."

"Dirt?" Hank said, his face tightening into a frown. "Are you serious? Dirt?"

Ada nodded vigorously. "Dirt ain't nothing. I've seen them gnaw on fence posts. Even seen them eat rocks."

Hank stood and finished off the last of his coffee. "Well. I've certainly learned something new today."

"Just tell them you need a salt block. They'll know exactly what you mean."

When Ada got up from the table and headed toward the sink, Hank knew exactly what she had in mind. The little metal coffee can in the windowsill from five years ago still occupied the same spot. Hank couldn't help thinking about the twenty dollars he'd "borrowed" and then put back the time he'd decided to hitchhike to Denver. He later learned the can contained his grandmother's hard-earned egg money.

Ada popped the plastic lid off the can and pulled out a folded ten-dollar bill. When she tried to hand it to Hank, he emphatically waved her off. "I don't need any money, Grandma."

"Yes, you do," she said firmly, pushing the bill in his direction. "Now take it."

Hank crossed his arms in defiance. "Nope. I'm not taking it."

"I don't expect you to pay for the things I need, son. I've got a little money saved up."

Slipping his arm around his grandmother, Hank pulled her close. "Remember me saying I was coming here to help?

Ada nodded.

"Then all you have to do is let me do it."

Hank slipped on his shoes and a shirt then grabbed the truck keys off the nail sticking out of the kitchen doorframe. He dropped the keys in his pocket, kissed his grandmother on the cheek, and told her he'd be back soon.

"Don't you want to eat a bite first?"

"I'm not hungry," he said. "Are you sure you don't need anything else?"

"I can't think of a thing right now." Hank had started to turn away when Ada held up an index finger. "Wait a minute. On your way back, stop by Ferguson's and pick up three ripe bananas. Oh, two cans of condensed milk and a large package of vanilla wafers. I've a good mind to whip up an old-fashioned banana pudding."

"Sounds good to me," Hank said with a convincing nod.

"You're sure you don't need any money?"

"I'm positive, Grandma."

~

HANK TOOK HIS TIME DRIVING INTO CROSSCUT. NOT BECAUSE HE had to, but because he wanted to. He had grown to love and appreciate the landscape he'd found so distasteful when his grandparents first brought him here. Jake had taught him that farming was an honorable profession. An essential profession. If farmers farm, people eat. If farmers don't farm then people don't eat. A plain and simple fact.

Leaving Louisiana in the first place had been a mistake. As much as he hadn't wanted to be a burden on his grandparents, the situation with Becky Rayburn probably played the biggest role in helping him decide. Once Hank got settled in Denver and started school, coming back had never seemed like an option.

After school, it had been the army and then, of course, the war in Vietnam.

Hank was back, bound and determined to put down roots. Living in Denver hadn't been so bad, but having spent the better part of his life in big cities, he was more than ready to make a change. The flatlands of the Bayou State would suit him just fine.

While at Craft's, Hank would try to find out where Ernie had been laid to rest. If he sensed an appropriate opening, he might ask if there were any details on how his friend died. Maybe his grandmother had left out something important.

First, he would have to tell them who he was. Though he knew Ernie, Hank never got the opportunity to meet his father, Homer. Today, with any luck, he would. Hank would offer his condolences and tell Mr. Craft how much he thought of his son and what a fine young man he was.

Instead of backing up to the loading dock like Jake used to do, Hank parked in front of the store. From Ada's description of a salt block, he should be able to handle it without needing any assistance.

Hank checked his watch. Eleven o'clock and the hot July sun beating down in typical Louisiana fashion. He thought it odd there were no other vehicles parked out front. Being the first of the week, maybe Monday just happened to be one of their slower days.

Grabbing onto the metal handrail, Hank quickly cleared the seven blue concrete steps leading up to the porch. The front of the store had been decorated with many colorful signs and banners advertising everything from the latest hybrid seed corn to mouth-watering hog and cattle feed. The biggest of the bunch was long and rectangular, perched high above the entrance and displaying the name of the business in tall, white lettering on a deep blue background. Each end featured the well-known red and white checkerboard pattern. For the benefit of some well-placed advertising, Hank figured the sign most likely had been generously donated.

Craft's store had matching double front doors, each featuring a large, thick pane of shining, tempered glass. They were closed, and though both had a handle, only the one on the right appeared to be ready for use. About eye level, a small red sign with white flowing letters read *Welcome. Please come in.*

Hank pulled the door open and a small brass bell jingled high above his head. From somewhere out of sight, a young woman with a pleasant-sounding voice called out, "Good morning. Be right with you."

Once inside, Hank found himself facing a long, wide, wooden counter complete with an old-style cash register probably from the 1930s. An assortment of catalogs, brochures, and pamphlets advertising the latest innovations in feed and seed development were scattered about on the countertop. Behind it, he noted another door leading into what appeared to be a small private office. The friendly voice he'd heard had come from inside.

Less than thirty seconds later, a young woman with shoulder length blond hair, wearing jeans and a short-sleeved blue denim shirt, appeared in the doorway. Head tilted slightly downward, she walked toward the counter. "Sorry to keep you waiting," she said, her words sounding sincere and apologetic. "I was checking on my..."

In the middle of her sentence, the woman had looked up and seen Hank standing on the other side of the counter.

Hank swallowed hard in stunned silence, as if his eyes were playing tricks on him. The woman he found himself face to face with was none other than Becky Rayburn. The same Becky Rayburn who'd stolen his young heart some five years earlier.

Just the night before, Hank had thought about her and wondered if, at some point, he might run into her. He never dreamed it would be this soon. And certainly not here, of all places. Things had changed quite a bit since he'd been gone. Before he left, he hoped to have the answer to the question swirling around in his head. What in the world was Becky Rayburn doing behind the counter at Craft's Feed and Hardware Store?

Becky was the first to find words. "Hank Goodman?" she said, awkwardly. "Is that you?"

Still slightly in shock himself, Hank threw his hands up. "Guilty as charged."

"What are you doing here?" Becky quickly brought her hand up to her forehead. "I'm so sorry, Hank. What I mean is, what are you doing in Crosscut? Mr. Taylor told Ernie you'd moved to Colorado. The last we heard you'd been shipped out to Vietnam."

"All true," he said, nodding. "I came back about a week ago to help take care of my grandma. Grandpa passed away last year, and she's by herself now."

"I see her every now and then," Becky said. "Your grandma's a good woman."

"Thank you."

Becky ran her hands down the front of her shirt as if to smooth it out. "It's so good to see you again," she said, her face now glowing. "How have you been?"

A baby's cry from inside the room Becky had just come from stopped Hank from answering.

"Hang on just a minute," she said, raising an index finger. "I'll be right back."

She soon returned bouncing a small child on her hip. Certainly no expert on children, Hank knew this one couldn't be more than nine or ten months old. Regardless, the little fellow was cute as a button and appeared to be quite content now that Becky was holding him.

Judging by the color of his hair, and the obvious bond of affection, Hank felt relatively confident the baby was hers. Just to be on the safe side, he thought he'd better ask. "He's adorable," Hank said, placing both hands on the edge of the counter. "Is he yours?"

"He's mine, all right." Hoisting the baby even higher, Becky said, "Hank, I'd like you to meet my son. Say hello to Little Ernie."

CHAPTER THIRTEEN

*B*ecky's announcement gave Hank quite a jolt, and he took an involuntary step back. Ada told him Ernie's wife had been about four months pregnant when Ernie was killed, but Hank had never even bothered to ask the poor woman's name. Not once had he considered the possibility Ernie had married Becky Rayburn. The many times he'd discussed Becky with the big guy, Ernie had shown no interest whatsoever. The fateful night at the carnival, Ernie seemed to have a greater affinity for shooting free throws than buying kisses from pretty girls. Maybe back then Ernie had felt a little more comfortable tossing a basketball into a hoop. So, Ernie Craft married Becky Rayburn. Good for him. No, good for them.

Hank cleared his throat. "I heard what happened to Ernie."

Becky took a deep breath and nodded as she blew it back out. "Grandma told me."

"It's been a little over a year," Becky said, bouncing her baby gently up and down. "But it's still pretty tough."

"I bet."

"Ernie wanted a son so bad." Becky sighed then forced a barely noticeable smile. "He never even got to see him."

Hank dropped his head. He couldn't even begin to imagine how she must feel.

The jingling bell over the door surprised both Becky and Hank, but Little Ernie's eyes lit right up. He laughed and clapped his hands when he saw the tall, balding man in bib overalls and a bright red western shirt walk through the door. The old fellow made a beeline for Becky and the baby, saying, "I'm gonna get you. I'm gonna get you." This seemed to amuse the already delighted youngster even further.

Little Ernie extended his arms, and the man reached across the counter and took him with a hearty laugh. He held the child high and gave him a little shake, resulting in immediate squeals of approval. The connection between the two was undeniable.

"Mr. Craft," Becky said, gesturing toward Hank. "This is Hank Goodman. Mr. Jake Taylor's grandson."

Moving the child to his left arm, Homer Craft reached out with his right. "Nice to meet you, son."

"Nice to meet you, Mr. Craft."

Now Hank knew where his friend got his height. The elder Craft had to be every bit of six-four, maybe six-five. Hank couldn't help wondering if Mrs. Craft was tall as well. Hopefully, at some point, he'd get to meet her, too.

"My boy used to talk about you all the time." Homer's face had lit up, his son's memory obviously touching a soft spot deep in his heart. "You're from Detroit, right?"

At the question, Hank flashed back to five years earlier in back of the same feed and seed store. Ernie's dad had just said Dee-troit, pronouncing it the same way his son had so very long ago.

Homer Craft continued. "Ernie loved baseball. My boy used to eat, drink, and sleep Detroit Tigers. Lots of nights when he was supposed to be asleep, I'd ease up to his bedroom door and he'd have the ballgame on the radio."

"My parents named me after one of the players."

"Ernie told me." Homer redirected his attention to Becky. "I'll stay with the little man here if you want to run get a bite. I never even thought about bringing you something back."

Becky slapped both hands lightly on the countertop. "Would you like to run grab a burger with me?" she said to Hank. "I'm starving."

"I'd love to."

"Let me grab my purse."

~

HANK AND BECKY LOADED UP IN HER TRUCK, AND SHE DROVE THEM to the Tasty Cream. In front of the little eatery, he asked what she wanted to eat and then climbed out to place the order. The gray-haired lady inside, wearing an all-white uniform and a suspicious, menacing frown, slid a pencil out from behind her ear and narrowed her eyes. While he dictated his request, she huffed and scribbled it all down on a small, green, lined pad. She told him in no uncertain terms it would take at least fifteen minutes and he could either wait in the truck or stand there at the window. Didn't matter to her one way or the other. She'd let him know as soon as the order was ready. Hank opted for the truck and the company of Becky.

Over the past five years, Hank had tried to convince himself he'd only left to make it easier for his grandparents. In his heart, he knew he would have gladly stayed if Becky had offered any encouragement at all. But she hadn't, and he didn't.

Hank had always assumed Becky would be married by now. Married and maybe even living somewhere far away from Crosscut. But here she was, still in the same little town and still just as lovely.

So, Becky had married Ernie Craft, and he had been killed. She'd had a baby and named him after her late husband. It would take a while for all the information to process.

"Fifteen minutes," Hank said, hopping back into the truck.

Becky tucked her hair behind her ears as she nodded.

Knowing Becky had endured terrible tragedy in the not too distant past still didn't negate the fact she was one of the most gorgeous women he'd ever laid eyes on. Detroit and Denver both had their share of beauties. But in his mind, none held a candle to Becky. Right or wrong, she was the standard by which he judged all others.

Hank cocked his head. "Remember the first time I rode in a pickup with you?"

"I certainly do."

Borrowing a phrase from Ada, Hank said, "Wasn't that something?"

Becky chuckled. "It was something all right."

"When I told you who I was, you couldn't get rid of me fast enough."

"Things were a lot different back then," Becky admitted. "I was young and still living at home."

Hank couldn't help wondering if Bill Rayburn—or Bill's father—had softened their stance any since Jake passed away. "What do you think your dad would say now if he saw us together?"

"If he knew who you were, you'd be Jake Taylor's grandson and nothing else would matter. But I'm a big girl now. And he knows it."

Sighing, Hank said, "I can't understand how Grandpa could be a Christian and still hold a grudge for all those years. If Christianity is a religion of forgiveness, I can't help wondering why he never did."

"Just because we're Christians, doesn't mean we're perfect," Becky said.

"Maybe you're right."

"What I can't understand is why Daddy feels the way he does.

I mean—it was Grandpa's sister who drowned, and Daddy never even knew her."

Hank threw his hands up slightly. "It's important to his dad, so it's also important to him."

"I guess so," she agreed with a shrug.

If Becky didn't want to share the information, Hank could understand. Still, he couldn't help wondering what chain of events led to her and Ernie getting together. Of all the different scenarios Hank had tossed around over the years, their being a couple was one he'd never even considered. If she didn't want to talk about it, surely she would tell him.

"Can I ask you a question?" Hank said.

"Sure."

"How did you and Ernie end up together?"

Becky eyes brightened and she coughed into her hand. "A few months after you left, Daddy sent me by Craft's to pick up a couple of things. Ernie was working the front counter, and when I asked if he'd heard anything from you, he said he hadn't. We talked for a while, and then it suddenly struck me just how handsome he was. Not to mention the sweetest person you'd ever want to meet."

Hank nodded. He knew that to be a fact.

"To make a long story short, I wasn't dating anybody at the time, and since there were no others in the store, I asked if he wanted to go out with me."

"You mean you asked him?" Hank said with a chuckle.

"I know." Becky threw her hands up slightly. "I couldn't believe it myself. Just sort of popped out."

"You think it scared him?"

"It probably did." Becky wrinkled her nose. "Just a little."

"So, what did he say?"

"Oh, you know Ernie. He said, 'Sure. Why not?'"

It was exactly the sort of thing Hank could have heard the big guy saying. Now he wanted to hear the rest of the story.

"So, what happened next? You guys went out and…"

Becky nodded. "One date led to another, and pretty soon we were madly in love."

"And I guess the rest is history."

"Not exactly."

Hank frowned, not expecting this development.

"We dated for about a year, and then Ernie graduated and went off to college. I still had a year of high school left and finally it got to the point where we rarely ever saw each other. Then, we sort of started to drift apart. Ernie came home one weekend, we talked a while, and then afterward broke the whole thing off. We agreed to stay friends and nothing more."

"So, what did you do then?"

"Do you remember Carl Walker?"

"No," Hank said, rubbing at his forehead. "The name doesn't ring a bell."

"He's the guy who jumped you the night of the carnival."

It being dark when the confrontation took place, Hank never got a good look at the guy. But he definitely remembered. Five years later, he would more than welcome a rematch. At the time, he was just a scrawny teenager, and Walker had caught him off guard. Now, it would be a completely different story.

"Oh, him," Hank said dryly.

Becky nodded. "Idiot I was, after me and Ernie broke things off, I hooked back up with Carl. By the time I realized what a mistake I'd made and I still loved Ernie, I had already gotten in way too deep."

"So, how'd you get out?" Hank said, shifting positions in the seat.

"One Saturday night, me and Carl and couple of our so-called friends were parked on the courthouse square. Carl always considered himself a tough guy but he'd had a few beers and was feeling ten feet tall and bulletproof. Then he saw Ernie's car pull in here at the Tasty Cream."

Hank didn't know how this story would end but he knew exactly where it was headed. "Go on."

"Ernie got out to place his order, and Carl started yelling at him, telling him he was gonna come over there and kick his—well, you get the picture. Anyway, Ernie did his best to ignore him but, finally, I guess he just got fed up with it. Carl didn't even have to bother crossing the street. Ernie came to him."

Hank had witnessed Ernie Craft pick up a hundred-pound sack of chops and toss it into the back of a pickup like it was nothing. And at the summer carnival, he'd done the same thing to Carl Walker. Hank's old friend had nailed it down himself. "Nobody messes with Big Ernie."

"So, what happened next?" Hank said, crossing his arms. He had a feeling things were about to get good.

"Carl just wouldn't shut up, and when I grabbed his arm, he slapped me as hard as he could."

"He slapped you?"

"Right across the face."

Hank narrowed his eyes. He had never hit a woman and never would. The fact Carl Walker would told him pretty much all he needed to know. In all likelihood, his slapping Becky was something Carl still wished he could take back.

"Worst mistake he could have ever made," Becky said. "Ernie picked him up by the throat and before the other guys could pull him off, he had slapped Carl about five times. Just like Carl slapped me."

"Did anyone call the police?"

"One town cop and a deputy sheriff showed up. Carl kept rubbing at his face, saying he was going to have Ernie arrested. I told the police if he pressed charges against Ernie, then I was pressing charges against him. Once Carl got wind of what I said, he decided just to go on home. Since he'd been drinking, they called his daddy to come pick him up. One of the other guys drove Carl's car. Needless to say, Ernie took me home."

"What did your dad think about it?"

"He never found out. If he had, he would've probably killed Carl."

"Your face wasn't bruised?"

"Just a little," she said, "but I kept it covered up pretty good with makeup."

"So, after that, the rest is history?" Hank asked cautiously.

"After that, the rest is history."

CHAPTER FOURTEEN

*F*ifteen minutes ended up being more like twenty. Hank and Becky had been so wrapped up in their conversation, they hadn't given the food a second thought. They also hadn't noticed the snaggle-toothed young fellow who'd just walked up to the passenger side window until he tapped lightly on it. Hank rolled the window down.

"Miss Wanda Jane said to tell y'all if you want this mess while it's still hot you better get on up here and get it."

Hank laughed out loud. "She said all that?"

"Yes, sir. And she gave me a whole nickel to come tell y'all."

The boy started to walk off when Hank called him back. "Hold up a second." Hank dug a quarter out of his pocket and handed it to the lad for his trouble. Thirty cents richer, the young fellow ran all the way back to the dark blue hardtop parked three spaces down.

The second time Hank walked up to the little sliding-glass window, he fully expected to face the wrath of an angry Miss Wanda Jane. And, he did. She scowled and said, "If this stuff's cold, I don't want to hear nothing about it. I've been standing up here waving like a maniac for ten solid minutes, and neither one of y'all would even look up. You owe me two dollars and seventy-five cents." She took Hank's money, rang up the total, and handed him his change. Not one time did she crack a smile or offer so much as even a "thank you." Hank bit his tongue and quietly walked away.

Shaking his head from side to side, Hank set the grease-stained paper sack on the red vinyl seat between himself and Becky. "Boy, she's a real piece of work," he said. "Wonder what's eating her?"

"She's just an old sourpuss," Becky confirmed. "Been that way ever since I can remember. If you can overlook her, the food here's pretty good."

"If it tastes as good as it smells," Hank said, "we should be in for a treat."

Both of them had ordered the deluxe cheeseburger, fries, and a chocolate shake. When Hank asked what made a regular cheeseburger a deluxe, Becky said a deluxe had two slices of melted cheese where the regular only had one. The battered French fries were, according to Becky, the tastiest and crunchiest she'd ever eaten.

Hank wanted to find out more about Ernie's accident and hear an account other than his grandmother's. Accidental firearm discharges were probably not uncommon, especially in rural areas where hunting was so prevalent. Even in Vietnam, it wasn't unusual for soldiers to be wounded occasionally. Guys dropping pistols, cleaning loaded weapons, and just general carelessness. Luckily, most of the incidents he'd heard about were non-fatal. Not wanting to upset Becky, he'd approach the subject as gingerly as he could.

Taking a big bite of his burger, Hank chased it down with a generous sip of chocolate shake. "I'm glad you and Ernie got together. It's just hard to believe he's gone."

"I know," Becky said, the sparkle quickly disappearing from her eyes. "Biggest shock of my life."

"How did you find out?"

"Sheriff Mayes told me."

"Grandma said Mr. Craft found him."

"Another terrible part of this whole thing. It was getting late in the day, and I hadn't heard a word from Ernie. When I called Mr. Craft, he said he hadn't either but would take a ride and see if he could spot Ernie's truck."

Hank nodded.

"Once he found the pickup, it was only a matter of time before he found Ernie. Like to have killed his daddy, too."

"I'm sure it did," Hank said.

"Can you imagine?"

"Grandma said Ernie was crossing a fence, and they think his dog knocked the gun over."

"The sheriff said it wasn't the first time he'd seen something like that happen."

Hank took a deep breath and blew it back out slowly. "Grandma said he took the gun in case he saw a snake."

"Ernie was deathly afraid of them, and I am, too. He always took a gun with him."

"I bet he liked to hunt, too."

Becky nodded emphatically. "Oh, he was crazy about it. Rabbit, squirrel, deer. Didn't matter to Ernie. He just loved being outdoors."

Hank dropped the rest of his burger and fries back into the sack. The food wasn't bad, he just hadn't been as hungry as he'd thought. He'd hold on to the shake and finish it off while he and Becky continued their conversation.

"Where is Ernie buried, if you don't mind me asking? I'd like to go by sometime and pay my respects."

Becky pointed straight ahead. "Craft Cemetery. About two miles east of here on Craft Road."

Hank didn't know why he found it a little surprising the

Crafts had a road and a cemetery named after them. He didn't have long to wait for further clarification.

"It's the family cemetery," she said. "The Crafts have been in Lee Parish for more than a hundred years. They own quite a bit of property out where we live."

"Wow."

Becky sighed. "You know what's funny though?"

"What?"

"I can't remember much of anything about Ernie's funeral. It's all like one big blur to me now. I know a lot of people were there and I hugged a bunch of necks. But, apart from family, I couldn't tell you who came and who didn't. Same thing for his visitation the night before."

"I'm the same way about some of the things I went through in Vietnam. Maybe it's just a built-in coping mechanism of some sort."

Hank wasn't about to tell her he woke up in a cold sweat most nights, shouting after a dream so terrifyingly real it was like being there all over again. Each time, it would be exactly the same, and he'd have to relive the agony of helplessly watching his best friend take his last, long, labored breath. He often wondered how long the dream would haunt him and if he'd have to deal with it the rest of his life. The thought of such a thing shook him to his core.

"Must have been quite an ordeal." Becky cleared her throat. "Being in the war, I mean."

"A lot of good men have lost their lives over there. Hopefully, it'll all be over soon, and the rest of our guys can come home."

"What branch of the service were you in?"

"Army."

"I hate to say it," she said glumly, "but a lot of people in this country don't appreciate our soldiers. It's not too bad around here, but I've seen some pretty awful things on television."

Hank nodded, directing his attention to the window by his

head. "What they don't seem to understand is soldiers follow orders. It's what they do. They go where they're told and do what they're told. None of the guys I met ever asked to be over there." He turned back to Becky. "I'll tell you what I think. The ones who don't appreciate our troops are the ones who've never had to fight for anything their entire life. They take their freedoms for granted then sit around all fat and happy, criticizing the ones who do their fighting for them."

Hank realized he'd gotten upset, and from his tone, Becky had probably picked up on it as well.

"I bet you're glad to be home," she said, somewhat changing the subject.

You have no idea, he thought. *Especially here.* "I am," he confirmed.

Becky took another petite bite of her burger. After giving her time to wash it down, Hank said, "So where do you live now?"

"We—I have a house on Craft Road, too. Matter of fact, it's just down the road from Mr. Homer. It's the one they lived in before they built their new one. It's a little on the small side, but I absolutely love it." She dropped her head slightly. "We were planning on building a bigger one in a few years. As soon as we could save up the money. We had such big plans for the future, but now none of that's ever going to happen."

Seeing the emotion starting to sweep over Becky, Hank knew it was his turn to redirect the conversation. "So, were you working at the store before Ernie's accident?"

Becky cleared her throat again. "A little," she said. "Once I got pregnant, Ernie wouldn't let me do much of anything."

"What about now? Are you full-time or part-time?"

"Full-time. Ernie dropped out of college to come home and help his daddy with the store. After he died, I wanted to do all I could so Mr. Craft wouldn't have to hire any more help. We could use some now, but we just can't afford it."

"What about Mrs. Craft? Does she work, too?"

Becky shot him a funny look. "Mrs. Louise? Not hardly. She's a sweet lady but strictly a homebody. She's offered to keep Little Ernie for me while I work, but I want him with me as much as possible."

"That's understandable."

"Of course, when he gets a little older I'll have to either leave him with her or hire a babysitter. For now, he can stay in his playpen at the store, and I can keep an eye on him myself."

Hank couldn't help wondering how big Little Ernie might turn out to be. His dad had been six-six. His mother, somewhere around five-five, five-six. But then, Homer Craft was a tall man, too.

"You think Little Ernie'll be tall like his dad?"

"Wouldn't surprise me any," she said. "Kind of runs in the family—the Craft family, I mean."

Hank had only wanted to talk about Becky and Ernie. To find out what had been going on with them since he left. He never wanted the conversation to be about him. Becky, however, had other ideas.

"So, what about you?" she asked. "I know you were in the army but not much else."

Hank shrugged. "Not a lot to tell, actually."

Becky cocked her head and narrowed her eyes. "You never got married?"

"Who, me?" he said, suddenly realizing how stupid it sounded since only the two of them were in the truck.

"Yes, you, silly."

"No. I never got too involved with anyone."

"Surely you had girlfriends."

"I had a couple of—well, only one I ever got serious about."

How could Hank forget the one-page letter he'd received from Debra Sue Mills just a couple of months after arriving in Vietnam? Other than Becky, she'd been the only girl he ever cared about on somewhat of a deeper level. He knew all along, however, that Debbie had wandering eyes. The letter then hadn't come as much of a surprise. When he made it back home, he found out she'd hooked up with a used car salesman who'd somehow managed a military deferment and they were now happily married. Well—married anyway.

"Didn't work out."

"Oh," she said.

"It happens," Hank said, throwing both hands up. "Just one of those things."

Becky hadn't been able to finish all her food and dropped her leftovers in the paper sack along with Hank's. Hank hopped out of the truck and tossed the bag into the open-top, fifty-five-gallon trash barrel sitting in front of the building. The entire time, Wanda Jane watched him like a hawk.

When Hank climbed back into the truck, Becky said, "I'd better be getting on back. Mr. Craft'll think I got lost or something."

"You're probably right."

"Plus, Miss Wanda Jane's been known to run people off when they stay too long. Her motto is 'Give me your money, eat your food, and then hit the road.'"

Hank laughed out loud.

"Don't laugh," Becky said, shaking her head slowly. "She's been known to chase teenagers off with her broom. Some of them say they've seen her flying around on it, too. Especially when there's a full moon."

"Maybe she does," Hank managed, laughing even louder.

Becky started up the truck and shrugged. "Maybe so." She shifted into reverse. "Wouldn't surprise me one little bit."

CHAPTER FIFTEEN

*B*ecky held the front door open for Hank and watched from the porch as he carefully navigated the blue concrete steps with his grandmother's fifty-pound block of salt. Just before he made it to the rear of the truck, she noticed the tailgate wasn't down and he'd never be able to open it without a little help. She'd have to do it for him.

"Hold up!" Becky shouted, rushing down the steps. "Let me give you a hand with the tailgate."

Hank looked on with both hands full as she unhooked the chain on the right. Hurrying to the other side, she did the exact same thing. Not sure if he was in a bind, she quickly lowered the tailgate then reconnected the left side chain to hold it securely in place.

"Now, then," Becky said, rubbing her hands together briskly.

After sliding the salt block into the bed of the truck as far as his arms could reach, Hank closed the tailgate and reconnected the chains. He thanked Becky for the help, and as he climbed up into the cab, said to her, "I certainly enjoyed our visit today." He turned the key, and the old truck came to life. "See you later."

Becky nodded then headed back up the steps. At the top, she

waved goodbye, but Hank was already backing out. Looking over his shoulder, he had never even seen her. Sighing and embracing herself, she watched in silence as the old truck slowly picked up speed and then finally faded out of sight.

"See you later," Hank had said. Did he honestly mean those words, or was he simply repeating the same old parting cliché folks used every day without giving it a second thought? Time would tell, she guessed.

Earlier in the day, when Becky had realized it was Hank standing on the other side of the counter, she'd momentarily been at a loss for words. Though his appearance wasn't exactly the same—taller, thicker through the chest, and broader through the shoulders, hair a good bit shorter—she'd recognized him immediately. And when he smiled, her heart fluttered just as it had five years earlier. The day she picked up a good-looking young hitchhiker walking down a hot, bubbly Louisiana blacktop.

Becky knew then she had feelings for Hank, but in the foolishness of youth, she'd overreacted to certain things and pretty much pushed him right out of her life. By the time she realized her mistake, the damage had been done and he had already left for Colorado.

If Hank had stayed in Crosscut, Becky couldn't help wondering how much different her life would have been. Surely, they could have worked around her daddy's stubbornness. Even if it meant going behind his back like Hank had suggested. Maybe they could have pulled it off until they were old enough that it simply didn't matter anymore. By the time he finally found out, they would have been madly in love, and marriage would have been inevitable. But it had been all her fault. She'd been the one too afraid to even try.

Becky stuck her head in the office door and, seeing Little Ernie still sleeping soundly, a feeling of satisfaction worked its way from the top of her head to the tip of her toes. Regardless of all the ifs, maybes, and might have beens in her life, she'd fallen in love with a wonderful man, and together they'd created a beautiful baby boy. When it was all said and done, things had worked out exactly the way they were meant to. Oh, how she missed her husband.

Though it had been a little over a year since Ernie's untimely death, Becky still lay awake at night thinking about it. Wondering why something so terrible had to happen to him. Why it had to happen to them. Losing her husband had been devastating enough, but the thought of her son growing up without a father —his own father—was almost too much to bear. Just recently, when her mother told her she was still a young woman and needed to get on with her life, Becky took exception. She'd grabbed Little Ernie up and left her parents' house hurt and angry. An entire week had passed since then, and she hadn't spoken to either one of them.

How long did it take to get over the loss of a loved one? A year? Two years? Five years. Never? Her grandfather's sister died some fifty years ago, and he hadn't gotten over it yet. Becky had thought long and hard about her mother's words. Right now, she simply wasn't ready to move on. And nothing was going to change the way she felt. Why in the world did Hank Goodman have to come back now and complicate things?

Becky had never said a word about Hank to her mother. As far as she knew, Susan didn't even know he existed. Since he'd come back, and his grandfather had passed away, maybe Becky could confide everything to her. After work today would be the perfect time.

The first thing she'd do was apologize for overreacting the previous week. Then she'd tell her mother the Hank Goodman story in its entirety. How she'd picked him up hitchhiking and how, in fearfulness of her father, she'd pretty much run the poor boy off.

~

WITH LITTLE ERNIE SQUIRMING IN HER ARMS, BECKY KNOCKED anxiously on her parents' front door. Her mother, a forty-plus version of herself, answered in short order, clapping her hands and making no attempt to conceal her excitement.

"There's my baby," Susan said enthusiastically. "I have missed you so much." She was not referring to her daughter.

Susan took Little Ernie and squeezed him tightly. Becky honestly did feel guilty about not coming around for an entire week. She'd kept him from his grandparents when she knew it wasn't the right thing to do.

"Come on in," her mother said. "I haven't seen y'all in ages."

Becky frowned. "It's only been a week, Mama."

Susan sighed. "I know, but it sure seems a lot longer."

If her mother had a significant shortcoming, it would be her tendency to exaggerate. She didn't mean any harm by it; it was just something she did. Something she'd always done. The family had grown so accustomed to it over the years, now they pretty much expected it.

"Come on in the kitchen," Susan said. "I just set a pan of blueberry muffins out to cool, and they'll be ready to eat shortly."

The bluish stains on the white cooking apron over her bright yellow sundress had already given it away. Trailing along behind her mother, Becky said, "They're my favorite, you know."

Susan chuckled. "Well, ain't that something?"

"What? Blueberry muffins being my favorite?"

"No, silly. How I baked muffins and didn't even know y'all were coming."

As much as she loved her mother's cooking, Becky had stopped by for completely different reasons. They sat down next to each other at the small breakfast table, Susan bouncing Little Ernie on her knee.

Becky glanced down at the fingers she had just locked

together. "The other day when I stopped by, you told me I needed to get on with my life."

Susan nodded. "And you got pretty mad about it, if I remember correctly."

"I'm sorry about the way I acted, Mama. I've given it a lot of thought since then and, well, even though I don't agree with what you said, I shouldn't have gotten so upset. You were only trying to help."

"Apology accepted," her mother said, giving Little Ernie a gentle poke in the belly and making him laugh out loud.

Becky sensed the opening and went for it.

"Mama, you probably won't remember, but a few years ago I tried to find out why our family and the Taylors didn't get along."

Susan shrugged, obviously not remembering anything about it at all.

"Anyway, the reason I was asking was..." Becky looked left then right. "I had met this guy."

At that bit of information, her mother's ears perked right up.

Becky then told her about the young hitchhiker she'd picked up and how she'd managed to shoot everything down before it even got off the ground. She told about him moving to Colorado. About joining the army and being in the war. How he'd come back to Crosscut to help out his widowed grandmother.

Susan had listened intently and never once interrupted. Talk about a shock. When she failed to respond at all, Becky finally said, "Well?"

"Well, what?"

"You're not saying anything."

Susan sighed. "What do you want me to say? You've talked to him already, haven't you?"

"He came in the store this morning, and we rode up town to get a burger."

Susan shot her daughter the strangest look and drew back. "Becky Marie."

"What?"

"People are gonna talk," Susan said, transferring Little Ernie to her other knee. "You know how they are."

Becky took a deep breath but blew it out rather quickly. Her mother thought she needed to move on but didn't want her to be seen in public with anybody. Obviously, it bothered Susan much more than it bothered her. "Well, if they can't find anything better to talk about, let them talk."

"Does this boy still have feelings for you?" her mother said, raising an eyebrow.

Becky crossed her arms. "You know, Mama, I guess I forgot to ask. You think I should call him?"

"What about Carl? Didn't you tell me he's been stopping by the store a good bit lately?"

Rolling her eyes in exaggerated fashion, Becky shook her head and said, "I wouldn't touch him with a ten-foot pole, and you know it."

"His family's pretty well off, you know."

"I don't care if they own half the parish."

"They pretty much do," her mother said haughtily.

"I don't care if they own the entire state of Louisiana." Becky crossed her arms in defiance. "I wouldn't be caught dead with him."

When it came to Carl Walker, Becky knew exactly where she stood. Still, she had to give the guy credit. He was persistent to a fault. Even before Ernie died, he would stop by the store when she was there by herself and make somewhat less than subtle suggestions. She'd never mentioned it to her husband because she knew exactly how he would react. After Ernie passed away, Carl's trips by the store became more frequent. It hadn't surprised Becky one bit when she found out his wife, Rita, had run off and left him. She couldn't see Carl being faithful to anyone for too long. Not to mention being meaner than a rattlesnake. Knowing they'd stayed together nearly three years was quite an accomplishment in itself.

"You know your daddy would never approve of this Goodman boy," Susan said, heaving an exaggerated sigh. "Him being related to the Taylors and all."

"There's nothing to approve, Mama, and he's not a boy. Anyway, I'm just telling you this because I thought you might enjoy the story. Me meeting him years ago and him being back in town."

"You know it wouldn't bother me a bit. But your daddy…"

Becky shook her head adamantly. Sometimes, her mother could be the proverbial brick wall. "Listen, Mama. He just stopped by the store this morning to pick up something for his grandma. We rode up to the Tasty Cream, got a burger, and then talked in the truck a little while. Then I went back to work, and he left."

"Uh, huh," her mother said, winking in dramatic fashion.

"If I ever do start seeing somebody, Daddy will be fine with it. Regardless of who it is."

Susan raised an eyebrow. "Oh, he will, will he? How can you be so sure?"

"Because he loves me." Becky crossed her arms and threw in a curt nod. "And he loves his little grandson."

CHAPTER SIXTEEN

*W*hen he left Ada's house earlier, Hank had no idea how the day would unfold. So, Becky Rayburn was the four-months-pregnant wife Ernie had so tragically left behind. Now she had a beautiful baby boy and had named him after his father.

Hank wouldn't even try to convince himself he wasn't still attracted to Becky. Certainly, he felt terrible about what happened to Ernie, but with her being a young woman, at some point she'd probably try to move on with her life. He wouldn't pressure her or anything, but if he ever sensed the time being right, he might just ask her out. She hadn't mentioned being involved with anyone.

One event in a person's life could change everything. If anyone knew about such things, Hank did. Sometimes the changes could be for the better. Other times, not so much. He'd never even dreamed of living in Louisiana. Off course, he didn't know his parents were going to die either. But they did. And him being sent off to Vietnam meant the girl he would have most likely married ended up tying the knot with someone else. Now, with Ernie Craft being tragically killed, Becky's life would never be the same. And neither would her son's.

Ada's old truck ran smoothly until about five miles out of town when Hank felt a sudden, significant jerk. The engine leveled back out, and he blew it off as just an anomaly. The old girl trying to catch her breath. One mile later, the truck jerked again. This time, the engine died completely. Hank stepped on the brake, got the right side tires just off the edge of the pavement, and rolled to a stop.

The distance from Crosscut to Hurt Road was almost exactly ten miles. From the highway to his grandmother's house, another mile and a half down a hot gravel road. Hank had already come six so, yeah, another five and a half miles yet to go. It would be a long, difficult walk under a blistering Louisiana sun. Lugging a fifty-pound block of salt along would no doubt make it feel even longer.

Hank quickly made up his mind. He would walk if he had to, but the bulky chunk of sodium chloride would have to stay behind with the truck. If someone thought they needed it worse than Ada, then so be it. He'd just have to run back up to Craft's later and pick up another one. Assuming they got the truck repaired.

Hank slid the keys in his pocket—though they wouldn't be of use to anyone—and hit the road walking. At that moment, if he could have had anything—not counting a new truck—it would be a hat to cover his exposed head. His old, well-worn boonie would work just fine. Something cool to drink would be nice as well.

After walking nearly a mile, Hank had seen only two other vehicles. Neither of which were traveling in the same direction as him. Both drivers, however, had taken the time to honk their horns and wave enthusiastically as they passed him by. Just because Hank was physically in the best shape of his life didn't mean he wouldn't drop dead from a heat stroke before ever making it back to Ada's.

Hank stopped walking momentarily just to catch his breath. He had just bent at the waist and put both hands on his knees when he heard a vehicle coming up from behind. By the sound of things, whoever it was at least planned to slow down a little as they passed him by. And, no doubt, wave and smile.

Stepping completely off the pavement, Hank figured he should probably take a look. Once he did, he never took his eyes off the black step-side Chevrolet pickup as it came to a stop, and the driver—an older gentleman wearing faded overalls and a stiff, gray straw cowboy hat—took his time climbing out.

"Looks like you might need a ride, young fellow."

Welcome words, indeed. "Yes, sir," Hank said, nodding fervently. "I sure do."

The man extended his hand, wrinkled on the top and calloused the on bottom. "Harvey Ellis."

Hank gripped it firmly. "Hank Goodman, Mr. Ellis. Nice to meet you."

"Don't believe I know any Goodmans." Harvey looked upward, rubbing at his chin. "Not around here anyway."

"I'm not from here."

Harvey furrowed his brow. "I could tell right off. Sounds like you've got a good bit of Yankee in you."

"I'm originally from Detroit."

"Detroit, huh?"

"Yes, sir." Hank couldn't help but chuckle. There it was again. Dee-troit.

"If I didn't know better, I'd swear that old truck back there on the side of the road belonged to Ada Taylor."

At the mention of the familiar name, Hank knew he'd just found a friend. "You're exactly right. She's my grandmother."

"Well, I'll be hornswoggled," Harvey said, pausing slightly between each word. "You must be Linda's boy."

The extreme heat suddenly didn't seem so extreme anymore. This old fellow even knew his mother.

"So, how are you planning on getting Ada's truck home, son?"

"To be honest, I'm not quite sure."

"I've got a pretty decent chain there in the bed of my truck. Let's run back up there and see if we can't drag her in. I'd bet dollars to donuts it's just the fuel filter."

Less than thirty minutes later, they had towed the disabled pickup back to his grandmother's house. Ada walked out onto the porch and covered her mouth with her hand. Seeing her truck hooked to the back of Harvey's must have been quite a shock.

Harvey put his arm out the open window and waved vigorously. "What you say there, Ada?"

Ada pulled her hand away from her mouth and waved back.

Hank unhooked the chain and put it back in Harvey's truck exactly as he'd found it. He thanked the helpful old gentleman for his timely rescue and told him if he ever needed anything, all he had to do was call. Ada stuck her head out the back door and asked Harvey if he'd like to come in for something cold to drink. He declined, saying, "I'd better be getting on along. Got a few things back home need tending to."

∾

HANK PULLED OUT A CHAIR FROM THE KITCHEN TABLE AND dropped down in it. Still hot and somewhat exhausted, he stared straight ahead as Ada poured tea into the two glasses she'd just filled with ice and set down in front of him. He picked one up and took a sip. "So, how well do you know our friend, Mr. Ellis?"

Ada sat next to him and sighed. "Let's see. How well do I know him?" She giggled. "Why I've been knowing Harvey pretty much all my life. We grew up just down the road from each other."

Hank nodded and then took another sip of tea.

"Matter of fact, we were kind of sweet on each other once upon a time," she remembered with a smile. "Before your grandpa came along."

"Did he ever try to win you back?"

"For a while he did, but I'd fallen so madly in love with Jake, Harvey finally gave up and married my younger sister, Evelyn."

Hank set his glass down hard, nearly spitting out his mouthful of tea. "He's your brother-in-law?"

Ada's head bobbed up and down.

"Wow," he said, "I don't guess I even knew you had a sister."

"I had two sisters," she said reflectively. "Evelyn and Doreen."

Hank frowned. Had, in this case, was not a good thing.

His grandmother took a deep breath then blew it out slowly. Growing up in a family of five, she was the only surviving child. "Doreen was only twelve when she died from pneumonia. Evelyn passed away fifteen years ago from breast cancer."

Hank shook his head. She'd had a rougher go of it than he had ever imagined. "I'm so sorry, Grandma," he said, lightly touching her arm. "So, Harvey's been by himself all this time?"

"He has."

"You see him on a regular basis?"

"Once or twice a week he'll stop by and see if I need anything. He's been a great help since Jake passed away."

"I like him," Hank said. "He seems to be a good, honest man."

"He is."

Hank was glad to hear someone cared enough about Ada to keep a check on her. At the moment, though, other issues needed his immediate attention. Hank stood and said, "How much you think a new truck would cost?"

Ada's old pickup could probably be repaired but Hank wanted something more dependable to drive. Something of his own.

"I don't know, son," Ada said with a shrug. "A lot more than I can afford right now."

"I meant for me," Hank confirmed. "I've got some money saved up. I just need to transfer it to one of the banks down here."

Actually, Hank had quite a bit of money saved up. Not only had he managed to hang on to most of his military earnings, on his twenty-first birthday, he'd gained full access to his trust fund. When his uncle sold his parents' house and all its contents, a lump sum payment had been set aside for him. From the fund alone, he had netted close to thirty thousand dollars.

For the next hour, Hank tinkered on Ada's old truck. Since Harvey had mentioned the fuel filter, Hank figured he'd check it out first. Once the engine cooled down, he unscrewed the filter from the carburetor and blew through it rather convincingly. He was amazed at the amount of trash—and what appeared to be water instead of gas—he'd blown out the other end. He screwed the filter back in, crossed his fingers and gave it a try.

The engine turned over at least ten times before even making an effort to start. When it finally did, the old truck roared to life and then purred just like a kitten. Hank marveled at how something so small—among the probably hundreds of other moving and non-moving parts of an engine—could be so important in the grand scheme of things. This, he surmised, could be said of many other so-called "small" things in life.

Excited over his good fortune, Hank headed back inside to share the good news with Ada. She met him at the door with an excited look on her face. Wiping her hands on a dishtowel, she said, "I thought I heard the old girl running."

"Fuel filter," Hank said, nodding. "Just like Harvey said."

Ada glanced upward and clasped her hands. "Praise the Lord."

"Now we've got the truck running, would you like to ride back into town with me?"

"Back to town for what?" Ada asked, looking at him curiously.

"To transfer the money I told you about. Once it's done, I'm headed to the dealership to buy a new truck."

Ada cocked her head. "You're sure?" she said. "You're more than welcome to use mine."

"I appreciate the offer, Grandma, but I'll be needing my own set of wheels. For getting back and forth to work."

"To work?"

"Well," Hank said with a shrug. "I do have to find a job first."

~

ONE HOUR LATER, HANK AND ADA WERE SITTING IN THE LOBBY OF the Crosscut National Bank. One of only two in the town of Crosscut, the small bank had gained national celebrity in 1932 when it was robbed by the infamous outlaw couple, Bonnie and Clyde. During the robbery, young bank teller Cleveland Edwards was abducted at gunpoint. Edwards spent the next two days supposedly carousing with the pair who eventually dropped him off unharmed somewhere around the Dallas/Ft. Worth area. Though forty years had passed, Cleve still happily shared the tale with anyone willing to stop long enough to listen.

They'd been in the bank only a few minutes when the young woman who'd initially greeted them walked up. "Mr. Edwards will see you now," she said politely. She led them across the wide lobby, and Cleve Edwards, now president of the old bank, met them at his office door.

"Ada," he said, greeting Hank's grandmother with a lively hug. "So good to see you."

"You too, Cleve." Ada put her arm around Hank and made the introduction. "This is my grandson, Hank Goodman."

The banker grasped Hank's hand firmly. "Nice to meet you, son. Cleve Edwards."

A big, imposing man, Edwards' cheekbones were high-set and his hairline had retreated close to the back of his head. He wore a suit probably one size too small, and judging from his cherry-red face, his colorful tie came dangerously close to cutting off the circulation to his mostly bald head.

"Have a seat," Cleve said, pointing to a green vinyl couch which—on a good day—might seat three exceptionally thin people. "So, what can I do for you folks today?"

Hank glanced over at Ada, who nodded, then back to Edwards. "I have money in a Denver bank I'd like to transfer here."

The banker took a breath, exhaled, and picked up the gold fountain pen off the desk in front of him. With a raised eyebrow, Edwards said, "And just how much money are we talking about here? A couple hundred? A thousand, maybe?"

"Forty-five thousand," Hank said. "Give or take a little."

Edwards' pen dropped from his hand, and his eyes widened. Looking directly at Hank, he said, "Quite a bit of money." Edwards cleared his throat. "For a young man like yourself, I mean."

Ada's turn to speak up. "Can you help us out, Cleve, or do we need to take our business elsewhere?"

"Now just hold on, Ada." Edwards coughed into his hand. "Certainly, I can. I just have to make a few phone calls first."

Hank left the bank sporting a brand new checking account with a balance of forty-two thousand, nine hundred twenty-seven dollars and fifty-three cents. Not to mention the other three thousand he'd folded up neatly and tucked in his front pants pocket. It was quite a bit of money for a young man, and he planned to use every dollar of it wisely. Next stop, Crosscut Motors.

～

HANK AND ADA'S FEET HAD BARELY TOUCHED THE GROUND WHEN they were approached by a tall man with thin graying hair wearing a white shirt, striped tie, and neatly-pressed khaki pants.

He introduced himself as Alex Stewart and shook hands with them both. Hank told him he wanted to look at a new truck and asked what time the dealership closed.

It surprised Hank to learn the dealership had only four new pickups on the lot to choose from. Two were Chevys. One a solid olive green color and the other, blue with a white top and sides. The GMCs were identical. Both red with white tops and sides. With the exception of the grills, he could see no remarkable difference between the two General Motors brands.

"We're open until you buy your new truck," Stewart said cheerfully. "And, as you can see, we have a pretty good selection."

Four was a pretty good selection? In a town the size of Crosscut, maybe so.

Stewart said, "See one you might be interested in?"

"I do," Hank said confidently. "I'll take the blue and white Chevy."

The tall man chuckled, but just a little. "Don't you want to take her out for a test drive first? See how she handles?"

"What size engine does it have?"

"It has, I believe, a…" He paused just long enough to glance at the sheet of paper in his hand. "A three-fifty. Yes, a three-fifty."

"Does it have an air conditioner?"

"It does have an air conditioner. She's top of the line."

Hank nodded. "The only question, then, is what will you take for it?"

"The sticker on it is thirty-five hundred." Stewart craned his neck to get a better look at Ada's old truck. "Were you looking to make a trade?"

"He won't be trading my truck," Ada said firmly.

"I have three thousand dollars cash in my pocket," Hank said. "Will you take it?"

The salesman nodded slowly then stuck out his hand. "I believe we can work something out, yes sir."

In less time than it had taken to transfer the money, Hank

now held the keys to his own shiny new pickup. He'd never owned a vehicle at all, much less a new one. He was proud but, other than Ada, had no one to share the good news with. Not to mention it was starting to get a little late. Hank would be back in town the next day to trade in his Colorado license and to start looking for a job. Time permitting, he might just run by Craft's and see what Becky thought about his brand new pickup.

CHAPTER SEVENTEEN

*C*arl Walker had been standing in front of Harper's Rexall —talking with Burt Evans and sipping on a tall, icy-cold bottle of Coca-Cola—when Becky Craft's truck passed by. He nearly spewed the mouthful of Coke right into Burt's face when he noticed the guy with the close-cropped hair sitting on the passenger side, a quirky sort of smirk on his face. For the past year, ever since her goofball of a husband managed to get himself killed by his own dog, Carl had been trying to hook up with her himself. And, for the most part, she wouldn't give him the time of day. Now here she was in broad daylight chauffeuring some character around town he'd never even seen before.

Three years earlier, Carl broke down and married Rita Jean Hastings. What a mistake that had been. He figured if he slapped her around enough, sooner or later, she'd get the message and move on. Being a hardheaded country girl, however, she just needed a little extra push. Now, with her out of the picture, he was free to play the field. And there was only one field he was interested in playing.

Carl and Becky had a history going all the way back to high school. Sure, it had been an off and on thing, but each and every time he'd managed to charm his way back into her good graces. At least until Ernie Craft came along. Ernie Craft. What could she have possibly seen in the guy? Oh, well. It really didn't matter now anyway. With him six feet under and Rita long gone, sweet little Becky was his for the taking. Shame she had to go and have the guy's kid and all.

Several times before Ernie died, Carl had stopped by Craft's store. Just to see if he could get a little something going with Becky on the sly. No such luck. And now, even without a husband looking over her shoulder, she'd barely even speak to him. Until today, it hadn't much mattered. With nobody else vying for her affection, Carl had just been biding his time. With some new guy suddenly in the mix, he couldn't afford to wait any longer. The sun wouldn't set on this day until he knew all there was to know about the moron he'd just seen in the pickup with his future bride-to-be.

~

CARL WAITED UNTIL THE MIDDLE OF THE AFTERNOON BEFORE stopping by Craft's. The slowest time of day for most local businesses, it just might be the perfect opportunity to catch Becky at the store by herself. He couldn't believe his good fortune when he pulled up and saw no other vehicles parked out front. Lady Luck was definitely on his side.

Snatching the door open, Carl heard the annoying little bell jingling high over his head. Becky had her back to him, sitting on a three-legged stool in front of a long row of wire bins as she sorted through multi-colored tubes of carpenter's caulk. Before she could even respond to the bell, Carl called out, "Well, hello, darlin'."

"What do you want, Carl?" she said flatly, still going about the business at hand.

Carl moved closer. "Now is that any way to greet an old friend?"

Becky stood as she turned to face him. "And what did you expect me to say? 'Hello darlin' back?"

"Wouldn't bother me none," Carl said.

Becky rolled her eyes. "Yeah, I bet."

Carl stood in place for a moment and studied Becky. She was still just as pretty as ever and not one ounce heavier than she'd been before she let herself go and get pregnant.

"Back to my original question," Becky said impatiently. "What do you want, Carl?"

"I think you already know, sweetie. I want things the way they used to be. Before your dead husband came along and screwed it all up." Carl pointed to Becky then to himself in quick succession. "You and me, baby. You know. Just like old times."

Becky shook her head then turned her attention back to the bins where she'd been working, mumbling something to herself.

"Don't tell me you don't want the same thing." Carl took another step forward. "I know you do. A man knows these things."

"Just keep on dreaming," Becky said, still facing the opposite direction. "It's never going to happen."

Moving quickly, Carl grabbed her by the arm and spun her around. "Oh, really? Wouldn't have anything to do with you riding some guy around town today, would it?"

Becky jerked away. "Let go of me, you idiot."

Carl threw his hands high in the air. "Okay. Okay. I shouldn't have done that. I'm sorry."

"Right on both accounts," Becky said, shaking her arm out. "Especially the last one."

Carl's eyes narrowed. "Just tell me who was in the truck with you today, and I'll leave you alone."

Both hands now firmly on her hips, Becky shot him a hard look. "And what makes you think it's any of your business?"

"When some guy's spending time with my girl, I have a right to know."

Shaking her head and vigorously pointing to the door, Becky said, "You need to go, Carl."

"Not before you tell me what I want to know."

"No, you don't understand. You need to go now."

Carl had just started to reach for Becky's arm again when a loud, booming voice from behind them filled the entire store. "Is everything alright up here?" Homer Craft had walked in from the warehouse in back.

Becky locked eyes with her unwelcome visitor. "Everything's fine, Mr. Craft. Carl was just leaving."

After Carl left, Homer placed a soft hand on Becky's shoulder. "What's going on?"

"Oh, nothing," Becky said to her concerned father-in-law. "You know Carl. Just a big blowhard."

"I don't mean to pry, but didn't Ernie tell me you and him were pretty close at one time?"

Becky bit her bottom lip then let it go quickly. "He was my boyfriend once." She cleared her throat. "A long, long time ago."

Homer heaved a heavy sigh. "They say he used to slap his wife around quite a bit. Before she finally got enough and left."

"I certainly wouldn't put it past him. He did the same thing to me once when we were dating. One night, Ernie had to put him in his place."

Over the years, the Walkers had been valued customers of Craft's Feed and Hardware. Donald, the patriarch of the family, was one of the wealthiest and most respected cattlemen in the state of Louisiana. The same could not be said for his only son, Carl.

The pattern had always been the same. Carl getting into trouble, and his father getting him out. Not just once or twice. Or even every now and then. But time after time after time.

Carl was a one-man wrecking crew who always got his way.

Had it not been for his father and his close circle of friends, he would no doubt be serving time in the state penitentiary or even worse.

Some of Carl's friends believed he had nine lives. He had managed to survive numerous car wrecks, boating accidents, and even an infamous single engine plane crash that killed two of his best friends. He was a hothead, well known for his quick and violent temper. He'd been arrested countless times over the years for fighting and disturbing the peace. Each time only to be bailed out by his father. By intervening, Donald never seemed to realize he wasn't doing his reckless son any favors.

"You watch yourself around Carl," Homer said. "I hear tell he's a heavy drinker and I trust him about as far as I can throw him."

Becky nodded in absolute agreement. She knew Carl Walker like a book.

~

CARL OPENED THE DOOR OF HIS PICKUP, SWUNG HIMSELF IN, AND slammed the steering wheel hard with both hands. Just his luck, old man Craft showing up and cramping his style. Becky was just being a stubborn, hardheaded brat. A few more minutes alone with her and she would have been eating out of his hand.

One of the biggest mistakes Carl had ever made was slapping Becky in front of Ernie. At the time, she was completely over the guy. All he'd accomplished was driving her right back into the big meathead's arms. Otherwise, he would have never been stuck with the likes of Rita Jean Hastings in the first place.

Rita grew up in Arkansas, the oldest in a large and dirt-poor family of sharecroppers. Her mother died when she was young and later, at only sixteen, she'd been forced to quit school to help support her low-life father and five other useless siblings. Relocating to Crosscut, she took a two-bit waitressing job at the Twelve Point Café. Rita sent most of her money home, and still her family barely managed to scrape by. She wasn't the sharpest tool in the shed by any stretch of the imagination, but she was pretty easy on the eyes. No matter how you sliced it, Rita was no Becky Rayburn. Not by a long shot.

For three long, grueling years, living with Rita had been nothing but a nightmare. Carl often wondered if other men felt the same way. Longing for the woman they actually loved while being stuck in a marriage with some second rate, last minute substitute.

But now, Rita was gone. Good riddance. With her out of the way, it would be smooth sailing from here on out. Regardless of the guy he'd seen in the pickup with Becky. Just another bump in the road he'd end up running right over.

～

HANK HADN'T NEEDED A ROOSTER OR AN ALARM CLOCK TO WAKE him. He'd slept two, maybe three hours, and it had absolutely nothing to do with the dream. He had a lot to do that morning and couldn't get any of it off his mind. And then there was Becky.

The first order of business would be to change his driver's license from Colorado to Louisiana. Shouldn't be a problem. He still dreaded having his photograph taken. No particular reason. Next would be his dreaded job search. Something he certainly wasn't looking forward to.

Since he joined the military straight out of high school, Hank had never been job hunting in his life and didn't even know where to start. In a small town like Crosscut, he supposed he'd just go door to door until someone said yes. If they said yes. Being new in town certainly wouldn't help his situation any.

And where in the world would he start? What practical skills did he even bring to the table? Of all the things he'd learned in the army, which of them would be of any use in civilian life? Sure, he could shoot an M-16 rifle with deadly accuracy. He could take one apart and put it back together in a matter of minutes. He could even open a can with a P-38 can opener. All valuable skills for a soldier. But he wasn't a soldier any more.

Ada had suggested Hank stop by and talk to the sheriff. Maybe fill out an application. She'd known Abel Mayes since he was a child and would certainly put in a good word if Hank wanted her to. Hank told her he didn't know, but would give it serious consideration on his way into town.

Changing states on his driver's license went off without a hitch. Not counting the fact that it took nearly an hour to complete the simple process. With his first task solidly behind him, Hank could spend as much time as he needed looking for a job. Surely someone was hiring.

Hank went to five different places and each time, the response was exactly the same. "Check back with us later."

What was he supposed to do? Not a soul in town was hiring. Or at least they weren't hiring him. Hank had even considered the law enforcement thing but wanted to try a few other avenues first. Those avenues, so far at least, had all been nothing but dead ends.

Sitting in his truck—pondering what to do and what he'd already done—Hank was beginning to think a little visit with Sheriff Abel Mayes might not be such a bad idea. He couldn't do any worse with the sheriff than he had already.

Abel Mayes. Hank considered the name, and for some reason, he quite liked it. He thought it sounded like a good name for someone in law enforcement. It had a certain ring to it.

The little parish courthouse at Crosscut sat smack dab in the center of the town square. Four large, round columns graced the front of the old blond brick structure built somewhere closer to the turn of the century than present day. Hank parked in one of the many open spaces and climbed out of his truck.

Hank quickly located the door marked "Sheriff's Department," opened it up, and went inside. There behind a counter stood a smiling older lady wearing a starched khaki uniform shirt and dark green skirt. Over her left pocket was a five-pointed golden star. Over the right was a rectangular gold nametag with the name "Erma Frost" printed on it in bold, black lettering. In addition to his law enforcement duties, Ada had told Hank, the sheriff was also responsible for collecting property taxes. More than likely, the job belonged to her. That and welcoming curious visitors such as himself to the sheriff's office.

"Hello there," Hank said, trying to remain cheerful after a frustrating morning of rejection after rejection. "Is Sheriff Mayes in?"

Erma eyed him closely, probably accustomed to answering questions from strangers off the street. "He is," she said. "Do you have an appointment?"

Hank shook his head. "No, ma'am."

"How about a name? Got one of those?"

Erma Frost chuckled under her breath at her own question. But Hank didn't mind. Long as he got to see the sheriff.

"I do," he said. "I'm Hank Goodman."

"I'll see if he's busy."

Less than five minutes later, Hank found himself eye to eye with Sheriff Abel Mayes.

Not a young man by any means, Mayes appeared to be around forty-five to fifty years old, stood maybe five-foot-eight, and weighed at least a couple hundred pounds. His thick dark hair held only the slightest touch of gray around the edges and probably hadn't seen a comb in at least a couple of days. He was broad and thick through the shoulders, and his face bore a strong, determined look. The man fit the part to perfection. He left little doubt that he was the duly elected sheriff of Lee Parish, Louisiana.

"Abel Mayes at your service," he said kindly, extending his right hand.

Hank gripped it firmly as the two men shook. "Hank Goodman."

"I wondered if you were going to stop by and see me."

Hank frowned momentarily, a little surprised. Then, it hit him. "Grandma called, didn't she?"

"She did, son, but don't say anything to her about it." Mayes chuckled. "I've been knowing Mrs. Ada since I was knee high to a grasshopper."

Hank followed Mayes into his office and took a seat in the oversized brown leather chair across from the sheriff's desk. The wall behind it displayed the various plaques and certificates of achievement the lawman had accumulated over the years. Prominently displayed on the desk was a picture of him in civilian attire with his arm around a lovely, petite woman of about the same age. Her auburn hair was thick and long, her eyes dark and penetrating. Another smaller frame held a photo of two children, a boy and a girl of about nine or ten. Based on their ages, he could only assume the little cuties were the sheriff's grandchildren.

Mayes leaned back in his chair and locked his fingers together. "Mrs. Ada's already told me a good bit about you. Said you're fresh out of the army and looking for a job."

"Yes, sir," Hank said, nodding. "Pretty much sums up my life at the moment."

"I like hiring young men who've been in the service." Mayes leaned forward in his chair. "They're the ones you can depend on. Matter of fact, I'm an old Navy man myself."

So, they had a military connection. It certainly couldn't hurt his chances.

"And what draws you to law enforcement?"

Hank glanced around the room before answering. "I'm a little embarrassed to say it, Sheriff, but this wasn't exactly my first choice. No one else around town seems to be hiring at the moment."

Mayes fell back in his chair and his face lit up. "I see," he said with a chuckle.

Before Hank could continue, Mayes leaned forward for the second time and cut him off. "Good answer. I halfway expected you to say you'd wanted to be a policeman all your life and this would be the perfect opportunity to make your dreams come true."

Hank drew in a breath and shook his head. Not the case at all.

"Above everything else, I expect my deputies to be honest."

"I've got no reason to be otherwise," Hank said. "My life's pretty much an open book."

Mayes leaned back in his chair again, hands out in front, bumping his fingertips together. After about thirty seconds of silence, he stopped abruptly and smacked his lips. "I like you, Hank. And it just so happens I have a vacancy. I've been holding on to it for quite a while but—well, to be honest, I just haven't had any qualified candidates."

Hank cleared his throat.

"Tell you what," Mayes said. "Fill out an application. Give me a week or so to check things out. If we don't run into any snags along the way, I'd say you have yourself a job."

CHAPTER EIGHTEEN

*H*is head still in the clouds after a successful interview with the sheriff, Hank drove straight from the court-house to Craft's Feed and Hardware. He couldn't wait to give Ada the news, but being in town, he wanted to stop by and share it with Becky first. Not only would he fill her in on his pending employment, but it would also give him a chance to show off the new truck he'd purchased the previous day.

Hank entered the front of the store only to find Becky busy with a customer. She acknowledged him with a silent finger wave, and he occupied his time by pretending to study the various nuts, bolts, and washers filling the long, metal rack of bins along the wall. So many nuts, bolts, and washers. So little time.

As soon as Becky thanked the man for his business and bade him farewell, Hank headed toward the counter.

"Good afternoon, madam," he said, picking a catalog up off the counter.

"And good afternoon to you, too, sir."

Hank had convinced himself he could stand in one spot for

quite a long time and just stare at this gorgeous woman. She was oh, so beautiful.

"So, what brings you into town this fine day? Need another salt block already?"

"Not today," he said. "Unfortunately, I've been out job hunting."

"Job hunting, huh?" Becky crossed her arms. "Sure sounds like fun."

Hank shook his head. "You have no idea."

"To be honest, you're right," Becky said. "I've never had to look for a job. Once I married Ernie, this one sort of landed in my lap." She walked over to the office door and peeked inside at her sleeping son. "I know you've been looking. The question is whether you found anything or not."

Hank moved closer to the counter. "It didn't start out too well, I have to admit. But I did get lucky."

"So, you found something," she said, her eyes lighting up. "I'm so happy for you."

"As long as everything checks out, you're looking at Lee Parish's newest deputy sheriff."

"A deputy? Wow. You certainly picked an honorable profession. Daddy said he always wanted to be a policeman, but he had the family farm to look after. Mama wouldn't have stood for it though. She's way too jumpy."

Hank knew as well as anyone police work came with a certain amount of danger. He'd only recently left a place where he'd faced such things on a daily basis. Many times, he felt pangs of guilt—knowing he survived the ordeal when so many of his fellow soldiers had not. Could guilt be the reason the dream interrupted his sleep on such a regular basis? After all, his best friend had been sent home in a body bag.

Steve McMillan's death was one of those things Hank couldn't wrap his head around. Hank wasn't a Christian by any stretch of the imagination, and after two long combat tours, he had made it home safe and sound. Steve, a devout follower of Christ, lost his life on the very first go-around. To Hank, it just didn't make sense.

"If you have a minute," Hank said. "There's something I'd like to show you."

Becky eyed him curiously.

"Won't take long." Hank pointed to the door. "It's right out front."

"Okay."

Becky followed Hank outside and onto the porch. When she saw the brand-new blue and white Chevy pickup parked out front, she clapped her hands like a delighted schoolgirl.

The two of them ran down the steps side by side. At the bottom, Becky said, "So this is yours?"

"It is indeed," Hank replied. "Bought and paid for."

Becky let go of his hand and then ran hers down the side of the truck's still warm hood. "Oh, Hank. It's gorgeous."

Hank stood a little straighter and puffed his chest out a bit. "I thought so, too."

Moving on to the driver's side door, Becky pulled it open. She pushed down on the seat and said, "I love it. When did you get it?"

"Late yesterday."

Hank then told her the story about how he'd left with the salt block and only made it a few miles out of town when Ada's old truck broke down.

"I needed a reliable set of wheels," he said, "and at the time, I didn't know I'd end up driving a sheriff's cruiser. Guess I'll still need a ride to the courthouse every day."

"A deputy friend told me their patrol cars run twenty-four hours a day, seven days a week. When it's time for him to get off, he has to stop by and pick up his relief. Then the guy coming on duty takes him home."

"Sounds like a lot of wear and tear on a vehicle."

Hank showed Becky a few of the truck's features and promised to take her for a ride sometime soon. She agreed and said she'd better get back in the store to check on Little Ernie. And in case the telephone might ring.

Back at the counter, they'd been busy talking and hadn't even noticed Homer come in from the warehouse. "How's it going?" the big man said, walking over to Hank and slapping him on the back.

"Fine, Mr. Craft. How about you?"

"Right as rain."

Becky said, "Hank was just telling me he's going to work for the sheriff's department. And he got a brand new truck."

"Sounds like you've been a busy fellow," Homer said. "When's the new job kick off?"

"It's not guaranteed, but Sheriff Mayes said if everything checks out—probably in a week or so."

The elder Craft glanced down at his feet and shook his head. "Wish I'd known you were looking for a job. I could sure use a little help around this place." He cleared his throat. "No offense to you, Becky. I meant back in the warehouse."

Hank remembered her saying she'd gone to work at the store full time to save Mr. Craft the expense of hiring any additional help.

"Tell you what," Hank said. "Since I'm not doing anything right now, I'd be happy to help out around here. Matter of fact, even if I start my new job, I can still stop by after work. On my days off, I can come up and give you a hand, too. Won't cost you a dime."

Homer's eyes met Becky's, and he nodded his approval. She took a deep breath and then blew it out shaking her head. "We couldn't ask you to help, Hank. It wouldn't be right."

"You're not asking me," he insisted. "I'm volunteering."

Becky said, "No matter how you phrase it, it's still the same thing."

"She's right, son," Homer said. "As good as it sounds, it wouldn't be fair to you."

"With all due respect, Mr. Craft, let me decide what's fair for me?"

Becky's brow furrowed when she said to Hank, "Are you sure about this?"

"I'm very sure."

"Okay, then," Becky said. "When can you start?"

"How about right now?"

"All righty then," Homer said, clamping down on Hank's shoulder. "We just got a big shipment of cattle feed in this morning, and every bit of it needs to be sorted and restacked."

Hank worked at Craft's the rest of the day and the next three days. Being so close to Becky had been great, even though the majority of his time was spent back in the warehouse. Occasionally he would take a break just to stick his head in and say hello.

Near the back of the store, Homer had set up a small wooden table to accommodate some of his older patrons and the children who occasionally accompanied them. Complete with a checkerboard, the table had two straight-backed chairs for the combatants and a high chair made especially for Little Ernie. Each day around eleven, Homer would go up town and pick up lunch for Becky and Hank. While Homer was gone, Becky would put her son in the high chair and feed him. When Mr. Craft returned, he would take the child into the office to play with him. And whether he'd done it intentionally or not, it gave Hank and Becky a certain amount of privacy while they ate. Thankfully, customers rarely showed up during the noon hour.

With each passing day, Hank found himself more and more captivated by Becky. She'd done nothing in particular to encourage him, but just being near her every day was having a tremendous effect. He could only hope, at some point, she might feel some of the same things for him. If he sensed anything positive, he'd take his time and not be pushy. Jake had told him once,

"Anything worth having is worth waiting for." Since he had no plans to go anywhere, he would wait for however long it took.

Late on Friday afternoon, Homer told Hank not to worry about coming in the following day. With it being a Saturday, the store would only be open until noon and what little needed to be done, he could easily handle himself.

"Are you sure?" Hank asked. "You know I don't mind."

Homer slapped Hank on the back. "Don't give it a second thought. We'll just plan on seeing you Monday."

❧

BECKY GENTLY LAID LITTLE ERNIE IN HIS BED AND PULLED THE blanket up snugly around him. She loved watching her young son sleep, his tiny chest rising and falling with each gentle, peaceful breath. Planting a soft, loving kiss on his forehead, she told him goodnight and how much she loved him. In all likelihood, he would sleep until morning. Ernie had always been a good baby, seldom fussing or crying. Becky was thankful. She'd heard horror stories from other parents about how difficult their own children could be at times. Homer had jokingly told her he thought she'd found herself a keeper. She couldn't have agreed with him more.

With her son put to bed, Becky headed to the kitchen table with a large album filled with old photographs. And a box of tissue. Most of the pictures were of her and Ernie during their wedding and the reception. Only a few of them had been taken while they were dating or after they were married.

Becky sat down at the table, and after only one photograph, she began to sob. She continued to cry while viewing the rest of the pictures then closed the album with a heavy sigh. For the longest time, she sat with her elbows on the table and her face buried in her hands. Thinking about Ernie and all the dreams they'd had. Suddenly, she straightened herself, wiped her eyes, and forcefully blew her nose. For her sake, and a certain little blond-haired boy's, the time had come to try and move on. Just like her mother had said.

Maybe it wasn't just coincidence Hank Goodman came back to Crosscut when he did and her being a single mother. Becky would be a fool to try and convince herself she didn't have feelings for him. And they were strong feelings. The more she'd been around him the past several days, the more she'd come to realize just how she felt. It also hadn't escaped her attention how he looked at her. How he conducted himself around her. He had to be feeling some of the same things, too. She just knew it. If only he would be bold enough to make the first move.

Becky would never get over Ernie and, in her heart, knew she wasn't supposed to. He had loved her, and she'd loved him. Still loved him. What happened to her husband had been tragic, but now, he was gone. And nothing she, or anyone else, could do was ever going to bring him back.

~

THE NEXT MORNING, BECKY DRESSED HERSELF AND THEN LITTLE Ernie. Around ten, she loaded him into the truck and headed out for Craft Cemetery. Being only a mile from her house, the drive would be a short one. Getting her son situated in the pickup would no doubt take a good bit longer than the actual trip itself.

After her decision the night before, Becky wanted to stop by and visit her late husband's grave. Regardless of what direction her life would eventually take, she would never forget the man she'd loved with all her heart. The man who had fathered the beautiful child she held dearer than anything else on this earth. She would make sure her son never forgot his daddy. The daddy he would never meet this side of Heaven.

Becky stood next to Ernie's grave in silence. Holding their young son tightly against her, she searched for the right words to say. Unsure where to start, she took a deep breath and began anyway.

"Hey, sweetie. I just wanted to stop by today and say hello. Catch you up on a couple of things. You won't believe it, but Hank Goodman's come back to Crosscut. I know. I can hardly believe it myself. He looks about the same, just a little bigger. Well, and a little older. Ernie, I don't know how to tell you this, so I'll just try to do the best I can. You know I still love you. So, so much. But I've been thinking a lot lately—about Little Ernie and how much he's going to need a daddy."

As she continued, painful, salty tears began to sting her eyes. "I wish you could see him, baby. He looks just like us. A little bit of me and you all mixed in together. I think he's gonna be tall like you."

Becky dropped to her knees, still clutching Little Ernie tightly. Getting through this was so much harder than she'd ever imagined.

"Oh, Ernie. I miss you so much."

For the next several minutes, Becky cried uncontrollably. Until her son started to cry as well. While she tried to console him and regain a little of her own composure, a warm summer breeze brushed lightly across her cheek. Softly, like a gentle, loving breath. Her husband's breath. A strange sense of calm came over Becky, and she exhaled all the air in her lungs. The timing of what had just happened couldn't have been more perfect.

Steeling herself, Becky stood back up. "Don't worry, Ernie. I'll be the best mother I can possibly be. I promise. And I'll never stop loving you. Thank you for letting me know you understand."

CHAPTER NINETEEN

To say Ada was happy about her grandson's decision to join the sheriff's department would have been quite an understatement. The following Sunday, she asked if he would like to attend church services with her, and after quite a bit of coaxing, he reluctantly agreed. The pride in her eyes was evident as she introduced him to the pastor and some of her closest friends. As with anything related to religion, Hank remained skeptical, but he paid close attention to the sermon. The message the pastor offered up had honestly been quite thought provoking. Still, Hank wasn't convinced.

The afternoon sky threatened a thundershower, but none ever managed to develop. An overabundance of clouds, however, had cooled things off significantly. Hank and Ada took advantage of the conditions by sitting out on the front porch and reminiscing about Jake. Ada told him his grandfather had been quite the jokester and shared several humorous stories about him. Hank had no idea Jake had been such a funny man.

Around one-thirty, the sound of a vehicle crunching along the dusty gravel road interrupted Hank and Ada's front porch chat. Only a couple of minutes later, a sheriff's department cruiser pulled up in front of the house and engulfed them in a massive cloud of angry, choking dust.

When the dust finally settled, a tall, lanky deputy of about thirty-five to forty climbed out of the car. With a head full of salt and pepper hair, he stood about six-feet-two, broad and thick through the shoulders. The uniform he wore was neatly pressed, and his collar brass and shoes shined like new money. Hank's initial impression of the guy—probably a former military man himself.

Hank and Ada stood as the deputy walked toward the porch. "How y'all doing?" the officer called out, a broad smile on his face.

Ada gave Hank a slight nudge. "Hey there, Jack. How are Lucy and the boys?"

"They're good, Mrs. Ada."

Jack Slater continued up the steps, and Hank extended his hand. "Hank Goodman."

"John Slater," the deputy said, gripping it firmly. "Folks around here call me Jack."

"Nice to meet you, Jack."

Ada gave Jack a convincing hug. "They call you Jack because your daddy's name's John, too. Am I right?"

Jack nodded. "Yes, ma'am."

"I figured as much. Hank, I've been knowing this fellow since he was just a wee sapling."

The deputy's face reddened, and he coughed into his hand.

Hank could see a pattern starting to develop. Everyone his grandmother introduced him to, she'd known since infancy.

"So, what brings you out this way?" Ada said. "And on a Sunday no less?"

"I could have stopped and called, I guess, but I wanted to come by in person to meet your grandson here." Jack then turned his attention to Hank. "Sheriff Mayes wants you in his office tomorrow morning at nine o'clock sharp to be sworn in. Said to tell you he's sorry about the short notice."

A surprising development to say the least. Hank distinctly remembered the sheriff telling him it would take a week or so. Though completely unexpected, the news was good nonetheless.

Hank said. "I wasn't expecting to hear anything this soon."

"The sheriff said you checked out fine, and he's ready to put you to work."

"I'll go put on a pot of coffee," Ada said. "Give you men a chance to talk in private."

Hank offered Jack the chair his grandmother had been sitting in then sat back down himself.

"I appreciate you coming by," Hank said. "There's something I wanted to ask the sheriff, but I can ask you instead."

"Fire away."

"Any idea what I'll be up against? You know—being young and all."

"I'll be honest with you," Jack said, nodding. "The first thing folks will notice is you're not from around here. And some of them will test you on account of it."

Hank took in a deep breath and blew it right back out. "I can understand," he said. "Me being from up north."

"You look like the sort of guy who can handle himself. The sheriff says you're fresh out of Vietnam."

"I am." Hank wanted to know if his suspicions about Jack were correct. "You were in the service, too, weren't you?"

Jack nodded vigorously. "Spent a year in Korea in '53. Was only eighteen at the time."

Hank had just met the guy, but he liked him already. Just something about him, the way he carried himself. He had a lot to learn, and he'd no doubt learn quite a bit from Jack Slater.

"You'll ride with me for a while," Jack said, "but as soon as they can get you in, you'll go through the basic police academy in Baton Rouge."

Police academy? Wasn't this breaking news. No one had ever mentioned attending an academy. Army boot camp had been bad enough.

"You couldn't be mistaken, could you?"

"No doubt about it. It's on the LSU campus."

"So, how long is this...academy?"

"Six weeks," Jack said, "but you get to come home every weekend."

Not the best news in the world, but what could he do? At least he'd be back on weekends.

"You said I have to be there tomorrow, but when do I actually start work?"

"If the swearing in's tomorrow, I'd say probably Tuesday. It's not up to me, so I can't be too sure."

Hank thought about Becky. Six weeks. It would be a long time even if he did get to come home on weekends. What he'd have to do is make the most of their time together before he ever left.

What Hank wanted to do was to ask her out. And landing a new job might be a good excuse to do it. It would be a legitimate cause for celebration, and who better to celebrate it with than sweet, beautiful Becky? Assuming she'd even agree to such a thing.

Jack rose and slapped both knees. "Guess I'd better get going."

"Don't you want to stay for coffee?" Hank said, standing as well. "Should be ready any minute."

"I'll have to take a rain check. Give my apologies to Mrs. Ada."

"I will."

"See you in the morning at nine. And whatever you do, don't be late. The sheriff doesn't tolerate tardiness."

As the police car disappeared in another massive cloud of dust, Hank couldn't help wondering if he'd made the right decision. Oh well. Too late to turn back now. He'd just have to do the best he could. Hopefully, his best would be enough.

~

HANK DIDN'T SLEEP MUCH AT ALL SUNDAY NIGHT. AROUND ELEVEN, he'd been awakened by the dream, and afterwards, it had been downhill all the way. He'd spent the better part of the night staring at a dark ceiling and wondering how God—if He truly did exist—could sit back and let one of His own perish like He had Steve. It just didn't make sense.

Another thing keeping him awake had been thinking about the law enforcement academy he'd just recently learned about. Six weeks wasn't all that long, but being away for any extended period of time would be difficult. He'd miss his grandmother, of course, but also a certain little blonde and her son he was becoming quite attached to.

Hank wanted Ada there for the swearing-in ceremony and didn't even have to ask. She told him in no uncertain terms she wouldn't miss it for the world.

"You ready, Grandma?" Hank called out from his bedroom.

"I've been ready," she said, rubbing her hands briskly together. "I can't wait."

The drive into Crosscut was quick and uneventful. They'd made the trip in Hank's new truck, laughing and talking all the way. He told his grandmother if plans changed and the sheriff wanted him to go to work immediately, she would have to drive his pickup back home. After witnessing her near miss with the church steps, he honestly hoped she wouldn't have to.

The first order of business was Hank signing a lengthy oath of office. Then having a picture taken for his identification card. Hank cleared his throat uncomfortably when instructed to place his right hand on a Bible, raise his left, and repeat after the sheriff. Fortunately, this oath proved to be a much shorter version than the one he had to sign.

Attending the brief ceremony were Ada, Sheriff Mayes, Chief Deputy Mike Hall, Erma Frost, and Jack Slater. Hank learned Lee

Parish had six deputies, including Jack, who worked patrol, and one full-time investigator. Clyde Hicks, the lone detective, doubled as the department's crime scene specialist and its official photographer.

Chief Hall instructed Hank to come with him, and Ada followed Sheriff Mayes into his office. The chief presented him with a shiny, five-point, star-shaped badge and then measured him for his uniform pants and shirts. Hall said he would order the items before the end of the day, but it would take almost a week to get them in. Same for the nametag. Being almost the exact same size, Jack had brought a couple of his own uniforms to loan to Hank. Hank thanked his new friend profusely for his more than generous offer.

Also issued to Hank was a black leather gun belt complete with a tarnished brass buckle, one pair of handcuffs and case, and a holster for his pistol. He would have to purchase his own pair of black, smooth-toed leather boots. From the bottom drawer of his filing cabinet, Chief Hall dug out a small blue cardboard box and opened it to reveal a four-inch nickel-plated Smith & Wesson Model 19 revolver. This would be Hank's official sidearm, the one he'd have to carry to the range and qualify with.

The chief dropped into the big leather chair behind his desk, and Hank took a seat directly across from him. Jack remained propped against the doorframe.

"I've talked with LSU," Hall said, "and their next academy doesn't start until September 11. That's on a Monday, so you'll need to plan on driving down the day before. We'll give you one of our cars, so you won't have to run up the miles on your new pickup."

Hank listened intently, nodding occasionally. He wasn't thrilled about having to do the Baton Rouge thing. But having it put off until September was good news indeed.

"Until then, you'll be riding with Jack here," Hall said.

When Hank acknowledged Jack over his shoulder, Jack responded with a snappy two-fingered salute.

Hall cleared the phlegm from his throat. "The guy behind you is quite good at what he does. You couldn't have asked for a better teacher."

"So, when do I actually start?"

Chief Hall told him the next day, Tuesday, would be his first on the job. Just as Jack had predicted. They'd be working the six-to-two day shift, and his partner would pick him up around five-forty-five.

～

HANK FINISHED UP HIS BUSINESS AT THE SHERIFF'S OFFICE THEN drove his grandmother back to the farm. He felt a pang of guilt for questioning her driving skills but was still grateful it hadn't been necessary for her to get behind the wheel of his new truck.

Changing into work clothes as quickly as he could, Hank told Ada he wanted to head up to Craft's to see if they needed any help. When she asked why he didn't just call first, he kissed her softly on the cheek, patted her on the shoulder, and told her he'd be home a little later.

Though extremely anxious to get there, Hank drove the speed limit all the way back into Crosscut. Now an officer of the law himself, he needed to set a good example. Hank couldn't wait to get to Craft's to tell Becky he'd officially been sworn in and would be starting his new job the next day. She would be excited for him, too. Of that, he had no doubt.

Pulling up at Craft's, Hank parked in front of the store and next to the only other vehicle there. The black, jacked-up Ford pickup couldn't have been more than a year or two old. Hank had never seen the truck before and had no idea it would soon become one he'd be all too familiar with. One he would come to loathe the very sight of.

Hank walked in just past the door and then stopped. Some guy he'd never seen before was leaning over the counter and doing his best to talk to Becky. From all indications, she was doing her best to ignore him. The guy never even budged when the bell over the door jingled. Sensing the tension, Hank called out in a loud voice, "Hey, Becky! How's it going?"

This got the leaning guy's attention. He stood up straight then spun around to face Hank. A couple of inches shorter than Hank, he had dirty blond hair and icy light-blue eyes narrowed in a cold stare. Slender built with little muscle development, he might have weighed a hundred and fifty pounds soaking wet. Hank felt confident he could handle the guy regardless of his physical attributes. Or lack thereof.

"Well, well, well," blondie said, tossing his head back. "If it ain't Miss Becky's mystery man. The one she likes to drive around town and show off."

"Shut up, Carl," Becky said from behind the counter.

So, this was Carl Walker. The same Carl Walker who'd jumped Hank out behind the Crosscut gym some five years earlier. Carl had managed to shove Hank to the ground and punch him in the face before Big Ernie showed up and saved the day. That night, it was dark and he hadn't gotten a good look at the guy. But now, his face would forever be etched in Hank's mind.

"It's okay, Becky," Hank said.

Carl took two steps forward and then stopped. "You sure made this easy for me, friend. I figured I'd have to come looking for you."

Hank narrowed his eyes. "You must have me confused with someone else. Last time I checked I didn't have any idiots for friends."

"So, you've got a smart mouth, too," Carl said, cocking his head slightly. "You obviously don't know who you're talking to."

"I know exactly who I'm talking to."

Now it was Hank's turn to move forward. Once he got within striking distance, the guy would no doubt throw a punch. Carl didn't disappoint.

In one quick movement, Hank caught Carl's fist in his hand, stopping it in mid-air. Then, he started to squeeze. In Vietnam, sometimes for fun, other times for a friendly wager, the guys would hold strength contests. When it came down to sheer gripping power, no one ever held a candle to Hank Goodman. He never backed down from a friendly challenge, and he'd never lost a contest.

Hank continued to squeeze until Carl dropped to his knees and cried out in pain. "Okay, okay. I'm sorry." Hank squeezed a little harder. "I said, I'm sorry. Now let go of me, you freak."

"Say 'please.'"

"Please."

Hank kept the pressure on for a few more seconds, until Carl's eyes began to tear up. Then, mercifully, he let go.

Still grimacing from the pain, Carl tried desperately to flex the fingers on his throbbing right hand. When he managed to stand, he brushed off the front of his jeans with his good hand and then locked eyes with Hank. "You may not know it, but you just made the biggest mistake of your life."

"I doubt it," Hank said calmly, crossing his arms. "I've made some pretty big ones."

Carl turned back to Becky and stabbed at her with his finger. "I'll deal with you later."

Hank never moved. As Carl stormed past, he said, "And I'll deal with you later too, hotshot. You can count on it."

"Good," Hank said, his brow deeply furrowed. "I'm looking forward to it."

~

As soon as Carl stomped his way out the door, Becky stepped from behind the counter. "I am so sorry."

Hank shook his head. "Don't be. Not your fault the guy's a jerk. What was he doing here anyway?"

"Just before you came in, he demanded to know who you were and what the two of us were doing together. He saw us in my truck the other day and thinks we're dating or something."

A date with Becky was certainly something Hank wasn't opposed to. And, if he played his cards right, he might just be able to make it happen.

"Does he know I've been working here some?"

"I'm sure he does," she said, nodding. "Word travels pretty fast around here."

Hank walked over to the long plastic hanging strips separating the front of the store from the warehouse. He parted them and, when he didn't see any activity, headed back to the counter. "Where's Mr. Craft? I thought he might need a hand today."

"He's been out running errands all morning." Becky checked her watch. "Should be back any minute now."

Hank could see the tiny muscles in her face tightening as they locked eyes. "You need to watch yourself," she said. "Carl will hurt you if he gets a chance."

"Thanks for the heads-up. I'll be careful."

The brief run-in had dampened his excitement just a bit, but he still wanted to share his good news with Becky.

"Everything's official now," Hank said sprightly. "I'm a full-fledged Lee Parish deputy sheriff. Duly sworn to protect and serve."

At the news, Becky's face lit up. "Wonderful, Hank. When do you start?"

"First thing tomorrow morning," Hank confirmed. "Jack's picking me up and we're working the day shift."

Reaching over the counter, Becky gave his hand a firm but gentle squeeze. Before letting go, she said, "I'm so happy for you."

Despite her recent encounter with Carl, Hank couldn't help noticing an upbeat sort of glow about Becky. Not one to beat around the bush, he said, "There's something about you today I can't quite put my finger on. You seem to be more..."

Becky lifted an eyebrow. "At peace?"

"Those are exactly the words I was looking for," Hank said, his head bobbing up and down. "At peace."

CHAPTER TWENTY

*H*ank crossed his arms and with an eyebrow flash, said, "I've been seriously thinking about a little celebration tonight."

"A celebration, huh?" Becky cocked her head slightly. "Meaning?"

"Oh, you know. A big meal at the Twelve Point. Then home and a good night's sleep."

Becky couldn't help laughing at Hank's "big" plans.

"Don't laugh," he said. "I have to get my beauty rest. Got a big day ahead of me tomorrow."

It was then Becky realized she didn't know much at all about the guy she was developing quite a thing for. Did he drink? She didn't think so, but she certainly didn't know for sure. Did he smoke? She'd never seen him light up, but so what? And what about cursing? While she hadn't heard him say a vulgar word, that still didn't mean anything. Becky had a feeling he was about to ask her to join him for his little "celebration." If he did, she would accept, and hopefully some of her questions would be answered.

"Sounds like fun, doesn't it?" Hank said.

"Not if you're celebrating by yourself."

"I'm glad to hear you feel that way. Maybe you can help me out."

Becky swallowed hard. Here it comes.

"I'd be honored to have you there with me," Hank said. He cleared his throat. "You know, to help me celebrate."

She'd almost agreed when she realized she wouldn't have a babysitter. "As much as I would love to, Hank, I'd have to find a sitter. Being a Monday and on such short notice I—"

"Why would you need a babysitter?" he said, cutting her off mid-sentence. "I bet the little guy enjoys a good celebration just as much as the rest of us."

Hank might not know it, but with Becky, his stock had just risen dramatically. She knew if she were to ever fall in love again, it would have to be with someone who accepted her son. That they were a package deal. All or nothing. Not saying this would be an actual date or anything.

"Then I'd love to," she said.

HOMER RETURNED, AND HANK FINISHED OUT THE DAY WORKING IN the warehouse alongside him. Hank had been ecstatic ever since Becky agreed to take him up on his offer. Sure, he was starting a new job and everything, but just being with her would be more than enough reason to celebrate.

Hank told Becky he would pick her and Little Ernie up around six-thirty. It would give them both enough time to get home, get cleaned up, and get ready. Especially Hank. He'd be filthy from working the better part of the day in the dusty, grimy warehouse. He'd already gone to the trouble of placing an old towel on his new truck seat to try to keep the dust off. The rest of the interior would have to be wiped down before heading out to pick up his guests for the evening.

When he got home from work, Hank told Ada not to bother cooking anything for him. He would be eating supper at the Twelve Point with Becky and her son.

Ada sighed and then slowly nodded.

Hank came out of his bedroom already dressed and ready to go. Ada sat quietly at the kitchen table, hands clasped in front of her and glancing down at them.

Walking over and putting a soft hand on her shoulder, Hank said, "Is everything all right, Grandma?"

Ada reached up and placed her hand on top of his. "Everything's fine," she said, giving him a gentle pat. "Just sitting here thinking about your grandpa."

Hank cleared his throat. He knew exactly what she had on her mind. "What he would say about me and Becky?"

"He wouldn't like it one little bit," she said, "but you know what? He'd be wrong."

Hank was surprised to hear her say so, but grateful nonetheless.

"I told you a long time ago, it was nothing against her personally. But he knew if you got involved with her, at some point he'd have to deal with the rest of her family. My husband took his bitterness to the grave with him, Hank, but I don't intend to. If Lester Rayburn has a problem with me, well, all I can do is ask the Good Lord to change his heart. I forgave him a long time ago."

Hank didn't know about the Good Lord part, but the rest of what she said made an awful lot of sense. He gave his grandmother a thoughtful kiss on the cheek and told her if he didn't leave soon, he'd be late picking up his guests for the evening. And he certainly didn't want to make a bad impression on their first date. After all, this was a date. Wasn't it?

~

HANK HAD BEEN PRIVILEGED TO DINE AT MANY FANCY EATERIES IN his lifetime. There was certainly nothing fancy about the Twelve Point Café. Located only about a mile north of town and just off the main highway, other than the reputation of its food, its easy in and out access could possibly be its greatest attribute. The moderately sized rectangular building had been painted light gray with a black, shingled overhang covering the front door and windows. One of the windows was long and featured three large panes of glass. This gave patrons an excellent view of the gravel parking lot outside and traffic passing by on the highway. The other two windows were much smaller, but all three were flanked by black plastic louvered shutters. Next to the front door sat a white pull-down newspaper box holding the latest edition of the weekly *Lee Parish Gazette*.

After pulling on the door, Hank held it open for Becky and Little Ernie. A bell overhead, similar to the one at Craft's, jingled their arrival. Hanging on the wall across the room was the large, mounted head of a thick-necked twelve-point buck. The lone waitress, who'd been facing the opposite direction behind the long, shiny white counter, greeted them when she heard the jingling bell.

"Well, my-y-y goodness," she said, a genuinely welcoming smile filling up her full, round face. "Look who's here." She plucked the blue-and-white-checkered dishtowel from her front apron pocket and quickly dried her dripping hands. "Y'all sit anywhere you like. I'll be with you shortly."

Along with the counter and its seven attached bar stools, the little café featured six square dining tables, each with four matching chairs, and four back-to-back booths lining the front wall. The stools, chairs, and booths were thickly padded and covered with black, plastic material somewhat resembling leather. Over time, some of plastic had dried out and split open, exposing the faded yellow foam padding underneath.

On a quiet Monday evening, this proved to be more than enough seating. Besides Hank, Becky, and Little Ernie, the only other patrons in the place were a couple of older gentlemen sitting next to each other at the bar. In the middle of a spirited debate over half-eaten slices of coconut pie and coffee, they'd stopped long enough to see who had interrupted their exclusive hold on the place.

Hank pointed to a table and Becky nodded. The smiling waitress soon joined them with a long-legged chair made just for infants and a couple of menus. "You'll be needing this high chair, I suppose."

Becky got her son situated and secured him in the chair. She glanced back up and said, "Thank you so much, Miss Helga."

Helga Streeter was a tall woman, close to six feet, strong and thick through the middle. Her eyes were a deep shade of blue and her long hair, blond mixed with alternating streaks of white and gray, had been pulled into a tight bun behind her head. She spoke fluent English but with a distinct German accent.

After taking their drink orders, Helga turned and walked away. Hank motioned at her with his chin and said, "You two seem to know each other quite well."

Becky's eyes brightened, as though a pleasant memory had just popped into her head. "I've known Miss Helga forever. Matter of fact, this is where Ernie brought me for our first date."

Hank nodded slightly, but afraid she might get upset thinking about her late husband, quickly steered the conversation in a different direction. "So, she's worked here for a long time?"

"She has. But not only does she work here; believe it or not, she owns this place."

Hank found this a bit confusing. Ada had told him the owner had killed the large twelve-point buck and named the café after it. He'd just assumed the person was a man. When he shared his thoughts with Becky, she laughed out loud. The two older men at the counter craned their necks to see what the fuss was about.

"Women hunt too, you know," Becky promptly informed him. "Around here, anyway."

"Do you?"

"No, not anymore," she said, shaking her head slightly. "Not since Ernie died."

Hank nodded weakly.

Becky sighed. "Daddy introduced me to shooting years ago. But it was Ernie who taught me how to hunt."

"Do you prefer a rifle or shotgun?" Hank asked.

"Shotgun," she said, "but I'm pretty good with both."

"You don't say." Hank had just used one of his late grandfather's favorite lines without even thinking about it.

Hank had never even considered the fact some women hunted. Or that Becky even knew how to use a gun. For him, being able to shoot had been quite a useful skill. He'd never fooled with guns much growing up, but once he joined the military, firing a rifle just seemed to come naturally. Good thing for him because not only had it saved his life, it had also saved the lives of his comrades on more than one occasion. Accuracy with a gun was a must. Knowing when to pull the trigger was just as important, if not more so.

Helga returned with the drinks and took the rest of their order. Extra hungry, Hank ordered a sixteen-ounce rib eye, medium rare, and a baked potato with extra butter. Becky chose the smaller eight-ounce sirloin, medium, and a baked potato as well. Both came with house salads. For Little Ernie, his mother ordered a small portion of mashed potatoes with just a touch of gravy.

Though he hadn't ordered them for himself, when Becky told Hank they were her son's favorites, he couldn't help sharing his own love for his grandmother's mashed potatoes. This, of course, meant he also had to tell her about the first time he'd tried his hand at peeling the stubborn spuds. He honestly didn't mind a good laugh at his expense, especially when it was her doing the laughing.

Little Ernie's potatoes arrived well ahead of the steaks, but the salads soon followed. Hank offered to feed the child while his mother ate, but she emphatically turned him down.

Becky told Hank she had her own system for getting them both fed. First, she offered a spoonful of potatoes to Little Ernie, which he gladly accepted, and then she took a bite of her salad. And so it went. She'd also poured some of her own tea into Ernie's little cup and after each bite, would offer him a drink. There were times when he would stubbornly refuse the tea, but not once did he turn down a spoonful of mashed potatoes.

When Little Ernie finished eating, Becky cleaned the potatoes from his face and hands. Afterward, he seemed content just to play with his rubber-coated spoon while the grownups talked and enjoyed their own food. Hank had a feeling Becky had set out on a fact-finding mission of sorts when she brought up several topics. But always in an indirect manner.

Becky: "I've never been much of a drinker. Have you?"

Hank: "Never cared for the stuff myself."

Becky: "I smoked a cigarette once and it dang near killed me."

Hank: "Never even had the urge to light up."

Becky: "When I was little, Daddy used to cuss like a sailor. But after he got saved, he changed his ways."

Hank: "I've never had any use for coarse language."

Becky: "Have you heard Carl used to hit on his wife quite a bit?"

Hank: "Any man who hits a woman is no man at all."

Though she'd brought them up in a roundabout way, he had addressed each subject as directly and truthfully as he could. First of all, he hoped she knew he'd been honest. And, secondly, even though he wasn't perfect, he didn't have too many bad habits.

Hank paid the tab and left Helga a more than generous tip.

On the way out, she thanked them for coming, and they thanked her for being such a great hostess. The evening had been a resounding success. In Hank's mind, anyway. He wouldn't know whether Becky enjoyed it or not until he asked her out again. Hopefully sooner rather than later.

CHAPTER TWENTY-ONE

*A*fter a wonderful evening with Becky and Little Ernie, and the dream not rearing its ugly head, Hank had gotten a pretty good night's sleep. Good thing. By five-forty-five, Jack Slater was already sitting in front of Ada's house, apparently ready to go. Hank's grandmother had cooked a big breakfast, but eagerly anticipating his first day on the job, he hadn't eaten much at all. Ada told him how nice he looked all dressed up in his uniform and how proud she was of him. Hank grinned and blushed all at the same time.

Hank kissed his grandmother on the cheek and headed for the door. "I love you," he told her. "And thanks for everything."

"What time did you say you get off?" Ada asked.

"Two."

"Just be careful, sweetie." Ada gave Hank a soft pat on the shoulder. "People can get a little crazy sometimes."

"I will." Jack honked the horn with one quick blast. "Got to go, Grandma."

Hank hurried to the passenger side and greeted his partner as he climbed in. Jack frowned and said, "Sorry."

"About what?"

"I wasn't trying to rush you or anything. I accidently bumped the horn with my elbow."

"Not a problem, man. Not a problem."

"Good deal. You ready to get this party started?"

Hank laced his fingers and cracked his knuckles. "Ready as I'll ever be, I guess."

Jack nodded and slid the car into reverse. "Alrighty, then."

~

HANK SOON LEARNED POLICE WORK INVOLVED MORE TIME RIDING in a patrol car and looking than actually putting bad guys in jail. By ten o'clock, they'd probably logged a hundred miles just traveling the scenic back roads of Lee Parish. Both were surprised when the dispatcher's voice interrupted the radio silence and asked them to investigate an actual breakout.

Jack and Hank quickly cornered the two suspects on the main highway and chased them back into the pasture from which they'd recently escaped. Afterwards, they spent a great deal of time trying to locate the owner. Just to let him know a portion of his fence had come down and a couple of his cows had gotten out. Hank laughed out loud when the man asked Jack if he had a hammer and any fencing staples.

"How many traffic tickets do you write a day?" Hank asked. "On average."

Jack shook his head. "None. We leave ticket writing to the state boys. We don't work wrecks either, but we do help out with traffic and such."

"So, what exactly do we do?"

"Everything else, my friend," Jack said with a chuckle. "You name it. Domestic squabbles. Barroom fights. Chasing cows off the highway."

Hank laughed as well. "I bet you've seen a little of everything, haven't you?"

"Most of what we deal with is serious but sometimes, it can be downright funny."

"Such as?"

"One time there was a drifter bothering customers out in front of Ferguson's store. I picked him up, took him to the next parish over, and dropped him off. A few minutes later, he's back at the same store hitting people up for money. When I asked how he got back so quick, he said one of the deputies in the other parish saw me drop him off and brought him back to the store."

Hank laughed again, even louder. "What did you do then?"

"I took him right back over there," Jack said. "Only this time, I made sure nobody saw me."

"Now that's funny stuff."

"If you think that's funny. Just stand by. You'll be amazed at some of the things we run into."

All morning, Hank had wanted to ask Jack a question. He'd been hesitant because he didn't know if they might be friends or have some other connection. He couldn't see it but wouldn't know for sure until he asked.

His gaze fixed to the side window of the car, Hank said, "What can you tell me about Carl Walker?"

Jack didn't immediately respond. At the intersection with the next gravel road, he wheeled in and brought the heavy cruiser to an abrupt, sliding stop. Jack shoved the car into park and then adjusted himself in the seat to face Hank. "Why do you want to know?"

Hank cleared his throat. "I had a little run-in with him at Craft's a while back."

Jack raised an eyebrow. "Oh, yeah? Tell me about it."

"Not much to tell," Hank said. "We were talking, and the guy just took a swing at me."

"And what did you do?"

"I squeezed his hand until he begged me to let go."

"Good for you," Jack said with a chuckle. "But you'd better

watch your back from now on. You can trust him about as far as you can throw him."

"Somebody else told me pretty much the same thing."

"If you knew him a little better, you'd understand."

"He gives you guys trouble sometimes?"

"No, not sometimes. All the time. Now you're a deputy, you'll be seeing a lot more of Carl Walker. Trust me."

"So, what's the deal with this guy anyway?"

"For one thing, he likes to slap women around. And he likes his booze. I felt sorry for his poor little wife. I'm glad she finally got enough of him and hit the road."

"Has he ever been arrested?"

"More times than I care to think about," Jack said, "but his old man's got connections. And money. Far as I know, he's never spent a night in jail. Carl can get away with anything, and he knows it."

"Sounds like I need to be ready, then," Hank said matter of factly.

"We'll run into him soon enough, and he'll be strutting his stuff. He'll be drunk and looking for a fight. We'll take him in, and before the ink's even dry on the booking log, his old man will have him out. It never fails, Hank. Never."

"You seem pretty sure about it."

"Just hide and watch, my friend. Just hide and watch."

BY THE END OF HIS SECOND WEEK ON THE JOB, HANK HAD GROWN accustomed to wearing a uniform and a gun everywhere he went. Working six-to-two, his first few days on the job had been mostly uneventful. So far, he and Jack had made only two arrests and answered just a handful of legitimate calls. Most of what they'd encountered they had handled with simple, commonsense solutions. People, he was quickly learning, often needed input from a third party to help settle their disputes. Probably just a matter of time before they'd have to deal with some hardhead who would change everything. Though they'd yet to have the inevitable run-in with Carl Walker, he seemed to be the most likely candidate to do just that.

Getting off at two each day allowed Hank to put in a few hours stacking feed and assisting customers in the back of Craft's store. He'd also been able to spend short amounts of time with Becky as well. The previous weekend, they'd attended a movie at the Magnolia Theatre, accompanied by Little Ernie. The movie house featured a "cry room" for those with small children, and with her son not being a particular fan of the big screen, they'd spent the majority of the evening studying its friendly confines. For Hank, it hadn't mattered in the slightest. Every day he was falling more in love with this beautiful woman, and every minute of the day when he wasn't with her he found himself thinking about her. He could only hope she'd been feeling some of the same things.

Late on a Friday evening, Homer tossed the last fifty-pound sack of feed to Hank, and he stacked it neatly on the pallet with all the others. "About time we call it a day," Homer said, wiping his sweaty brow with an already dripping handkerchief. "Don't you think?"

Hank reached up high and stretched his tired, aching muscles. "You'll get no argument from me," he said.

Both men laughed, and Homer slapped him on the back as he walked past. "Let's get out of here then."

The men walked up to the front of the store and found Becky getting ready to close up for the day as well. Homer said, "Why don't you two take off. I'll lock up."

"Two?" she said, cocking her head.

Homer's face quickly changed to red. "Well, I meant to say three."

They had a good laugh then Becky disappeared into the office. Minutes later, she was back with Little Ernie in her arms.

The sheriff's office had given Hank the next four days off. Jack had told him they wouldn't have to report back to work until Wednesday afternoon, and then, they'd be on the evening shift for the next two weeks. During his days off, he would have to try to spend as much time with Becky as he possibly could.

Hank walked Becky to her pickup. While she strapped Little Ernie in, he said, "So what are you guys up to this weekend?"

She stopped and faced him. "I have to be here tomorrow," she said with a slight frown. "But just until noon. Afterward, not much of nothing."

"Me either."

"What did you have in mind?" she said, raising an eyebrow.

Hank shrugged. "Nothing in particular. I thought it might be nice if we could do something together though." He cleared his throat. "If you want to, I mean."

Becky rubbed at her chin as if having to think it over. Then, shaking her finger in the air at nothing in particular, she said, "I know exactly what we can do. Why don't you come over to my house tomorrow evening? I'll cook supper for us."

Hank couldn't help smiling at her thoughtful suggestion. He'd never heard a better plan in his entire life. "Count me in. Do I need to bring anything?"

"Just your appetite," she said convincingly. "I'll call Mama and see if she can keep Ernie."

Hank laid a hand on her shoulder and shook his head. "No need. Anything we do, he needs to be right there with us."

Becky's eyes lit up as she nodded in agreement.

"What time do you want me there?" Hank asked.

"How about six?"

"Sounds good to me," he said. "Be there with bells on."

To be honest, Becky's plan sounded better than good. It

sounded great. The downside for him would be the wait, but it would be well worth it.

~

FOR BECKY, THE TIME ON SATURDAY MORNING SEEMED TO BE moving in slow motion. The steady stream of customers had kept her rather busy, but being preoccupied with her plans for later, she'd had several undeniable hiccups along the way. First, she'd put Mr. Kleinpeter's items in Mr. Jacobs's bag. And vice-versa. Then, she'd mistakenly rung up a two-dollar package of sheet-metal screws as two hundred dollars and thought Mrs. Jefferson had suffered a light heart attack when she announced the amount. After closing the store, she'd driven nearly a mile toward home when suddenly remembering she hadn't locked the front door. So far, it had been one of those days. Hopefully, her streak of bad luck wouldn't continue into the evening.

Why in the world had she ever offered to cook? And what in the world was she going to cook? She hadn't even bothered to ask Hank what he liked. Or what he didn't like. He'd mentioned at the Twelve Point how much he loved his grandmother's mashed potatoes. She made those for Little Ernie all the time. But what were the chances hers could stand up to Mrs. Ada's? Well, she'd try her best, and that's all she could do. But what else? If man could not live by bread alone, he probably wouldn't get too far on just mashed potatoes either.

Racking her brain, Becky suddenly remembered the package of deer steaks she had tucked away in the back of the freezer. Her father killed the animal the prior fall and had given her a few packages of the highly sought after meat. Now, less than a year later, she found herself already down to one.

Early on, Becky's mother taught her how to prepare venison without simply serving it fried. First the meat had to be seasoned and floured, then browned in a heavy, cast-iron skillet. The contents were then dropped into a pressure cooker, a little water added, and allowed to cook for about fifteen minutes. This process produced the most tender, succulent steak a person would ever want to wrap their lips around. Not to mention, the best tasting gravy on the face of the planet. Whip up a pan of biscuits, along with the potatoes, of course, and you had yourself a meal fit for a king. Hopefully, her honored guest would think so, too.

Not expecting Hank until around six, Becky was surprised to hear a vehicle pull up in front of her house around five-thirty. If he'd made it a bit early, that wouldn't be a problem. She hadn't started the meal yet, but maybe he could watch television or entertain Little Ernie while she cooked. Since her son usually kept himself occupied in his playpen filled with toys, Hank might even be willing to pitch in and help.

Becky pulled back the curtain to take a peek and gasped. Instead of Hank's new blue and white Chevy sitting in the driveway, she saw the familiar black Ford pickup she'd come to despise.

Taking a long, deep breath, Becky reluctantly walked out onto the porch. She didn't know what the madman had in mind, but whatever he had to say to her, he could say it just fine outside. He wasn't about to set foot inside her house.

Carl climbed down slowly from his truck. "Told you I'd see you later, didn't I?"

Becky just stood there. Silent. Arms crossed, staring right at him.

"Well, here I am," he said with his usual swagger.

"I don't know what you think you're doing here," she said, "but you'd best get back in your truck and hit the road."

Carl shook his head slowly and continued toward the porch. "Now is that any way to talk to the guy you're so madly in love with?"

Becky held her ground. "You set a foot on this porch, you psycho, and I'm calling the cops."

"And what are the cops gonna do, sweetie pie? Huh? Haul me off to jail? I'll just get right back out. And, then what?"

"You might," she said convincingly, "but at least you'll have it to do."

Carl eyed her closely, apparently taking notice of the fact she wore makeup. "What are you so dolled up for? You been expecting me?"

Becky rolled her eyes. "Not hardly."

"Wait a minute," Carl shook an angry index finger in her direction. "I know what's going on here. Lover boy's coming over. Ain't he?"

"And what if he is? It's nothing to you."

Carl took another step closer, still shaking his finger. "See, that's where you're wrong. It's everything to me. Let's face it, Becky. I'm single. You're single. It's just a matter of time before it's you and me again, baby. Just like it's supposed to be."

"Can't you get it through your thick skull? It's never gonna be you and me." Becky reached for the screen door handle. "And you need to leave right now."

"Go on in and call the cops. I'll be standing right here when they show up."

"I'm not calling the cops, Carl," she said, her voice sounding low and gritty. "I'm calling an ambulance."

"Why do you need an ambulance?"

"It's not for me," she said. "It's for you."

"And why do I need one?"

"Because I'm going inside to get my shotgun."

Carl crossed his arms defiantly. "You wouldn't shoot me, and you know it."

Becky stopped dead in her tracks. Slowly, she turned and locked eyes with him. She was strictly business. "Let me tell you something. My baby's in there, and I'll do anything I have to, to protect him. And if it means killing you, Carl Walker, then so be it."

Throwing both hands in the air, Carl took a quick step back. "Hold on there, Annie Oakley. If you want me to leave, I'll leave. But this ain't over by a long shot. I always get what I want, and you know it. It's just a matter of time, sweetheart." Carl took another step back. "Just a matter of time."

Carl snatched the door of his truck open and swung himself inside. Through the open window, he shouted, "And tell your friend Goodman he'd better watch his back."

Gravel slinging everywhere when he backed out, Becky sat down on the steps, her eyes quickly filling with tears. Seemed like no matter what she did and how hard she tried, it was always something. Always.

CHAPTER TWENTY-TWO

*H*ank hoped Becky wouldn't mind him showing up early. By four-thirty, he'd already dressed, splashed on a little aftershave, and was ready to go. After pacing the floor for nearly an hour, he could wait no longer. Time to get this show on the road.

When Hank pulled up in front of Becky's house, he'd done a double take. There she was, sitting on the front steps with her elbows on her knees and her face cradled deeply in her hands. Apparently in tears.

Something must have gone terribly wrong. His first thought was she'd run into trouble with the meal. Burned the biscuits or something. Whatever it was, it had upset her in a big way.

When Hank sat down next to Becky, she never moved or said a word. He put his arm around her and gave her a firm, comforting hug. "What's the matter?" he said softly. "Why are you crying?"

Becky never looked up. Between sobs, she managed, "Carl just left."

Hank's pulse quickened, and he could feel the heat rushing to his face. "He didn't hurt you, did he?"

"No," she said, barely shaking her head. "Nothing like that."

"You want to tell me what happened?"

"He just won't leave me alone." Becky lifted her head slightly. "Things were bad enough after Ernie died, but with his wife gone he—he somehow he thinks we're going to get back together."

"Let's get you inside," Hank said, urging her to stand, "and out of this heat."

What Hank wanted to do was to catch up with Carl and beat him within an inch of his life. After he got through with the guy, Carl would wish he'd never even heard of Becky. But he couldn't do that. First of all, he couldn't leave her alone in her present condition. And secondly, he was now a sworn officer of the law. Any dealings he had with the guy would have to be handled on a professional level. If the opportunity ever presented itself, he'd give Carl an open invitation and hope he'd be stupid enough to accept it. If he ever laid his grimy hands on Becky, lawman or no lawman, Hank wouldn't be responsible for his actions.

Inside the house, Becky told Hank she would be okay and just needed a few minutes to freshen up. He sat down on the living room couch, grabbed a magazine off the coffee table, and started slowly flipping through the pages. Less than ten minutes later, she'd made it back with Little Ernie bouncing on her hip. Becky appeared refreshed and, with her ruined mascara removed and replaced, absolutely gorgeous.

Hank tossed the magazine back on the table, got up, and walked over to her. "You sure you're okay?" he said softly, brushing her hair back.

Becky took a deep breath and blew it back out. "I'm fine, but I haven't even started supper yet."

Rubbing his hands together briskly, Hank said, "So what can I do to help?"

"I don't know." Becky managed a slight chuckle. "Can you cook?"

"Not so much, but I'd certainly be willing to try."

"I'd planned on deer steak and gravy with mashed potatoes. With homemade biscuits, of course."

At this revelation, Hank's eyes immediately lit up, and he raised his hand like a fifth grader. "I'll peel the potatoes," he said.

"Are you sure you remember how?"

"Of course I do," Hank said confidently. "Just like riding a bike."

"Well, let's see if you've still got it then."

Becky dragged Little Ernie's playpen into the living room and put him in it along with his favorite toys. Her house featured an open floor plan, and from her vantage point in the kitchen, she could keep an eye on him while preparing meals or cleaning up afterwards.

Hank busied himself whittling on the six good-sized potatoes Becky had laid out. By the time she seasoned the steak, floured it, and put it in the cast iron skillet she'd been heating, Hank had already finished. Now he was ready to cut them up into smaller pieces for boiling.

"Well look at you," Becky said, clapping her hands lightly together. "You do pretty good work."

"Why thank you," Hank said. "You're not so shabby yourself."

Becky narrowed her eyes. "Watch it, mister."

Hank watched closely as Becky raked the browned contents from the skillet into the pressure cooker, added some water, and then made sure the lid was on good and tight. Next, she lit the gas burner and brought the flame up to its highest setting. A few minutes later, when the small metal object on top of the cooker began to steadily bob up and down, she walked back over to the stove and lowered the heat.

Having seen one of these contraptions at his grandmother's house, he'd never had too much interest. But that was then. "What do you call that thing anyway?" Hank said, raising an eyebrow.

"That?" Becky pointed to the steaming pot on top of the stove. "It's a pressure cooker, silly."

Hank shook his head. "No, not the pot itself. I mean the little metal gadget jumping up and down on top."

"Mama says it's what controls the pressure."

"I figured as much," he said, nodding, "but what do you call it?"

Becky shrugged. "I don't know the official name. We've always called it a jiggler."

"A jiggler?" Hank laughed out loud. "Are you serious?"

"You wanted to know, and I told you." Becky placed her hands firmly on her hips. "And what's so funny?"

"I'm sorry" Hank said, now laughing even louder. "But a jiggler?"

"And I suppose you have a better name for it, Mr. Smarty-Pants?"

"I don't, but let me call my grandma. I bet she does."

Soon, Hank had Ada on the line. "Grandma—quick question. What do you call the little metal thing on top of a pressure cooker? Yeah, it bounces up and down. Oh, I see." He glanced over at Becky, his face contorted. "Yes, ma'am. Okay. Got it. Yes, ma'am. All right. Okay. Thanks a lot. Okay, I will. Bye."

"Well," Becky said, crossing her arms in defiance. "What did she say?"

"You sure you want to know?"

"Not only do I want to know, I want to know now."

After a few moments of hesitation, Hank finally threw his hands up. "A jiggler."

Becky cackled. "I told you, didn't I?" she said, giving Hank a playful poke in the ribs.

～

WHILE HANK HAD BEEN PEELING POTATOES, BECKY PROMISED TO

teach him how to make homemade biscuits. When she told him she was ready, he pulled a chair from under the table and moved it closer to where she would be working. By the time she had both hands completely covered with flour and gooey, sticky dough, Little Ernie began to fuss in his playpen.

"Oh, my goodness," she said. "Would you mind getting him?"

"Not at all."

Working the sticky biscuit dough, Becky never took her eyes off the scene unfolding in the living room. Little Ernie reaching up from the playpen, and Hank taking him into his arms with a bright and genuine smile. Once again, she could feel her heart flutter.

The truth of the matter couldn't be denied. Becky had fallen head over heels for Hank Goodman. Seeing him interact with her young son only served to strengthen her feelings. Possibly, he felt the same way, but at this point, she couldn't be a hundred percent sure. Before the end of the evening, she sincerely hoped to find out.

Becky couldn't help wondering what the rest of her family—the Rayburns and the Crafts—would think about her being with Hank. Her mother would be okay with it, but her father was the wild card. Though she'd recently told Susan he would be fine with whomever she wanted to date—because he loved her and her son—that didn't necessarily make it so.

As for the Crafts, she honestly couldn't see them having a problem with it. In fact, Homer thought the world of Hank and appreciated his contributions down at the store. Mrs. Craft, such a sweet and caring lady, would be happy just to go with the flow. Anything her husband approved of would no doubt be okay with her, too.

And what about Carl Walker? How do you deal with a guy who can do anything he wants and get away with it? What does he have to be afraid of? Threatening him with jail certainly wouldn't accomplish anything. Mentioning the shotgun had given him pause, but in reality, he probably thought she was bluffing. But, she wasn't. When it came to protecting the child Becky loved more than life itself, she would go to her own grave if she had to.

And Hank needed to be concerned about Carl, too. Even though she'd seen how he handled him in the store once, at some point Carl would retaliate and try to get even. She'd definitely taken to heart his parting remark about Goodman watching his back and would be sure to pass it on to Hank. He needed to take it to heart as well.

"Supper's ready," Becky called out from the kitchen.

Hank had settled in on the couch, and with some assistance, Ernie was standing up in his lap. He seemed to take great delight in tickling the child's belly and making him laugh out loud. Ernie, in the meantime, had developed quite a fascination for Hank's eyes and nose. The two were apparently enjoying one another's company so much they'd been oblivious to Becky's announcement.

She tried again. "I said supper's ready, guys. Am I the only one here who's hungry?"

Now, she had their full attention. "Man, that smells good," Hank said, arming up Little Ernie and heading into the kitchen. "If it tastes anything like it smells, I'd say we're in for a treat."

Becky dropped her head and let out a heavy sigh. "Speaking of treats, I didn't make the first thing for dessert."

"Oh, man," Hank said, snapping his fingers and feigning disappointment. "Are you serious?"

"Sorry."

"I know what we can do. After supper, we'll run into Crosscut and get some ice cream."

Becky wrinkled her nose and shook her head slightly. "It is Saturday night, you know. All the kids will be in town, and the Tasty Cream will be packed. I'm pretty sure I have some vanilla wafers in the pantry. Ernie just loves those things."

"Then vanilla wafers it is," Hank said.

After getting Ernie situated in his high chair, Becky gave him his own little rubber-coated spoon to play with. She and Hank fixed their plates from the stove, and once they were seated, she asked if he would like to say Grace.

Hank cleared his throat. "I'm afraid I wouldn't be too good at it. Haven't had much practice."

"Would you like me to say it?"

"Do you mind?"

Becky reached for Hank's hand and gently took it in her own. "I don't mind at all."

~

HALFWAY THROUGH THE MEAL, LITTLE ERNIE FELL ASLEEP. BECKY lifted him out of the high chair while Hank wiped the remnants of the mashed potatoes from his face and tiny fingers with a damp cloth. She carried her sleeping son into the bedroom, transferred him into his nightclothes, and laid him down for the evening.

When they'd finished eating, Hank couldn't stop complimenting Becky on how great the food was. As he helped put the dishes away, she asked what he thought about the mashed potatoes in particular. Her face took on a bright red shade when he said hers were every bit as good as, if not better, than his grandmother's.

"Let's go sit in the living room," she suggested, pointing toward the couch.

Hank made a sweeping gesture with his hand. "After you, my lady."

As far as Hank was concerned, the evening couldn't have gone any better. Carl Walker showing up had been a slight bump in the road, but afterward, everything seemed to fall right into place. The laughing and talking with Becky while he peeled potatoes, and playing with Little Ernie while she made biscuits and finished up the meal. Hank could see himself getting used to something like this.

Hank had never gotten over Becky in the first place. But since his return to Crosscut, he'd fallen for her big time. She would never know how hard it was being in the back of the store every day while she worked up front. So close and yet so far. He wanted to hold her in his arms. To kiss her and tell her exactly how he felt. Maybe now wouldn't be the right time. Maybe it was still too soon. Maybe she only considered him a friend.

"I had a great time tonight," Hank said.

Becky's head bobbed. "So did I."

"There's something I want to tell you, but I'm afraid I might end up disappointed."

"What do you mean?"

Hank blew out a labored breath. "What I mean is—I want to tell you how I feel about you, but I don't know if it's something you'd even want to hear."

Becky poked him in the chest rather convincingly. "I'm a big girl," she said. "Remember telling Mr. Craft to let you be the judge of what was fair to you?"

Hank nodded.

"Then let me be the judge of what I want to hear."

Swallowing hard, Hank tried desperately to remove the huge lump lodged in his throat. Not only was he heading into unchartered waters, quite possibly his boat had a huge, gaping hole in it.

"You know I had an awful big crush on you five years ago."

Becky clasped her hands together, and Hank was sure he could hear her heart beating. But maybe it was his.

"The day at the store, when you first stepped out of the office, I realized those feelings had never left. And ever since then I..."

"Yes?"

"Look, nobody hates what happened to Ernie more than I do,

and I know I've only been back a short while, but..." Hank hesitated. "Man, this is harder than I thought."

"You're doing fine."

"Then I'll just come right out and say it." Hank reached for Becky's hand. "I'm in love with you."

For the longest time, Becky didn't say a word. Hank was beginning to think he'd jumped the gun big time. That his leaky boat was indeed going down.

As Becky began to speak, her eyes found Hank's. "I loved my husband," she said. "More than you or anyone else will ever know. At first, I didn't think I was ready to move on, but these last couple of weeks have opened my eyes to a lot of things." She took a deep breath and blew it out quickly. "I'll just come out and say it, too. I love you, Hank Goodman."

When their lips met, feelings of love—of passion and desire—rushed through them. Consuming them. Then, as if right on cue, the unmistakable sound of a child's cries came from the bedroom just down the hall. Little Ernie had woken up.

～

CARL WALKER WAS FURIOUS WHEN HE LEFT BECKY'S HOUSE. JUST who did she think she was, anyway? He loved her and all, but he'd never let any woman talk to him like she had. Not without paying dearly for it. Once they were together again, he'd have to lay down the law. Then she would know what he expected of her and wouldn't have any excuses when it came time to exact a little discipline. And the time would come, of that he had no doubt. With stubborn, hardheaded women, it always did.

And what was the deal with the shotgun? She could count her lucky stars he'd played along with her nonsense. Becky shoot somebody? Yeah, right. Truth be told, she probably didn't know one end of a gun from the other.

After asking around, Carl found out the guy she'd been seeing

—the one who'd pretty much crushed his hand in the store that day—was Hank Goodman. Some Yankee transplant from Michigan and the grandson of Jake and Ada Taylor. Carl didn't know much about the Taylors, only that they were penniless dirt farmers who lived on Hurt Road down south of Crosscut. He'd heard through the grapevine the old man had died a year or so ago. And, if that was the case, good riddance.

Carl also learned Goodman had been in the army and had seen considerable action in Vietnam. Wasn't that just great? Now they had some baby-killing psycho working for the Lee Parish Sheriff's Department. What in the world would possess the idiot of a sheriff to hire somebody like Goodman in the first place?

Biding his time would be Carl's best option. The guy being a deputy might complicate things a bit, but sooner or later an opportunity would present itself. And when it did, Goodman would no longer be a problem and Becky would be his for the taking.

CHAPTER TWENTY-THREE

Over the next three days, Hank spent as much time with Becky as he possibly could. He worked Monday and Tuesday at the store. Both evenings, as soon as he made it home and cleaned up, he climbed back in his truck and headed straight for her house.

As much as Hank loved her, he still found it surprising to learn they had so many things in common. They enjoyed the same television programs, many of the same foods, and she'd even taught him how to play a fun, new dice game, new to him anyway, called Yahtzee. The one thing she'd forgotten to teach him, however, was how to win at Yahtzee. Hands down, she remained the champ and couldn't help rubbing it in every little chance she got. All in good fun, of course.

Hank's introduction to the evening shift had gone by without a hitch. The first night went by peacefully without a single call for assistance. The majority of their time was spent patrolling parish roads, checking locks on homes and businesses. They'd looked for anything suspiciously out of place and hadn't found much at all. Jack reminded Hank the inevitable "run-in" with

Carl Walker was still yet to come. "Just a matter of time," Jack said again. "Just a matter of time."

They didn't have to wait long for Jack's prediction to come true. Around eight-forty-five the following evening, they received a call about a disturbance at the Twelve Point Café. Helga Streeter reported some young people had "bunched up" in her parking lot, and it appeared as though a fight might be about to break out. She told the radio operator she recognized the "Walker boy" in the group, and he appeared to be the instigator.

Hank and Jack pulled in at the café to find a small group of about ten to twelve guys and girls gathered in the parking lot. Just as Helga had reported. They'd formed a crude circle, and in the middle stood Carl Walker and some other fellow Hank had never seen before.

"Step back," Jack commanded in a loud voice, pushing his way through the compact circle of people. "And you two break it up."

Carl whipped his head around. "You stay out of this, Slater. This is strictly between me and this idiot."

"I said, I didn't mean anything by it," the other guy pleaded. "I was just trying to impress Angie. I swear."

"Oh, no, big boy. You told her you were tougher than me, and we're about to find out if you're right."

"We're not about to find out anything," Jack said, stepping between the would-be combatants. "Unless it's who's going to jail."

"You're wasting your time, and you know it. My old man'll have me…"

Hoping to observe his partner and see how he dealt with situations such as this, Hank had been quiet the entire time. Once Carl took notice of him, his role as observer quickly changed to participant.

"Well, well, well," Walker said, looking Hank up and down. "Check it out, boys and girls. Looks like there's a new sheriff in town."

Hank gritted his teeth and held his ground.

Carl moved a step closer. "Good thing for old Roger here you showed up, Goodman. The beating I was going to give him, I'll give it to you instead."

Before Jack could intervene, Carl took a wild, lumbering swing at Hank. Instead of catching his fist and squeezing it as he had before, Hank simply sidestepped and grabbed Carl's wrist as it passed by his head. Seconds later, Hank had his would-be attacker on the ground with both hands securely cinched behind his back.

~

"I'LL HAVE YOUR JOB OVER THIS, GOODMAN," CARL SHOUTED FROM the back seat of the patrol car. "Mark my words."

Hank quickly decided not to say anything. Just let the guy run his mouth. With no one paying attention to the windbag, maybe he'd eventually sit back and shut up. No such luck.

"Are you deaf up there? I said I'm gonna have your job. My old man owns most of this parish. Meaning he pretty much owns you guys, too."

Hank had heard enough. Turning in his seat, he said, "If some idiot like you can get my job then I don't want it anyway."

"You talk mighty big with this cage between us." Carl leaned closer and lowered his voice. "Let me give you some good advice, old pal. Stay away from Becky. You understand? Stay away from her and her stupid kid."

Hank could feel his blood beginning to boil. Becky's name crossing Carl's lips was bad enough. But calling Little Ernie stupid? He wanted rip the guy's throat out.

Carl kicked at the cage. "Take these handcuffs off, and we'll settle this right now."

"Those handcuffs are the only thing saving you," Hank mumbled, barely audible.

"I'll take care of you, Goodman. And a whole lot sooner than you think."

Jack took a turn. "Just keep talking, tough guy, and we'll add more charges."

"Like it's gonna matter," Carl said defiantly. "I'll be sleeping in my own bed tonight, and you know it."

Hank had heard more than enough but knew his options were limited. He'd love nothing more than to give Walker a chance to put his money where his mouth was. He could ask Jack to stop the car, but it wouldn't be fair to his partner. Hank would bide his time. He took a long, deep breath, then blew it out slowly and evenly just to calm himself. Turning his gaze to the window and the night, Hank never said another word.

The rest of the trip to the courthouse was short and uneventful. With the exception of Walker running his mouth non-stop. Jack escorted Carl inside, holding onto his right elbow. The entire time, Carl never took his eyes off Hank.

Jack walked Carl over to the two folding, metal chairs next to the wall and removed the left handcuff. Bringing Carl's arms to the front, he ordered him to sit in the chair on the right and then attached the loose cuff to the empty one. If Carl got the bright idea to jump up and run, he'd have to take the extra chair with him.

Once inside the lockup, Carl finally quieted down and closed his eyes. His head bobbed up and down, apparently fighting a losing battle to stay awake. The sound of the heavy metal door opening less than ten minutes later snapped him right out of it.

A tall, thin man, wearing a stiff straw cowboy hat and dressed all in khaki, walked into the room. Falling ashes most likely made the hundreds of tiny burn holes covering his shirt. Hank based this assessment on the lit, hand rolled cigarette still dangling from man's thin, tight lips.

The fellow walked right past Jack and Hank and never said a word. Carl opened his mouth to speak, and before he could utter a single word, a hard, calloused hand slapped him hard across the face. Carl's eyes went wide, and he cowered as best he could while still handcuffed to the chair. This didn't stop the man from slapping him a second time. Carl cried out in obvious pain.

"Hold on there, Mr. Walker," Jack said, stepping forward. "That's just about enough."

Donald Walker nodded slowly, now focusing all his attention on the deputies. "Judge Wallace said I could sign his bond. You can call him if you need to."

Jack shook his head. "How'd you find out so quick he was up here?"

Walker grunted. "One of his so-called friends called me."

With the paperwork prepared and signed, Carl was a free man again. Just as Jack and Carl had predicted. When Carl caught his father not looking, he winked at Hank.

"Sorry for the inconvenience, men," the elder Walker said sincerely. He grabbed a handful of Carl's shirt and gave it a quick jerk. "Come on, boy."

∼

JACK DROPPED HANK OFF AT AROUND TEN-FORTY-FIVE AND THEN headed out to pick up their relief. The previous night, Ada had stayed up and waited for Hank to come home. This night, however, he found the house completely dark and still. Hank tried his best to be quiet, easing the front door open and carefully slipping inside. After only two cautious steps, his grandmother's voice broke the late night silence.

"Hank?" she called out. "Is that you?"

"Yes, ma'am," Hank said, in the darkness. "It's me."

"Your supper's on the table, sweetie. Just put your dirty dishes in the sink when you're done."

"I will," he said. "And thank you."

"You're welcome. Goodnight, Hank."

"Goodnight, Grandma."

Hank ate as quickly and quietly as he could. When he finished, he put his plate, fork, and empty glass in the sink just as his grandmother had instructed. Hank knew how truly blessed he was to have someone as sweet, thoughtful, and kind as Ada in his corner. Jake had certainly hit the jackpot when he found her. She was one special lady.

By midnight, Hank had already taken his bath and stretched out across his bed. Time to relax and reflect on the events of the day. It had been his nightly ritual even before he started the evening shift. Some nights, he would read until he got too sleepy to hold his eyes open. Others, he'd simply lie there and think about things. Things, more often than not, being Becky and Little Ernie.

Hank loved the mesmerizing drone of the huge attic fan at the back of the house and the cool, moist air it pulled in through his bedroom window. As much as he liked it, however, he knew air conditioning would be a better, much more comfortable option. He would discuss the matter with Ada and see if she had any interest. After all, the house belonged to her. If she did, he'd be more than happy to purchase a couple of the big window units. The electric bill would be quite a bit higher but nothing he couldn't take care of as well.

Around one a.m., Hank awoke to the sound of gravel angrily crunching in front of Ada's house. When he finally figured out what was happening, the vehicle in question had already cut several donuts in the middle of the road. Tiny pieces of rock showered the front of the house, hitting both the siding and the windows. By the time Hank made it to the door and flipped on the porch light, the vehicle had already sped away. Nothing remained but a massive cloud of thick, choking dust.

Hank thought about running out to his pickup and giving chase. But by the time he got to his truck and started it up, the chase would be pretty much over before it even started.

Out on the porch, Hank checked the extent of the damage. He'd plainly heard the tiny rocks hitting the windows, but fortunately none of them had been broken. The house sat far enough off the road that even though the gravel had made it that far, it had little momentum left when it did.

Ada joined Hank on the porch. "What's all the commotion?"

"Probably just some teenagers cutting up," Hank tried to assure her.

"And on a week night, too," she said, shaking her head in disbelief.

Hank didn't like being less than honest with his grandmother. The culprit, or culprits, could have just been teenagers making a statement to Lee Parish's newest deputy. But Hank knew better. Who, other than Carl Walker, would have any reason to do such a thing?

"We might as well go on back to bed, Grandma," he said, putting his arm around her and pulling her close. "Hopefully, that's all the excitement we'll have for one night."

～

AFTER TWO LONG, FRUSTRATING HOURS OF TOSSING AND TURNING, Hank finally drifted off to sleep. If he had known the dream would rear its ugly head, he would have chosen to stay awake.

Hank had met Steve McMillan at AIT school shortly after finishing a grueling eight-week boot camp. The two hit it off instantly, but finding out his new friend also hailed from Michigan pretty much sealed the deal. Having been assigned to the same duty, the two of them had even flown to Vietnam together for their first tour. Sadly, Steve's first tour would also be his last.

Steve became the brother Hank never had. Once overseas, they were inseparable. The two men worked side by side, ate side by side, and they fought side by side. And they shared everything.

Including each other's care packages. And letters from home. At quieter times, they reflected on what they missed most back in the States and even shared their well thought out plans for life after the war.

Pinned down a couple of times by heavy enemy fire, they'd held on to each other while Steve fervently prayed for their safety. On the several occasions when Steve had tried to share his faith, Hank would tell him that as good as Steve was at praying, it should be enough for the both of them. They'd made a vow to watch each other's backs. And under no circumstances short of death would one ever leave the other on the field of battle.

The day started out pretty much like all the others since they'd arrived in country. Rain, rain, and more rain. They'd been trudging through the soggy jungle on high alert for nearly thirty minutes, toward an objective none of them were quite sure about, when suddenly a murderous hail of machine gun fire erupted. A classic ambush. Amid the ensuing chaos, Hank saw Steve, just a few feet off to his left, fall to his knees, drop his rifle, and clutch his chest with both hands. Steve had been hit.

Hank rushed to his wounded friend's side. "Hang on, buddy. I've got you."

With bullet after bullet whizzing past his own head, Hank managed to drag Steve over to the side of the trail and behind the base of a tree just wider than Steve's shoulders. Plopping down behind it, Hank pulled his wounded friend close. With Steve's head now resting on Hank's lap, Hank desperately screamed for a medic. And then, just as quickly as it started, everything around them turned eerily quiet. The withering fire had stopped. The ambushing enemy had apparently fled.

By then, Steve's eyelids were fluttering wildly. "I see Jesus, Hank!" he cried out. Steve reached up, grabbed Hank's arm, and squeezed it tightly. "Hank, I see Jesus." Steve managed one last, labored breath, and by the time the medic got there, Hank's best friend had already left him. A lot of good Jesus had done.

Hank awoke with a gasp and, in the dim light, saw Ada standing at his bedside.

"Are you all right?" she said softly.

"I'm fine, Grandma." Hank raked his hand across his chin. "I didn't mean to wake you up."

Ada leaned over and planted a gentle kiss to Hank's sweat-covered forehead. "Why don't you try praying, son? See if that helps."

CHAPTER TWENTY-FOUR

By six the next morning, Hank had been up long enough to be working on his second cup of coffee. He hadn't slept much at all, thanks to Carl Walker's late night antics. And the dreaded nightmare he'd suffered through afterwards. Reliving the most horrific event of his life, almost every night, was starting to take its toll. Something had to give, and soon.

Working evenings, Hank had found he didn't need any extra sleep. Even on the day shift, he'd stayed up most nights past ten and many times until twelve o'clock or later. Once graveyards rolled around, in all likelihood, he'd have to sleep the better part of the day. Would the dream interrupt his daytime sleep as well? He'd just have to wait and see.

Hank had on his mind to run by the store and have a little chat with Becky. Fill her in on what happened with Carl and see if she'd experienced anything out of the ordinary at her house. If so, hopefully, she would have called. Either way, she needed to know about the incident. Not to mention how seeing her beautiful, loving face would more than make his day.

Walking into Craft's around ten, Hank found not only Becky standing behind the counter but another quite attractive woman as well. This pretty lady, looking remarkably like an only slightly older version of his sweetheart, busily bounced an excited Little Ernie on her hip. This had to be Becky's mother. The one he'd already heard so much about. The one Big Ernie had referred to five years earlier as "nuttier than a fruitcake."

The jingling bell over Hank's head got Becky's immediate attention, and when she saw him, her eyes lit right up.

Hank walked straight over to the counter and laid both hands on top of it. "Good morning, ladies."

"Morning," Becky replied with a smile. It disappeared when she cleared her throat to reluctantly make the introductions. "Mama, this is Hank Goodman. Hank, this is my mother, Susan Rayburn."

Susan extended her hand and Hank took it gently. "So nice to finally meet you, Mrs. Rayburn."

"Likewise," she said through tight lips.

Hank greeted Little Ernie with a gentle poke to the ribs, and the young fellow laughed out loud.

"My daughter here tells me you were in the service," Becky's mother said casually. "Is that right?"

"I was in the army, yes." Hank looked at Becky questioningly. She shrugged and rolled her eyes a bit but didn't say anything.

"And she told me you were also in the war."

"Yes, ma'am, I was."

Susan stopped her bouncing and shot him a hard look. "Then let me ask you something, Hank. Have you ever killed anybody?"

Becky winced. How could anyone be so crude? "Mama!"

"Well—I'm just asking."

Hank folded his arms and said, "Let me put it like this, Mrs. Rayburn. I never killed anyone who wasn't trying to kill me."

Susan's eyes went wide. "Oh."

Feeling as though all the air had just been sucked out of the room, Hank opted to bow out gracefully. He could always stop by later and catch up with Becky. When he didn't have to face the Spanish Inquisition.

"Just thought I'd stop by and say hello," Hank said to Becky. Turning to leave, he added, "Nice meeting you, Mrs. Rayburn."

"Likewise," she said for the second time.

～

WHEN HANK WALKED OUT OF THE STORE, SUSAN WAS GRINNING like a mule in a briar patch. "So is he the handsome young prince you were telling me about? The one you picked up hitchhiking?"

Becky's hands went straight to her hips, hard eyes cutting right through her mother. "You know he is," she said dryly. "And thanks for running him off."

"You don't have to be so snotty about it. I was just trying to make conversation. The boy's obviously way too sensitive."

Becky picked up a catalog and pretended to read, hoping her mother would either leave or simply remain quiet. But she knew better.

"He is cute, you know," Susan said.

"Yes, Mama. He's certainly is."

Becky knew her mother all too well. If she ever found out they'd gone to the movies or that she'd had him over for supper, she'd have them engaged and on their way to the altar. She loved her mother but sometimes her exaggerations simply went too far. Still, it wasn't like Becky was trying to keep any secrets. Being as Becky was madly in love with the guy, Susan was bound to find out sooner or later. Might as well fess up.

"I cooked supper for him last Saturday night," Becky revealed rather tentatively.

Susan took a surprised step back and clamped her free hand over her mouth. She quickly pulled it back and said, "Becky. Are you serious?" The words barely out of her mouth, she dropped her chin then glanced back up with only her eyes. "And when were you planning on telling me about it?"

"It was just the other night, Mama. Good grief. We ate, then talked a little, and he went on home." Becky wasn't about to tell her mother Hank had been over at her house every night since. At least up until he started the evening shift.

"I could've kept the baby for you, you know," Susan huffed.

"I know, Mama, but I wanted him there with us. Hank did, too."

Susan threw her hand across her heart, nearly dropping Little Ernie. "He did?"

"He most certainly did."

Becky's mother would have jumped at the chance to keep her grandson. No doubt about it. But Becky hadn't wanted her to know anything beforehand. A relentless grilling with never-ending questions would have been inevitable. Just like now.

"So-o-o," Susan said, dragging the little word out. "When are you two getting together again?"

Becky flipped a couple more pages in the catalog. "I have no idea, Mama."

"You're in love with the guy, aren't you?" Susan narrowed her eyes. "It's all over your face."

Becky answered her mother's question without reservation. Since the cat had already poked its furry head out of the bag, might as well let the rest of him out, too. "I am, Mama," she confessed with newfound boldness. "Yes, I am."

Susan cleared her throat. "I'm happy for you, you know I am, but when your daddy finds out, it'll most likely kill him."

"Ma-ma."

"Well, it's the truth, and you know it."

"How can you say how he'll react? Daddy doesn't even know Hank exists."

All too familiar with Susan's mannerisms, Becky could tell her mother had something on her mind. Susan might not want to share it, but—whether she wanted to or not—she was about to give it up.

"What is it you're not telling me, Mama?"

"What are you talking about?"

Becky crossed her arms. "You know exactly what I'm talking about. Now spit it out."

Susan dropped her head and sighed. "After you left the other day, I told your daddy all about Hank."

Becky's head dropped. "Oh, Mama. Why in the world would you want to tell Daddy?"

"Now just hold on, young lady," Susan said, wagging her finger in Becky's face. "You never told me not to."

Becky was fit to be tied. She'd shared confidential information with her mother, and Susan had betrayed that confidence. The fact it had been with the father she so dearly loved, still didn't make it right.

"You knew better than to tell him. If I'd wanted Daddy to know, I would have told him myself."

"He has a right to know these things, Miss Priss. He's your father."

"I'm a grown woman, Mama," Becky protested. "I've been married and I have a child. I'm not his little girl anymore."

"You will always be his little girl."

Becky gave her mother another hard look. "I didn't mean it like that, and you know it."

Now Becky would have to sit down with him and have one of those father/daughter talks. Something they hadn't done in years. Something she'd always dreaded.

"So, what did he say?" Becky said reluctantly.

Susan sighed. "Don't worry. I didn't tell him everything."

"What do you mean?"

"I never told him the boy's related to the Taylors. You'll have to do that yourself."

~

HANK PULLED UP AT CRAFT'S FOR THE SECOND TIME, HAPPY TO SEE no other vehicles parked out front. Though an empty parking lot wasn't exactly good for business, at least Becky's inquisitive mother had left the building. They would no doubt face off again sometime in the future, and when the day came, hopefully, it would be a lot less awkward than the first.

Becky was nowhere in sight when he entered the store. Moments later, she pushed through the plastic hanging strips separating the front from the warehouse in back.

"Can I help you, sir?" Becky called out.

Her silliness elicited a hearty chuckle from Hank. "I'm sure you can, miss."

They met halfway between the door and the counter and shared a long and passionate kiss. "We've got to stop meeting like this," Hank said, feigning a nervous glance around the store. "Someone might be watching."

Becky flashed her eyebrows.

Hank said, "Little Ernie asleep?"

"Yep," Becky said, "and Mr. Craft's not here either."

Another longer and more passionate kiss ensued.

Hank could have stood there and kissed her all day, but he had to go to work and so did she. Not to mention a customer might walk in unannounced from the back exactly like she just had. Hank reluctantly loosened his grip, and Becky took her place behind the counter.

"I have to apologize for Mama," Becky said. "Sometimes she can be so…"

"Annoying?"

"Worse than just annoying. The woman's a loose cannon."

"Don't worry about it. Grandpa used to say we can pick our friends but we can't pick our relatives."

Becky laughed. "Don't you have to be at work by three?"

Hank did have to be at work by three, but he still needed to tell Becky about Carl's arrest and the subsequent rock-slinging exhibition the guy had put on in front of his grandmother's house.

"We arrested Carl Walker last night."

Becky's eyes narrowed sharply. "You did?" she said. "What for?"

"Him and a few of his buddies had gathered up at the Twelve Point, and he was determined to pick a fight with some guy named Roger."

"Roger McCaffrey?"

"Sounds about right. Anyway, once we got there, he decided to go after me instead."

Becky gasped. "He didn't hit you, did he?"

"No," Hank said. "He's not quick enough. Not if I know it's coming."

"So, what happened next?"

"We took him to jail. His dad showed up, slapped him in the face a couple of times, then bonded him out and took him home."

"Typical," she said.

"Then…"

"You mean there's more?"

"Around midnight, somebody cut a couple of donuts in the road at Grandma's and slung gravel all over the front of the house."

"Sounds just like something Carl would do."

"Nothing similar happened over at your place, did it?"

Becky shrugged. "If it did, I guess I slept right through it."

Hank cleared his throat and took a step closer. "You'll let me know if anything should happen, won't you?"

"Of course, I will," she said, flashing a smile that nearly took his breath away. "Cross my heart."

~

BECKY LOCKED UP THE STORE AND LOADED LITTLE ERNIE INTO THE pickup. There would never be a good time to talk to her father, so she might as well go ahead and get it over with. She'd talked a good game with her mother, but how her father would react, she wasn't quite sure. Finding out his daughter had fallen madly in love with Jake Taylor's grandson was bound to elicit some sort of interesting reaction. Good or bad, it wouldn't change the way she felt. But to keep the peace, Becky would do her best to win his approval.

Pulling up in front of her parents' house, Becky saw her father's truck parked in the driveway. Her mother's car was nowhere in sight. Perfect. With Susan not there to butt in every other word, she might just be able to charm her father a bit. Certainly worth a try.

Bill met his daughter at the door and immediately took Little Ernie. "How's my boy?" he said, taking a step back and holding the child high. "And how's my favorite daughter?"

"I'm good, Daddy," she said brightly. "Where's Mama?"

"Mrs. Jacobs wasn't feeling well, and your mama went down to check on her and take her some soup. She shouldn't be gone long. Come on in."

Becky took a seat on the couch. Bill sat down in his well-worn recliner and propped Little Ernie on his knee. "I understand congratulations are in order," her father said.

"Sir?"

"Your mama tells me you've met a young man."

"Yes, sir, I have," Becky said, nodding. "I sure have."

"She said he's not from around here."

Becky squirmed uncomfortably. "No, sir, he's not. He's originally from Michigan, but then he moved out to Colorado." She conveniently left out the part about Hank's short stint in the great state of Louisiana.

"Susan said he just got out of the army and he's been to Vietnam a couple of times."

"Yes, sir, and just recently, he went to work for the sheriff's office. He's training with Jack Slater."

Bill leaned forward and kissed his grandson on the head. "She said something about him living with his grandparents for a while before moving up to Colorado."

So he did know about the Louisiana part after all. Becky's father remembered the story her mother told him quite well. Apparently, she'd only left out the part about the identity of Hank's grandparents.

"Who are his grandparents anyway, if you don't mind me asking? If they live in Lee Parish, I'm sure I know them."

Oh, you know them all right. Though she dreaded it with every fiber of her being, Becky was about to find out just how much her father despised the Taylors.

"Jake and Ada Taylor," she said softly, hoping he wouldn't drop Little Ernie on the floor or toss him through the ceiling.

For a long moment, the room remained eerily quiet. Only the low rumble of the ceiling fan overhead could be heard.

If Becky expected to hear the lion's roar, she was not to be disappointed. "Becky Marie. Are you out of your ever-loving mind?"

"Daddy, I..."

"No, no, no. A hundred times, no. Anybody else, I can deal with. But Jake Taylor's grandson? No, Becky. I won't stand for it." Bill shook an angry finger in her direction. "Your grandpa won't stand for it either."

"Daddy, there's absolutely nothing wrong with Hank. If you just get to know him you'll..."

"I don't want to get to know him. I said, no. And no means no."

Becky hopped up off the couch with hot tears streaming down her face. "Give me my son," she said coldly.

"What?"

"Give him to me. Right now."

Becky took Little Ernie and stared her father down. "What did Hank Goodman ever do to you, Daddy? And for the record, what did Jacob Taylor ever do to you?" She blew out a hard breath. "You and grandpa need to grow up and start acting like Christians. But if you're willing to let this stand between you and your grandson, it'll be your problem. It's certainly not mine."

Bill made no attempt to follow his daughter, and she slammed the door hard on her way out. Here it was again. Always something.

CHAPTER TWENTY-FIVE

*H*ank recounted the events of the previous night. Jack listened closely but kept his thoughts to himself. When Hank finished, Jack said, "No doubt it was Carl. Sounds just like something he would do."

"Yeah, but I could never prove it. Especially since I never got a look at the vehicle."

If something wasn't done about Carl, Hank knew incidents such as this would become commonplace. The question then was what to do about it? Arresting the guy would be an exercise in futility. Donald Walker made sure of it. But what if Hank could find some other way to put a little fear into the guy? He'd need some time to think it over. See if he could come up with a plan.

Jack made a tsking sound and shook his head. "He's got it in for you, Hank. Better watch yourself."

"I plan to."

Less than a mile down the road, Jack braked hard and made a quick left turn into an old abandoned service station. The heavy cruiser ground to a stop next to rusty gas pumps unused by paying customers in many long years. Hank couldn't help smiling when he remembered this being the same place Jacob came unglued the first time he ever mentioned Becky Rayburn to him. But why had Jack stopped here?

Jack took a long, deep breath then blew it out slowly and evenly. He adjusted his position in the seat to better face his partner. "What I'm about to tell you, Hank, I've never told another soul." He sighed. "Nobody."

"O-kay." Hank said, dragging the word out. If the intensity in Jack's voice was any indication, things were about to get interesting.

"When I heard what had happened to Ernie, I immediately thought about Carl Walker."

Hank narrowed his eyes. The exact same thing had crossed his mind a time or two. But, like Jack, he hadn't mentioned it to anyone either.

"I was working the night Carl slapped Becky on the courthouse square. Ever heard the story?"

"Becky told me," Hank confirmed.

"Then you know how it ended.

"From what I hear, not too good for Carl."

"Exactly. Anyway, while me and Elmer Jenkins were running around trying to figure out what to do with Carl, I overheard him say something about killing Ernie."

"Did Elmer hear it, too?"

Jack shook his head. "I don't think so. If he did, he never mentioned it."

Hank knew all too well, saying it and doing it were two completely different things. In the heat of the moment, people often said things they didn't particularly mean. When it came right down to it, maybe Carl had done the same thing.

Jack sighed. "At the time, I didn't think that much about it. To me, he was just a drunk kid running off at the mouth. My red flag didn't go up until Ernie actually came up dead."

"Why didn't you mention it then?"

"Everybody out there in the woods that day—Sheriff Mayes

included—thought it was an accident. And with no evidence of foul play whatsoever, who was I to be the odd man out? Deep down though..."

"I can't say I haven't thought the same thing. How do you feel about it now?"

Jack made a sound with his mouth somewhat like a whistle. "I still think it's a possibility," he said. "I just don't have anything to back it up. I could never prove it."

If Carl killed Ernie, Hank believed it had nothing to do with the slapping incident. More than likely he was just getting the big guy out of the way so he could have another shot at Becky. If so, now Hank had come along and upset Walker's apple cart. Big time. If Carl planned on taking out any competition for Becky's affection, Hank knew he'd do well to heed Jack's advice.

"So, what do we do now?" Hank said. "From a police stand-point, I mean."

"If we're gonna pursue this thing, I say we need to talk to Carl's ex-wife, Rita. But with her being gone from here, it won't be easy. Rumor has it she went back to Arkansas to be with her family. At least Carl's saying she did."

Hank rubbed his chin between his fingers and thumb. "So, nobody knows for sure."

"Not really."

Narrowing his eyes, Hank said, "Maybe he killed her too."

Jack shrugged. "One thing's for certain. If she is still alive and there's anybody who can get in touch with her, it'll be Helga at the Twelve Point. Rita worked there for a while before she hooked up with Carl."

"You think she'll tell us what she knows?"

"I don't see why not," Jack said, putting the car in reverse and looking over his shoulder. "When we stop by there later for coffee, we'll find out."

Jack and Hank pulled into the empty parking lot of the Twelve Point Café at exactly eight-forty-five. Jack had already told Hank that even though it was Friday, the café closed at nine o'clock sharp. Helga apparently saw the patrol car drive up and met them in the doorway with her arms crossed.

Furrowing her brow, Helga said, "This place closes in fifteen minutes, and I don't make exceptions. Not even for officers of the law."

Hank looked at Jack and shrugged. Helga's face suddenly lit up. "But for you two, I will. Come on in."

Jack said, "Got any coffee left?"

Helga stopped and cocked her head. "Now, Jack Slater. Have you ever known me to run out of coffee?"

Jack and Hank took a seat at the bar, and Helga brought over two steaming, hot cups. When she set them down on the counter in front of the men, Jack said, "As much as we love your coffee, Helga, we're actually here to pick your brain a bit."

"That shouldn't take too long," she said with a goodhearted chuckle.

"What can you tell us about Rita Hastings?" Jack coughed into his hand. "Walker, I mean."

Helga picked a dishtowel up off the counter and wiped her hands. "What's going on with Rita?" she said. "Is she okay?"

Hank picked up the hot cup and blew forcefully across the top. "We were just wondering if you've heard from her lately."

Looking up at the ceiling, Helga pursed her lips and made a funny face. "Not a word," she said to Jack. "Not recently, anyway. Once she hooked up with the Walker boy, I only got to see her every now and then. And when I did, he was always with her. I heard a while back she had left him and moved back to Arkansas to be with her folks. Couldn't swear to it though."

"Did she fill out an application before she went to work here?" Jack said.

Helga glanced at the ceiling again, now tapping her chin with an index finger. "I'm pretty sure she did. Don't know if I can put my hands on it though. I'll check if you want me to."

Hank and Jack turned to each other with raised eyebrows. "If you don't mind," Jack said. "We'd certainly appreciate it."

"I don't mind at all. You boys help yourselves to a piece of coconut pie while I'm gone."

After a brief absence, Helga returned waving a wrinkled, slightly yellowed sheet of paper. "Look what I found," she said, holding it high with obvious pride.

Jack reached for the application, and Helga swatted at his hand. She slipped on the glasses dangling from her neck, squinted, and then started to read. "Rita Jean Hastings, Route Two, Shadley, Arkansas. Nearest relative, Buddy Ray Hastings, Route Two, Shadley, Arkansas."

Hank frowned. "Where in the world is Shadley?"

"I ain't no expert on geography," Helga said, "but sounds to me like it might be in Arkansas."

Helga gave Hank a lively shove on the shoulder, then she and Jack exploded into laughter.

Hank rolled his eyes and shook his head. He'd run right into that one.

When Jack finally stopped laughing, Helga handed him a folded paper napkin to wipe his eyes. "Sorry, partner." Jack cleared his throat. "I've never heard of the place either."

"Me neither," Helga said, passing the application over to Jack, "but it seems like Rita told me once it was close to Fordyce. Or Little Rock, maybe. I can't remember."

Hank said, "What about a phone number?"

"Here's one," Jack said, pointing to the application. "Hopefully it's still good."

Hank nodded. "Only one way to find out."

Jack pulled a small spiral pad from his shirt pocket and hurriedly copied down the number. He handed the sheet of paper back to Helga and thanked her for her help.

"Y'all never did tell me why you're looking for Rita."

"We're not looking for her," Jack said. "Just want to talk to her."

Helga said, "Wish I could have been more help. Honestly, Rita's a good girl."

"You've been a big help, Mrs. Streeter," Hank said. "We appreciate it.

Helga's hands shot to her hips. "What about the pie?"

"We'll have to take a rain check." Jack stood then motioned for Hank to follow suit. "Come on, partner, let's get out of the way so she can close this place up."

Hank and Jack agreed it was already too late to try to contact the Hastings. As soon as Jack picked up Hank the following afternoon, they would head to the courthouse and use the sheriff's department phone. Being a Saturday, the office would be empty, and they could talk freely. Not that they had anything to hide. In all likelihood, no one would have said a word about two deputies trying to get in touch with some woman who'd supposedly left her husband and moved off to another state to be with her family. If, in fact, that was what Rita Hastings Walker had done.

∼

BEING THE MORE EXPERIENCED OF THE TWO, THEY AGREED JACK should do the talking. If they got lucky, the phone number from the application would still be good. If they got extra lucky, Rita herself would answer the phone. If not, hopefully whoever did would at least let Jack talk to her. Maybe it would be her father, Buddy Ray.

Hank took a seat on the edge of the desk, and Jack plopped down behind it. Jack picked up the receiver then dialed the number slowly and deliberately. A few seconds later, he pointed to the phone and nodded briskly. Bingo.

Jack was on the phone for less than five minutes. Best Hank

could tell, Jack did most of the listening, and the person on the other end, most of the talking. Hank couldn't wait for Jack to get off the phone and share what, if anything, he had found out.

Hanging up the phone, Jack blew a huge puff of air from his nose then slowly shook his head.

Hank threw his hands in the air. "Well?"

"That was her daddy, Buddy Ray. He said they haven't seen Rita in over two years. Said Carl brought her by once when they were passing through, and they haven't seen her since."

"Two years? Are you serious?"

"As a heart attack. Said as far as he knows, she's still married to that no account Walker so and so. I wasn't about to tell him any different either. Not yet anyway."

Hank sighed. "Did he even ask why you wanted to talk to her?"

"It never even came up. According to him, they disowned her the minute she'd stopped sending any money home."

Hank couldn't believe it. Maybe the poor girl had stopped sending money home because she was dead. If Carl had killed Ernie, he could have killed her just as well. Just so he could be with Becky. Until recently, Hank viewed Carl as just some spoiled little rich kid who always got his way and pulled stupid stunts to get attention. Now, he could quite possibly add murderer to the list.

"Now do you think he killed her?" Hank asked, wanting to get his partner's thoughts.

Jack stood. "If he had guts enough to kill Ernie, then taking out Rita wouldn't have been that difficult. And if he's killing anybody standing between him and Becky, man, you've got a huge target on your back."

"So, what do we do now?"

"As much as I hate to, we're gonna have to talk to the sheriff about this."

~

BECKY CRIED ALL THE WAY HOME AFTER THE HEATED EXCHANGE with her father. Though she still believed him to be a good man—and one she loved with all her heart—he could possibly be the most stubborn, hardheaded man on the face of the earth. Was he so dead-set in his feelings he would let them come between him and his grandson? That certainly looked to be the case.

Little Ernie had fallen asleep on the trip home, and Becky had just laid him down when a frantic knock at the front door startled her. She didn't even have to peek to know who the visitor was.

Becky jerked the door open without hesitation. "Can I come in?" Susan said tentatively.

"Of course you can come in, Mama. I've got no beef with you."

Susan entered, shaking her head from side to side, then gave her red-eyed daughter a hug. "Bill told me what happened, and I am so, so sorry. Can we sit down and talk?"

She led her mother into the kitchen, and they sat down at the table next to each other. Becky propped up her elbows and promptly buried her face in her hands. Susan said, "Maybe he just needs a little time to digest everything. Time heals all wounds, you know."

The comment stung like an angry yellow jacket. Becky raised her head and gave her mother a stern look. "He's had more than enough time to digest everything. Matter of fact, he's had years. How long can this craziness go on, Mama? Mr. Taylor's dead, for goodness' sake. Dead and six feet under. And what, pray tell, does any of that have to do with Hank Goodman? He didn't even know anything about it until I told him."

"Must be a Rayburn thing," Susan said, exasperatedly. "All this hard-headedness."

"I'm a Rayburn, too, you know."

"See what I mean?"

Becky crossed her arms and narrowed her eyes. "Well ain't you one to talk, Mama? I bet I get my fair share from both sides of the family."

"Look, Becky. Us getting into it ain't gonna help a thing. Let me talk to your daddy and see if I can soften him up a bit. He's a good, Christian man."

Without preamble, Becky jumped to her feet. "I know one thing," she said with conviction. "Christian or not, he won't catch me on my hands and knees any time soon. I tried my best to reason with him, and I'm done. If he wants to change his mind then he can come crawling to me."

"And what if he doesn't?"

"Then I think we already know what's gonna happen. Don't we?"

CHAPTER TWENTY-SIX

*H*ank stared out the window into a parking lot occupied by only his and Jack's patrol car. Jack was back behind the desk, only this time dialing Sheriff Abel Mayes's home telephone number. They had agreed, for better or worse and regardless of what his response might be, the sheriff needed to know what was going on. At least what they thought was going on. When the smoke cleared, he would be the one who decided whether to move forward or not.

Hank had asked Jack why they couldn't just discuss the matter with Chief Hall. His partner made a funny face and said they couldn't because of the chief's somewhat "close" connection with Donald Walker. Hall dealt in cattle himself but on a much smaller scale than the Walkers. Still, they made regular purchases from each other's herds, and over the course of time, the two men had developed quite a friendship. With the sheriff, Jack went on to say, there was no love lost. Mayes didn't necessarily dislike the man, he simply didn't appreciate him always rushing to get his reckless son out of trouble. The sheriff had been overheard to say a few nights in jail might just be what the boy needed. And, so far, it hadn't happened.

Some fifteen minutes later, a red-faced Able Mayes appeared in the doorway. He heaved a long, heavy sigh. "This better be good, boys. We were trying to spend a little quality time with the grandkids."

Hank and Jack frowned at each other then followed Mayes into his office. He plopped down in the big leather chair behind his desk, leaned back, and locked his chubby fingers together. Both deputies remained standing.

"So, let's hear it," the sheriff said.

Hank said nothing, happy just to listen and let his senior partner do all the talking.

Jack explained his suspicions about Ernie Craft's death, the comment Carl had made the night of the slapping incident, and the information he and Hank had recently acquired. The sheriff listened intently, his eyes widening and then narrowing as the story progressed.

By the time Jack finished, Mayes was leaning forward with both elbows propped on the edge of the desk. "So, let me get this straight," he said, sitting back in his chair again. "You have a gut feeling Carl killed Ernie based on some comment he made several years ago. And just because her daddy hasn't seen her in two years, you think he killed Rita, too. That just about sum it up?"

Hank and Jack glanced at each other and then nodded to the sheriff in unison.

"Look, fellows, I can appreciate your enthusiasm. And, trust me, I don't take any of this lightly. But if we don't have anything more to go on—then we have nothing to go on."

The two deputies exchanged glances a second time. Jack moved closer to the sheriff's desk. "Hank here's dating Becky Craft. If Carl is taking out anybody standing between him and Becky, don't you think Hank might be next?"

"What do you think, Hank?" Mayes said to his newest deputy.

"You've been awful quiet through all this. I'd like to know what's on your mind."

"I agree with Jack, but you bring up a good point. Other than our gut, we don't have a whole lot to go on."

The sheriff stood and stretched then joined his men on the other side of the desk. Mayes laid a heavy hand on Jack's shoulder. "Thanks for bringing this to my attention," he said. "I think what we need to do now is keep our eyes and ears open. If either one of you see or hear anything—and I mean anything—I want to know about it right away."

How could Hank and Jack not agree with the sheriff? With no hard evidence to support their suspicions about Ernie, and not even knowing for sure about Rita Hastings, they didn't have a leg to stand on. Hank knew all about being careful. In Vietnam, he'd grown accustomed to living in constant danger. At least there was only one Carl Walker for him to have to worry about.

Back in the patrol car, Hank stared out the window, quietly mulling things over. Wondering how Carl could have killed Ernie and made it look like an accident. Finally, he said to Jack, "How did they know it was Ernie's gun that killed him?"

"Mr. Craft identified it. And when we broke it down, it had a spent shell in it."

"Single-shot?"

"That's right."

"So, we know the gun had been fired but not who fired it. If Carl had been hiding close by, he could have easily grabbed it when Ernie got about halfway through the fence. No way the poor guy could have defended himself."

"Exactly."

"Did they check the gun for fingerprints?" Hank said. "Other than Ernie's, I mean."

Jack sighed and shook his head. "See, that's the thing. Nobody checked anything for anything. Like I said, to everybody out there that day, it was just a freak accident. One of those terrible things you deal with the best you can and then go on home."

Hank understood why they'd felt the way they did. If he had been there, he would have probably thought the same thing himself.

"The sheriff was pretty clear about his feelings. What do you think we should do now?"

"What he said, I guess. Just keep our eyes and ears open. I'm worried for you though. The guy's a time bomb just waiting to go off."

"I appreciate your concern." Hank drew a deep breath and blew it back out. "I'll be careful."

∼

JACK DROPPED HANK OFF AT ADA'S HOUSE AROUND TEN ON SUNDAY night. They wouldn't have to report for duty again until six a.m. on Wednesday morning. This would start another full week on the day shift. When Hank asked if they would be working grave-yard anytime soon, Jack assured him it wouldn't be until he completed the basic academy.

Up early the next morning, Hank headed into Crosscut to help Homer in the warehouse. His primary objective, however, was to be with his one true love, who he hadn't seen since Friday. He'd talked to her on the phone Saturday morning, but something hadn't been quite right. He couldn't put his finger on it at the time. Today, he'd do his best to find out.

Becky met Hank at the door and he picked her up. While she was still in the air, their lips met for a long, passionate kiss. Hank hoped Mr. Craft wasn't watching, but if so, he'd just witnessed quite an exhibition on kissing.

"You guys all by yourself this morning?" Hank said, setting Becky back on her feet.

"Mr. Craft's in the back. I told him you were coming, and he's looking forward to seeing you."

Hank nodded. "Does he even know about us?"

"He does."

"Has he said anything about it?"

Becky shook her head. "No, but any time I mention your name, he lights up like a Christmas tree."

"Oh, really?"

"He thinks a lot of you," she said. Becky let out a giggle she tried to suppress with her hand. "I think a lot of you, too."

Another extended kiss followed. After, Hank said, "At lunch today, we need to have a talk. Something's come up."

Becky took a step back, placing her hand over her heart. "Not with us, I hope."

"No, no," Hank said, shaking his head emphatically. "I just need to run a couple of things by you."

"Good." Becky ran her hand across the top of her head. "I need to run something by you, too."

~

WHEN HOMER RETURNED WITH LUNCH, BECKY AND HANK SAT down across from each other at the checkerboard table. They made small talk until they'd finished eating. Hank cleared his throat and said, "Should I go first or do you want to?"

"Better let me," Becky said, nodding slightly.

Hank propped his elbows on the table and locked his fingers together. He leaned forward and said, "Fire away."

Becky dabbed at her mouth with a napkin. "Friday evening after I closed the store, I stopped by to talk with Daddy."

"And?"

She dropped her head and sighed. "It wasn't good, Hank. Not good at all."

"How so?"

"He doesn't want me to have anything to do with you," she managed. "You're Jacob Taylor's grandson, and, to him, nothing else matters. I tried to reason with him, but he refuses to even listen."

Hank knew how hard this had to be on Becky. She'd not only been hurt by her father's reaction, it had embarrassed her as well. Here was another example of a professed Christian who couldn't even find it in his heart to forgive. Hank reached across the table and took her hand gently in his. "Maybe he just needs a little time to get used to everything."

Hank had no idea he'd just taken the same path of reasoning Becky's mother had.

"From what I've seen so far," she said, now sniffling, "I don't think it's ever going to happen."

Tightening his grip on her hand, Hank said, "But we love each other. And one way or the other, everything will work itself out."

"I hope so." Becky repositioned herself and sighed. "Now, what did you want to tell me?"

Letting go of her hand, Hank fell back in his chair. He took a deep breath, blew it out quickly, then leaned forward again. "I honestly don't know the best way to tell you this." He hesitated a moment. "But Jack and I have been talking." Another hesitation. "Jack thinks Carl may have killed Ernie."

Hank paused another beat, giving what he had said a chance to sink in. Finally, he added, "And so do I."

Becky looked away, staring at nothing in particular. "I thought the same thing at first but then I convinced myself even Carl couldn't do something so despicable."

Hank reached for her hand again. When she turned back to him, tears were streaming down both cheeks. "How could he do such a thing to my husband?"

"If he did, he's—well, he's just evil."

"But why would he kill Ernie?" she said, shaking her head

vigorously. "He couldn't be with me. He had a wife for goodness' sake."

Time for the rest of the story.

"You've heard the rumor going around?" Hank said, tsking. "How Rita left Carl and moved back to her family in Arkansas?"

"Yes. I've heard it."

"We called them, and they haven't seen her in two years."

Becky swiped the back of her hand across her face. "What?"

"Her father said as far as he knows, she's still married to Carl and living in Louisiana."

"You think he killed her, too, don't you?" Becky's eyes grew wider. "It's what you're saying, isn't it?"

"I think it's certainly possible. But right now, we don't know for sure."

Pulling her hand away, Becky quickly stood as if she'd had a revelation. "If he did," she said. "Then he's killing anybody who comes between me and him."

"Certainly looks that way."

Becky sat back down then reached for Hank's hand. "What are you going to do?"

"Not a lot I can do, I guess," he said with a shrug. "Other than staying on my toes."

"What about me?"

"You need to do the same," he cautioned. "If it's you he wants, then it's hard to imagine him hurting you. But you never know what's going on in a mixed up mind like his. If he's killed two people already, no doubt the guy's nuts. And who knows, maybe he's decided if he can't have you, nobody can."

When they stood in unison, Hank leaned in and kissed Becky tenderly. Laying even a finger on the woman Hank loved would be the worst mistake Carl Walker ever made.

~

AFTER THE GRAVEL-SLINGING DEMONSTRATION HE PUT ON IN front of Ada Taylor's house recently, Carl had kept a low profile. Not that her or her ignorant grandson could do anything about it. By the time those two clowns came to their senses, he was already making tracks. No way they could ever pin it on him.

Goodman needed to realize something, and the quicker he did, the better. For him anyway. In Lee Parish, the Walkers ruled the roost. Donald had all the local politicians—except maybe the sheriff—firmly tucked away in his back pocket. All three district judges were old hunting buddies, and he'd contributed nicely to each man's election campaign. The district attorney, Uncle Bud, had been married to Donald's sister for the past twenty-some odd years. Anyway you sliced it, they had all the bases neatly covered.

Donald Walker sat atop an empire, and with no brothers or sisters to stand in the way, one day it would all belong to Carl. And oh, how he longed for that day. All his life, he'd been nothing but a dog feeding off his father's table scraps. Someday, and probably in the not too distant future, it was all going to change. The old man certainly wasn't getting any younger.

Speaking of the old man, Carl had made up his mind. If his father ever slapped him again—like he did at the courthouse in front of Goodman and Slater—blood or no blood, he would pay dearly for it. If he knew what had happened to the last guy who'd done something stupid like that, Donald would stop and think twice about it. Blood or no blood.

CHAPTER TWENTY-SEVEN

S tacking bag after heavy bag of cattle feed in back of the stuffy warehouse had given Hank a chance to think things over carefully. With the dreaded training academy less than a month away, he couldn't help but be concerned. His being away from home couldn't be kept secret, and sooner or later, Carl would find out he was gone. And once he did, the guy would pretty much have free rein to harass Becky any time he wanted. He would have to ask Jack and the others to keep an eye on the store and her house while he was away. Especially at night.

Hank had considered discussing his suspicions with Homer but managed to talk himself out of it. After all, it was only specu-lation anyway. If Mr. Craft even suspected such a thing, there was no telling how he might react. Since Homer didn't trust Carl either, Hank would ask him to watch for the guy's truck and to let the deputies know if he saw it anywhere near Becky's place.

If Carl had even a snowball's chance of getting with Becky, Hank would have to be eliminated. He knew that, but then, so did Carl. If Carl had indeed killed Ernie, he had done a pretty good job of making it look like an accident. If he ever came after Hank, he might try something along those same lines. For all Hank knew, the guy could already be planning such a thing.

By five o'clock, Homer had already headed out, leaving Hank and Becky behind to lock up the store.

Becky slipped the key in the deadbolt and gave it a turn. "Are you coming over this evening?"

Hank moved a little closer, brushing his hand lightly across her cheek. "Do you want me to?"

She giggled and then poked him in the chest with her finger. "What do you think?"

"I think I'll be there as soon as I can knock a little of this dust off."

"I can't wait," she said with a wink.

~

BECKY GRIMACED WHEN HER HOUSE CAME INTO VIEW AND SHE SAW her grandfather's pickup parked in the driveway and him leaning up against it. As much as she loved the old man, he was about the last person on Earth she wanted to talk to right now. Lester was the reason her daddy felt the way he did about the Taylors. And if anybody thought Bill Rayburn was stubborn and bullheaded, his father could be that times ten.

After hopping out of the truck, Becky hurried to the other side to gather up her sleeping son. "Come on in, Grandpa. I need to get Little Ernie out of this heat."

"I can't stay but a minute," he said, slowly trailing her up the steps.

With Ernie squared away, Becky strode back down the hall for the inevitable showdown with her grandfather. His trips to see her being few and far between, she knew exactly why he had come. From the living room, she could see him sitting in the kitchen, both elbows propped on the table and an undeniable frown on his face.

"Can I get you anything, Grandpa?" she said with little enthusiasm. "A glass of tea, maybe?"

Lester shook his head slightly. "I don't think so," he said. "I'm good."

Becky took the chair closest to his and asked the question she already knew the answer to. "So, what brings you by today?"

Lester Rayburn cleared his throat. "Bill tells me you and Jake Taylor's grandson are getting pretty sweet on each other."

Her suspicions had been right on the money. Lester was there for one reason and one reason only. To talk to her about Hank. She started to speak, but after opening her mouth only slightly, she stopped.

"I sure hate to hear things like that, sweetie."

Is that right? What a surprise.

"Look, Grandpa, I love Hank Goodman, and that's all there is to it. I hate something happened to your sister, like what, a hundred years ago, but it has nothing whatsoever to do with me. And it certainly has nothing to do with him."

"He's got Taylor blood," Lester said, his voice trembling slightly. "Can't you see that?"

Becky's hand slapped the tabletop. "No, I can't see it, and apparently you and Daddy are the only ones who can. And honestly, Grandpa, what big difference does it make anyway?"

Lester rose from his chair and huffed. "Bill said he couldn't talk any sense into you. Looks like I can't either."

"You just need to go, Grandpa."

Near the door, Lester stopped. Without even looking back, he said, "You need to think long and hard about this, Becky. Family always comes first."

Yeah, right.

~

HANK FOUND HIS GRANDMOTHER STANDING AT THE STOVE

vigorously stirring a large pot of homemade vegetable soup. She hadn't heard him come in, and he briefly thought about slipping up behind her and giving her a playful scare. Not knowing if her heart was up to it, he quickly changed his mind. Not to mention the possibility of getting whacked over the head by a large metal spoon dripping with boiling hot soup.

"You'd better close the windows and doors, Grandma," he said. "Once a smell that good gets out, people will be coming from everywhere wanting to get a taste."

"Oh, Hank," she said, spinning around. "I didn't even know you were home."

"I just got here," he said.

"So, the soup smells good?"

"It smells great," he said, giving his grandmother a convincing hug and receiving a mile-wide grin in return.

"I'm making cornbread to go with it. I've got crackers but I'd much rather have cornbread. Wouldn't you?"

"No doubt about it. Especially yours."

"Why don't you get cleaned up?" Ada said, turning her attention back to the stove. "I should have everything ready by the time you're finished."

Twenty minutes later, Hank had washed off the thick layer of warehouse dust, slipped on a clean set of clothes, and dabbed on a bit of his best cologne. Ada had the soup and cornbread waiting on the table when he came out of his room. She'd poured two large glasses of sweet iced tea. Even peeled and sliced a fresh Vidalia onion.

"I guess you're headed over to Becky's after supper," Ada said, her knife slicing smoothly through the hot cornbread.

"Yes, ma'am."

"Harvey called a little earlier and said he might stop by. Once he finds out I made soup, I'll have to warm him up some." Ada covered her mouth to stifle her giggle. "I'm talking about the soup."

The entire day, Hank had been pondering whether or not to tell Ada what Becky had shared. His grandmother would have good insight on something like that, and getting her opinion might not be such a bad idea. He'd give it a shot.

Hank reached over and touched his grandmother's arm. "You know I'm in love with Becky. Don't you, Grandma?"

Ada nodded, smiling weakly, but said nothing.

"We've got a situation I wanted to run it by you. See what you think."

Sitting up a little straighter, Ada said, "I'm guessing you're talking about her daddy."

"Yes, ma'am."

"You know, Hank, I wish I could tell you how to fix this thing, but I'm afraid I can't. Even though she loves you, it don't necessarily mean her family will. What we have to do is hope and pray that someday, they'll come to their senses. And, they may never. If they don't, you and Becky will just have to be prepared to live with it."

"That would be tough," he said, shaking his head slowly.

"For the longest time, I didn't think my own mama would ever speak to me again. And it took Linda's being born for her to do it. She just couldn't forgive me for running off with Jake and not having the big church wedding she'd always dreamed of. By the time she finally came around, it was me who had to do the forgiving. See what I mean?"

"I guess we all have our share of difficulties."

"Just do right by Becky," Ada said, patting Hank's hand. "Be good to her and let the Good Lord work out the rest of it. If y'all get married and He blesses you with a grandbaby or two, the Rayburns will soften up. I guarantee it."

Hank could feel a great deal of his anxiety lifting. If he had anything to say about it, it would happen just like his grandmother predicted.

Ada picked up the little bowl with the sliced onion. "Try a

piece of this," she said. "I believe it's one of the sweetest I've ever tasted."

Hank laughed out loud. "Becky would never forgive me if I ate onion, Grandma."

∿

BY SEVEN, HANK WAS SITTING ON BECKY'S COUCH WITH HIS ARM draped around her shoulder. Little Ernie seemed content in his playpen, surrounded by a vast assortment of brightly colored toys and stuffed animals.

Becky placed a hand on Hank's knee and sighed as she slowly shook her head.

"What is it?" he asked.

"When it rains, it pours, don't it?"

"Meaning?"

"When I got home today, Grandpa was waiting for me. And I didn't even have to wonder why."

"Let me guess," Hank said, tapping his chin with his index finger. "He wanted to talk about me?" He coughed into his hand. "Or us."

"Yeah," she said. "He feels the same way Daddy does and thought he might be able to talk some sense into me."

Hank chuckled. "Did he have any luck?"

With the same hand that had just been resting on his knee, Becky playfully smacked him on the upper arm. "Oh, stop it," she said.

Hank was more than ready for their relationship to move forward. Regardless of how the rest of her family felt. He'd taken his grandmother's advice to heart, and from what Becky had told him earlier, she was prepared to do the same thing.

"They may never come around," Hank said, "but as long as we love each other, nothing else matters. I hope they accept me at some point, but if they don't, are you sure you'll be okay?"

"The three of us being together is all I care about. But one thing does have to change though."

Hank drew his head back, giving her a curious look. "What do you mean?"

"Regardless of how Daddy feels about you, I can't keep him away from Little Ernie. It's not fair to him, and it's certainly not fair to my son. He needs to spend time with his grandpa."

"I couldn't agree with you more."

"It won't be easy," she said with a frown. "I'm sure I'll have to bite my tongue from time to time."

Hank nodded in agreement. "You might, but it'll be okay."

"For Little Ernie's sake, I have to be the bigger person here"

Hank leaned in and kissed her tenderly. Oh, how he loved this woman.

～

BECKY'S PORCH LIGHT DIDN'T COME ON UNTIL NEARLY ELEVEN. FOR the past two hours, Carl had been parked just down the road with those two idiots not even having a clue. He'd backed under an old, abandoned tractor shed less than a quarter of a mile from her house and cut off his headlights. From this vantage point, he could see her porch and the front of Goodman's pickup. The view wasn't great by any means, but it was good enough. He couldn't do anything about the guy being there—not at the moment anyway—but at least he would know how long he had stayed.

Carl wasn't sure but thought he could make out the silhouettes of two people standing in the doorway. Probably swapping spit. He'd been sipping from a tall bottle of eighty-proof whiskey all evening, and by then, everything was starting to run together. All he had to do now was hold his position. When Goodman left, he'd be heading in the opposite direction. Even if he drove by the shed, he'd never see Carl's pickup hiding in the shadows.

When Goodman's truck finally left, Carl seriously considered driving over to Becky's and banging on the door. Maybe even kicking it in. But what good would it do? She'd already threatened to shoot him, even though he knew hot air when he heard it. As much as all this was killing him—some other man spending time with his woman—one day soon, Goodman would be out of the picture. Permanently. And how did he know such things? Because he was the one who would make it happen.

CHAPTER TWENTY-EIGHT

*A*bel Mayes sat on the edge of his chair anxiously thumbing through a thick stack of documents few had ever seen or would ever see. They were arrest reports, and there were quite a lot of them. In just the past five years, Carl Walker had been arrested twenty-seven times. The sheriff shook his head in disbelief. Twenty-seven times he'd been brought in handcuffed, and not once had he spent the night in jail. Such a thing even being possible simply boggled his mind.

Most of the arrests were for fighting but ranged anywhere from disturbing the peace to unlawful destruction of property. Then there was domestic abuse. In the three short years Carl and Rita had been married, he'd been arrested six times for battery—arrested half a dozen times, but deputies had been called to the residence over and over and over. Rita was quick to pick up the phone and call for help, but when officers arrived, she never wanted to press charges. Most likely, she remembered the further beatings she'd received after the other six times.

The sheriff's sudden interest in Carl's criminal history, or lack thereof, had been brought about by his recent meeting with Jack Slater and Hank Goodman. Both men strongly suspected Carl of killing Ernie Craft. And now, quite possibly, his missing wife. Like everyone else, when Mayes heard the girl had left her husband, it came as no surprise at all. But had she actually left?

Nearly three days had passed since he'd downplayed things with the guys. And probably a bit too much. With Rita's family not even knowing her whereabouts, she could have met with some sort of tragic end. The sheriff would have to do some investigating of his own. Maybe drop in on Carl for a little one-on-one. Unexpectedly, of course.

~

THE SHERIFF SPOTTED CARL'S PICKUP PARKED NEXT TO ONE OF THE family's catfish ponds and Carl walking down the levee carrying a long, flexible fishing rod. In addition to their cattle empire, Donald Walker had also established a quite lucrative business producing pond-raised catfish. Mayes watched from a distance as Carl abruptly stopped and then made a cast out near the middle of the pond.

Walking up to within twenty feet of Carl, Mayes stopped and said, "Little hot for fishing today, ain't it, Carl?"

"Heat don't bother me none," he said dryly, without looking up. "Just cops."

Mayes moved closer, squinting in the bright sunlight. "Oh? And why is that?"

Carl spun around and grunted. "Huh," he said, tossing his head back. "Like you don't know."

The sheriff knew all right, just like everybody else. Cops bothered the guy because he'd had so many run-ins with them over the years.

"So, what you been up to lately?" Mayes said. "Heard you got into a little ruckus down at the Twelve Point the other night." He cleared his throat. "Heard you might have it in for my new deputy, too."

Carl rolled his eyes. "What are you even doing here anyway? I ain't got nothing to say to you."

"Just passing by and saw your truck," the sheriff said, pointing back over his shoulder with his thumb. "Thought I'd stop and see how you're doing these days. Heard your wife left, and I was just wondering if you were okay."

"You don't give two hoots about me, and you know it. Now unless you're totally blind, you can see I'm trying to do something here."

The sheriff threw his hands up. "Don't let me hold you up. Oh, by the way. You haven't heard anything out of Rita lately, have you? We were talking to her daddy, and he said he hasn't seen her in quite a long time."

"Then he's the one with a problem," Carl said with a smirk. "Not me."

"Just asking," Mayes said.

Carl threw his fishing pole to the ground and stomped past the sheriff. "I told you I ain't got nothing to say to you."

"You think I don't know what you did," Mayes called out after him. "But I do."

Stopping in his tracks, Carl slowly turned back to face the sheriff. "Yeah, and just what did I do? Let's hear it. Tell me what I did."

"You know exactly what I mean."

"What did you think, you old fool? You'd come down here and trick me into confessing or something? You ain't got nothing on me, and you know it." Carl made two fists, put his wrists together, and extended his arms to the sheriff. "Put the cuffs on me then. Right now. If you've got something on me, cuff me and let's go. Put your money where your mouth is."

Mayes dropped his gaze to his feet and swallowed hard.

"See there," Carl said, nodding. "I knew it. You're just blowing smoke." He took a step closer to the sheriff, poking at him with his finger. "Remember this, old man. I don't like you, and my daddy don't like you. And if you don't start toeing the line, you're gonna be looking for a brand new line of work. Now if you'll excuse me, I have better things to do with my time."

~

CARL JERKED OPEN HIS PICKUP DOOR AND SWUNG HIMSELF IN. Stupid idiot. Just what he needed, some broken-down old lawman breathing down his neck. As much as he despised the sheriff, Goodman was probably behind this whole Spanish Inquisition thing. Oh, Carl had it in for Mayes's newest deputy all right. And sometime in the not too distant future, it was all going to come to a head.

Taking his time driving home, Carl thought about how great it would be when he and Becky could be together again. With Goodman out of the picture, she'd come crawling to him on her hands and knees. He'd make her sweat first. Maybe even beg a little. Finally, he'd relent and take her back. But not without her knowing he could have any other woman he wanted just as easy. Then things would be the way they used to be. Back before Ernie Craft came along and screwed everything up. Yes, sir, it would be the good old days all over again. Except for that stupid boy of hers. But then, kids could have accidents, too.

All Carl had to do was come up with a plan to get rid of the guy. Once and for all. Figuring out some way to make Goodman leave would probably be the easiest thing to do. Maybe he could start a rumor of some sort. Something so outrageous and terrible it would ruin the guy's reputation. Yeah, that ought to do the trick. If he could shame him enough or, better yet, get him fired, the guy would no doubt want to leave and never come back.

But who was he trying to kid? It would never work. And even if it did, such a thing could take forever to pull off. No, sir. He needed a more quick and permanent solution to the problem. He needed Goodman dead. Dead meant no chance of failure. Dead meant Goodman could never come back. Dead meant dead.

~

HANK SAT ON THE EDGE OF THE LOADING DOCK, HIS FEET DANGLING over the side. Abel Mayes drove up and, when the dust settled, stepped out of his car shaking his head. "Good grief, son. Do you ever not work?"

After slipping off his gloves, Hank slapped them solidly together and dust particles flew in every direction. "Idle hands are the devil's workshop," he said. "Or so I've heard."

"Something Mrs. Ada taught you?"

"Actually, it was Mr. Rockford," Hank said. "My old high school principal."

Mayes started the slow climb up the dock's concrete ramp. "Seems the older I get, this thing just gets steeper and steeper." He stopped midway. "I used to be able to run up this ramp. Hard to believe now, huh?"

"I'd offer you a seat, Sheriff, but this floor's pretty dusty." Hank patted the concrete with his hand. "It's pretty hard, too."

"I'll just stand." Mayes took his time, surveying the wide expanse of the warehouse. "You back here by yourself?"

Hank stood, groaning slightly. "Mr. Craft was here but he ran uptown to handle some business. He should be back soon."

"No big deal. It's you I wanted to talk to."

As the sheriff laid out the details of his recent encounter with Carl, Hank listened intently. He couldn't honestly say he hadn't thought about paying the guy a little visit himself. What was he supposed to do? Sit on his hands and wait for Carl to do something stupid?

"Did he say anything about me?"

"No," Mayes said, shaking his head. "He didn't."

"So, what did you want to talk to me about?"

The sheriff took a deep breath and blew it out slowly. "This thing's been driving me nuts ever since you and Jack brought it up. I know we don't have much to go on, but I just can't seem to get it off my mind. I've got a really bad feeling and I don't want you to get hurt."

"I'm certainly with you there."

"I've looked in the boy's eyes, and there's—" Mayes sighed loudly. "I don't know, Hank. There's something missing for sure."

"Are you saying he's crazy?"

Mayes shrugged. "I'm not sure what I'm saying. He certainly doesn't look right to me."

Hank remembered telling Becky if Carl had already killed two people, he had to be crazy. Now it seemed the sheriff thought so, too.

"Thanks for stopping by," Hank said, extending his hand. "It's good to know you're looking out for me.

"Don't take any unnecessary chances, Hank. It's not worth it."

AFTER WORK ON TUESDAY, BECKY AND HANK SPENT A COUPLE OF minutes discussing their plans for the evening. She had told him she'd be a little late getting home but still wanted him to come over. He said he would, but having to be at work early the next morning, he couldn't stay long.

What Becky had on her mind was stopping by and having a talk with her grandmother. She'd make a scouting pass first to make sure her grandpa's truck wasn't there. If she saw it, she'd keep right on going. He'd left no doubt as to where he stood. She had absolutely nothing else to say to him.

With Lester's pickup nowhere in sight, Becky pulled up in front of her grandparents' house and killed the engine. Rosalie walked out onto the front porch, wiping her hands on a red and white striped dishtowel.

"Becky," she said, her face lighting up. "What a surprise."

"Hey, Grandma," Becky said with a wave. "Thought I'd stop by and visit for a minute. Brought Little Ernie with me, too."

"Ya'll come on in the house where it's cooler."

Rosalie sat down in a padded rocking chair and then reached out for the baby. "Let me hold the little fellow," she said.

Becky sank down deep into the well-worn couch cushions. "Where's Grandpa?"

"I don't know for sure. Just out and about. Told me he'd be home around six. We'll see."

Becky checked her watch. Five-thirty already.

"Grandma? Do you remember the time I came by and asked why the Rayburns and the Taylors didn't get along? Would have been about five years ago."

Rosalie glanced upward, her eyes scanning the ceiling. "Can't rightly say I do, sweetie."

Becky understood. After all, it had been a long time ago. And, her grandmother was getting on up in years. She opted for a different approach.

"Did Grandpa tell you I have a boyfriend now?"

Rosalie's eyes went wide. "Why, no, he didn't. Who's the lucky young man? If you don't mind me asking?"

"Hank Goodman."

"Don't think I know any Goodmans."

"You wouldn't know him," Becky said, shaking her head, "but you would know his grandparents." She hesitated then cleared her throat. "Jake and Ada Taylor."

CHAPTER TWENTY-NINE

*R*osalie stopped rocking and ran her crooked fingers slowly through Little Ernie's hair. "How is it your grandpa knows about this and I don't?" she said, her voice calm and even.

"Daddy told him. I've tried talking to both of them, but they just don't understand." Becky leaned forward and touched her grandmother's knee. "I love him, Grandma."

Her grandmother nodded, and a warm smile crossed her face. "Well, if you love him, sweetie, then nothing else matters. These hardheaded men will just have to get over it."

"It doesn't bother you he's a Taylor?"

Rosalie brushed her off with a wave of her hand. "No. Let me tell you a little story. Not only did my folks not want me to marry Lester, they didn't want me to have anything to do with him."

This bit of information piqued Becky's curiosity, and she scooted to the edge of the couch. "Oh?" she said. "How come?"

"Back in his younger days, your grandpa was a pretty colorful character."

"He was?"

"Yes, he was," Rosalie said with a nod. "I thought he was the best-looking thing I'd ever laid eyes on. But Mama and Daddy didn't cotton to him. Not one little bit."

"So, what did you do?"

"One night at supper, he was all they talked about. Lester this and Lester that. Finally, I stood up and kicked my chair out from under me. I was just eighteen at the time."

"Then what happened?"

"I told them in no uncertain terms me and Lester Rayburn were getting married, and if they had any hopes of ever seeing their grandchildren, they'd best come to grips with it."

"Grandma!" Becky fell back into the couch, cackling.

Rosalie giggled. "They finally came around, and eventually, he became like a son to them."

Becky composed herself and said, "You think something like that could happen for me and Hank?"

"I don't rightly know, sweetie, but like I said. If you love the boy then nothing else matters."

Becky nodded her understanding, thankful for her sweet grandmother's soothing words.

"I know one thing," Rosalie said as she stood. "I'm about to have a talk with your hardheaded old grandpa."

~

THE PREVIOUS NIGHT, HANK HAD FALLEN ASLEEP ON BECKY'S couch with his head in her lap. She had woken him up just as a mortally wounded Steve McMillan reached up and grabbed him by the arm. Becky told him he had cried out in his sleep, and she was worried about him. Embarrassed, he told her not to be concerned and he'd better be going since he had get up early the next day.

The following morning, Big Ben's loud, five a.m. clanging caused Hank to sit bolt up in bed. The night had been a short one, and by a quarter to six, Jack had already pulled up out front.

"Morning," Hank said, pulling the sun visor down and settling into the seat.

"Morning, partner. You eat yet?"

Hank shook his head. "I just had coffee," he said. "I'm not hungry at all."

Jack chuckled as he put the car in gear. "Well, I'm starving. Let's stop by the Twelve Point and grab a quick bite. A short stack and some thick, smoky bacon ought to hit the spot."

The café was packed with the early-morning breakfast crowd. Nothing unusual there. With all the stools at the bar occupied, the deputies settled for the only empty booth in the place.

Helga greeted them with a wink from behind the counter, and minutes later she was at their table with two menus, two white mugs, and a steaming pot of coffee. She handed each of them a menu. "How about some coffee, boys?"

Both nodded. Someone across the room called out to Helga and held up his cup while she filled the two mugs. She spilled a bit on the table and muttered a mild expletive.

"Haven't seen y'all since you stopped by the other night," she said, wiping up the spilled coffee. "Any luck getting in touch with Rita?"

Jack shook his head. "Her daddy said they haven't seen her in a couple of years. As far as he knows, she's still married to Carl Walker."

Helga set the coffee pot on the table. "Rita was a good girl," she said, nodding. "Hard worker, too."

"You talk about her in the past tense," Hank said. "You know something we don't?"

She shrugged. "Don't suppose I do," she said. "But it wouldn't surprise me a bit if you found her buried out behind the Walker boy's house. I saw how he treated her. And so did everybody else."

Helga sighed dramatically and then shook her head. Nothing else was said about Rita Hastings Walker, and she quickly jotted down Jack's order. Hank told her he'd be fine with just coffee.

Hank leaned back against the hard, plastic seat and locked his fingers together. "Anything going on this morning?"

"All quiet, far as I know. Heard they had a little excitement on the graveyard shift. I wanted to wait till we got here to tell you about it."

"A little excitement, huh?" Hank said, raising an eyebrow. "So, what happened?"

"Clete said around one o'clock this morning, him and Owen had to go out to Carl Walker's house."

Who would have guessed it?

"He said Carl was outside his house in his underwear, running around in the yard and firing off a shotgun." Jack took a quick sip of coffee, spilled a drop, and wiped his chin. "Anyway, several of his neighbors called in complaining about it."

"Did they take him in?"

Jack shook his head slowly. "Clete said about the time they showed up, Donald did, too. Fit to be tied. When his daddy told him to get back in the house and get some clothes on, Carl mouthed something Clete couldn't quite make out. Whatever it was, the old man slapped Carl so hard he dropped the shotgun."

Hank chuckled. "I'm guessing he went back inside after that."

"Clete said he did, but not before getting up in the old man's face and telling him he'd better not ever do that again."

"Those two have a pretty strange relationship," Hank said. "I mean, his dad's always getting him out of trouble, but then he smacks him around."

"Maybe he's tired of dealing with Carl. You know it has to get old."

"I'm sure you're right."

Helga brought out the bacon and pancakes. When she set the plate down in front of Jack, his eyes lit right up. "Sure I can't get you something, Hank?" she said.

"I'm good, Miss Helga. Thanks anyway."

~

WITH THE BRIGHT SUNLIGHT SHINING DIRECTLY IN HIS EYES AND HIS head pounding like a big bass drum, Carl woke to a brand new day. Or what was left of it. Most of the headache could be attributed to the massive amount of whiskey he'd consumed the night before. For some of it, at least, he could thank the old man.

Carl climbed out of bed slowly. When his feet hit the floor, sharp, stinging pain shot up both legs. He walked gingerly down the hall to the bathroom, went inside, and closed the door behind him. With his eyes still closed, Carl reached for the cold-water handle. He cupped his hands under the cool liquid, filled them up, and then splashed a handful on his face. Repeating the process two more times, he opened his eyes, and the reflection in the mirror made him furious. There, on the left side of his face, was the perfect red imprint of his father's large hand.

Carl slammed his fist down hard on the edge of the lavatory. His face looked hideous. Not to mention something like that taking days to clear up. What was he supposed to do in the meantime, go into hiding? He certainly couldn't let his friends see him like this.

The straw had finally broken the camel's back. Never again would Carl feel the sting of his father's calloused hand. No matter the circumstances. Donald Walker had slapped his son for the very last time.

~

BECKY HAD A DIFFICULT TIME FALLING ASLEEP AFTER HANK LEFT. Whatever made him cry out in his sleep like that must have been something pretty horrendous. Since he was obviously embarrassed by it, she wasn't about to ask any details. Most likely, it had something to do with his experiences in Vietnam. She couldn't help wondering if it might be something he struggled with on a regular basis. She sure hoped not.

While getting ready for work, Becky found herself daydreaming about what it would be like to be married to Hank. About his likes and dislikes. She couldn't help smiling when she remembered the indirect grilling she'd put him through at the Twelve Point. She'd gathered some good information, but she had other questions as well. And though they didn't amount to much, they were certainly things a girl would want to know. Would need to know. Like which side of the bed he preferred. How he liked his eggs. Did he even eat eggs? What were his favorite colors? Becky hoped to one day have all the answers. When Hank asked for her hand and she answered with an emphatic "yes."

The sound of gravel crunching in her driveway brought Becky back to reality. Peering out the nearest window, she felt all warm inside when she saw the long white car with the familiar five-pointed star pasted on the side. The guys sworn to protect and serve had just arrived.

From the porch, Becky waved emphatically. Jack waved back from inside the car while Hank climbed out. Glad to see he was okay, she hoped he hadn't felt obligated to stop by and explain what had happened the night before.

Becky hurried down the steps to meet him. "Long time, no see," she whispered in his ear as they locked in a tight embrace. "I love you so much."

"I love you, too."

"So, what brings you by this early? You going to arrest me or something?"

"If we did, I'd have to frisk you first." Hank drew her even closer. "Departmental procedure, you know."

Becky pulled away and winked. "Maybe you can frisk me

later," she said. "Right now, I'm running a little late. Mr. Craft's probably wondering if I got lost."

"We can only stay a minute anyway."

Becky crossed her arms. "What's going on?"

"A couple of deputies went over to Carl's house last night. Seems he likes to fire off shotguns while he's running around in his underwear. Looks like his old man had to put him in his place."

"I'm not surprised," she said, shaking her head. "I've come to expect such things from him."

"Me too, but I have a feeling this guy may be about to go off the deep end."

Becky nodded. Something along those lines wouldn't surprise her either.

"Anyway. The sheriff talked to him yesterday and said he sensed something wasn't right. If the guy's crazy—and I don't doubt he is—I don't want him anywhere near you or Little Ernie. There's no telling what he might do. We don't even know for sure all the things he's done already."

"I've always been a little afraid of him," she said with a shiver. "Now, I really am."

Hank sighed. "We don't have to be afraid. We just have to be careful."

"So, what should I do?"

"Keep all your doors locked, and whatever you do, don't let him in your house. If you see him drive up, call the office right away. Even if he comes in the store, call us. Especially if you're by yourself. I don't want you taking any unnecessary chances. It's just not worth it. He could hurt you, and he could hurt Little Ernie."

"I'll be careful," she said, her head bobbing up and down. "I promise."

～

CARL STEWED FOR NEARLY TWO HOURS BEFORE FINALLY DECIDING to go for a ride. Not wanting the glaring handprint tattooed on the side of his face to be seen, he'd keep his distance and stay inside the truck. It was a tough pill to swallow, no doubt about it, but for the time being, he'd simply have to manage.

He'd left home with one destination in mind. Hurt Road. He'd been down it only once in recent years, the night he'd slung gravel all over old lady Taylor's house. This day, however, he would be gathering intelligence.

Carl drove slowly down the dusty road, mentally taking notes as he went. Scouting the place in the daytime would give him a better look at the layout. After seeing it, he should be able to come up with a pretty decent plan. When it was all said and done, this could be the place where he ended up taking Goodman out. More likely than not, it would happen at Becky's house. Either way, he would have all his bases covered.

Driving past the little farmhouse, Carl couldn't help thinking what a disgusting eyesore it was. Goodman's grandmother barely had a penny to her name and lived in what could only be described as a run-down pauper's shack located out in the middle of nowhere. People like her had no business wasting good air. She served no useful purpose. An absolute burden on society if he'd ever seen one. If he ended up killing Goodman here, maybe he'd do the rest of the world a favor and put the old wretch out of her misery, too. For his generous contribution to the public good, they'd most likely pin a medal on him. Carl laughed until it hurt.

CHAPTER THIRTY

*T*he remainder of the week went by without any noticeable hiccups. Each day after Hank got off duty, he would work at Craft's from around two-thirty until closing. He mentioned Carl Walker's latest escapade to Homer and suggested he not leave Becky in the store by herself for too long at a time. Homer assured him he wouldn't.

While on patrol each day, Hank and Jack did their best to be on the lookout for Carl's all too familiar black pickup. The only times they'd seen it was when they passed by his house from time to time. For some strange reason, since the Wednesday night incident with the shotgun, he'd been keeping quite a low profile. Ordinarily, they'd see his truck parked pretty much anywhere. But not this week. Hank couldn't help wondering what the guy might be up to. Whatever it was, it couldn't be good.

Hank and Becky managed to chat a little at the store each day, but had more intimate, in-depth conversations when they got together in the evenings. He loved her deeply and wanted to spend as much time with her as he possibly could. She'd told him in no uncertain terms she felt the same way. Hank would have to leave for the academy in the not too distant future, but as soon as he had his training behind him, he would ask Becky to be his wife. Regardless of how her family felt.

Becky's family was the last thing they'd talked about before he left her house on Friday night. She told him after she closed the store at noon on Saturday that she planned to spend the rest of the day with her folks. Since he got off at two, she suggested he swing by for a few minutes and meet her father. Hank, needless to say, was not too keen on the idea.

"Has something happened I don't know about?" he said. "Your dad have a sudden change of heart?"

Becky shook her head slowly. "No, but I thought if you just sort of showed up, he'd have to be okay with it. I know what I said about him having to come to me, but I can't stand the way things are now. I feel like I have to do something."

The lively discussion continued. Finally, Hank gave in. He would stop by but just long enough to say hello and goodbye. Nothing more. Once Becky made it back to her house, she would call, and he'd meet her over there.

～

JACK STEERED THE BIG CRUISER ONTO THE MAIN HIGHWAY AND pressed the gas. "So, you're actually going over there?"

"I guess so," Hank said with a shrug. "I'm not too happy about it though."

"You're gonna have to you know. Sooner or later."

Hank took a deep breath and blew it out forcefully. "I know," he said, "but later sounds like the better option."

"Surely it won't be too bad."

"I don't know, man. This thing's been building up for years. Going to the Rayburn's will be walking into a lion's den."

"Then you'd better be all prayed up, Daniel."

Hank shot Jack the strangest look. "What do you mean?"

Jack's foot slid off the accelerator and he tapped the brake slightly. "You mean you've never heard the story of Daniel? How he was thrown in with the lions and the Lord sealed their mouths? It's straight from the Bible."

"Sounds pretty farfetched to me."

"You don't believe the Good Book?"

Hank shook his head. "I've never read any of it. So, no. I don't guess I do."

"Then maybe you should."

When it came to a Bible, Hank didn't even own one. Never had. The story sounded somewhat interesting, but after all, it was only a story. If he wanted to read more about it, he could always borrow one of the books from Ada or Becky.

Hank directed his gaze to the window next to his head. "Maybe I'll look into it sometime."

❧

AT ELEVEN FORTY-FIVE, HOMER TOLD BECKY SHE COULD GO. HE would stay behind and lock up the store. Before heading to her parents' house, she'd wanted to stop by her own place and change her and Little Ernie's clothes.

When Hank finally agreed to stop by and meet her father, Becky couldn't have been happier. But now, the more she thought about it, the more her jubilation started to turn to dread. If he dropped in completely unannounced, Bill's reaction might end up being worse instead of better. Her great idea could turn out to be anything but. She should have at least talked to her mother about it first. When it all blew up in her face, she'd have no one but herself to blame.

The thought of going back home had even crossed Becky's mind. To just call Hank and tell him not to come. But he was on duty. She could always get the dispatcher to relay a message, but was it important enough for her to bother him at work?

Becky decided just to let it ride and see what happened. She would deal with the consequences of her poor judgment later. After all, it wasn't like her father and Hank were going to get into a fight or anything. Worst case scenario, it would be a little uncomfortable for everyone and then, it would be over. She hoped so anyway.

∾

BECKY HAD BEEN AT HER PARENTS' HOUSE ONLY ABOUT AN HOUR, and already her nerves were just about shot. Finally, she decided she had no choice. She would tell her mother Hank was coming over.

With her father and Little Ernie busy playing on the living room floor, Becky and her mother retired to the kitchen table to talk about cooking and various recipes handed down through the family over the years. And during the conversation, Hank Goodman's name hadn't come up once.

Nervously rubbing at her nose, Becky suddenly blurted out, "I told you Hank's stopping by today, didn't I?"

Susan, who'd been holding an index card with her fabulous banana pudding recipe hand-scribbled on it, let the little card drop from her hand. "What do you mean he's stopping by? Not here, he's not."

"I asked him to, Mama. He needs to meet Daddy. Once he sees what a good person Hank is, maybe we can put this foolishness behind us."

Becky's mother hopped up and pushed her chair back. "You just don't get it, do you?"

"Get what?"

"I told you I'd talk to your daddy, and I did. Till I was blue in the face. He feels like he feels, and there's nothing you or me or anybody else can do to change it."

"Grandpa could."

Susan crossed her arms. "Grandpa could? Are you kidding

me? Sweetie, your little old grandpa feels the same way your daddy does. Even more so."

"But Grandma said she would talk to him."

"She did talk to him, Becky, and now they're not even speaking to each other." Her mother pointed emphatically at the telephone hanging on the kitchen wall. "Get on the phone right this minute. Call your friend and tell him do not—under any circumstances—come over here. If you don't, things are gonna get ugly, and there's nothing I can do to stop it."

∼

HANK AND JACK HAD JUST WRAPPED UP WHAT WOULD HOPEFULLY BE their last call of the day when the radio unexpectedly crackled. Hank picked up the mike and told the dispatcher to go ahead. "Deputy Goodman," she said. A short pause. "You need to call Becky Craft at her house. ASAP."

Hank hung up the microphone and asked Jack to get him to the nearest pay phone as quickly as possible. His first thought was Becky might be in trouble. Carl Walker might be there trying to beat her door down. Or maybe she'd seen him drive by. But what would she even be doing at home? She was supposed to be visiting with her parents.

Becky answered after only the first ring, and Hank couldn't conceal the strain in his voice. "Are you okay?"

A moment of silence followed. "I'm okay," she said softly, "but there's been a slight change of plans."

Hank knew exactly what happened but couldn't help wondering what had brought it about. "Tell me about it."

"Mama said you coming over's not a good idea. She talked to Daddy, and he refuses to budge. And we can forget Grandpa, too. Mama said Grandma tried talking to him, and now they're not even on speaking terms."

Hank could hear the disappointment in her voice, and to

some extent, he was disappointed, too. He felt relieved he wouldn't have to go to the Rayburns', but still understood at some point all this foolishness would have to come to an end. One way or the other. A surprise visit—even though he had to agree with Becky's mother—probably wasn't the best way to go about it.

"It'll be okay," Hank assured her. "We agreed to move forward regardless. Looks like it's going to have to be that way."

He could hear her frustrated sigh over the phone.

CARL CHECKED HIS FACE IN THE BATHROOM MIRROR ONE MORE time before walking out to his truck. Nearly three days had passed, and for the most part, the handprint on his face had all but disappeared. A bit of redness still remained, but nobody would ever figure out what had happened. If anyone asked, he'd simply tell them he had some sort of allergic reaction. But why sweat it? Nobody in his tiny circle of friends would have guts enough to even mention such a thing.

Being a Saturday night, Carl had plans to do things up right. He'd pick up a couple of the boys, head over to Tiny's Bar just across the parish line, drink a bunch of beers, and then hook up with some hot little cuties.

Carl couldn't wait to get out and about again. For the past few days he'd felt like a caged-up animal. Other than riding around and throwing up a hand to a couple of his buddies, he'd stayed pretty much out of sight. Now, he was back in business and ready for action.

With the next day looking to be the grandest of his life, Carl wanted his night on the town to be one filled with wine, women, and song. Well, actually, beer, women, and song, but alcohol nonetheless. By the time the next day faded with the sunset, Hank Goodman would be nothing but a memory. He'd give

Becky time to grieve—a week or two at best—then he'd be in like Flynn.

After a great deal of thought and careful planning, Carl decided he'd better take Goodman out from a distance. Give the guy credit. Up close and personal, he was quite a formidable opponent. One shot from a high-powered rifle, however, would take the fight right out of him. He'd never even know what hit him.

The old barn just down the road from Becky's house would be the perfect spot for setting up such a thing. Goodman would get off work around two. He'd run home and change then hop into his pickup and head straight for Becky's. When he got there, Carl would have the candles on the cake already lit. Surprise, surprise, surprise.

Carl would take up his position during the early morning hours while darkness still prevailed. Then he'd have to wait out the rest of the day until Goodman showed up. He'd never been good at waiting, but with something this important, he'd simply have to suck it up. He'd always heard anything worth having was worth waiting for. And wasn't sweet little Becky worth waiting for?

The moment Goodman climbed out of his truck and started for the house, Carl would take the shot. It would be long and tricky, but he'd killed deer from a lot farther out. Missing meant Goodman would still be alive. Missing meant he could be caught and sent to prison for the rest of his life. Missing would not be an option.

Instead of driving his pickup to the barn, Carl would ride Leo, the horse he'd used on elk hunting trips in Colorado the last couple of years. Leo was steady, and the sound of rifle fire wouldn't bother him a bit. Once he finished the deed, he'd slip, unseen, out the back and light out for home. There and back, he'd keep to the thick, dark woods. The entire time, his pickup would be sitting in his driveway for all the world to see. What an alibi.

Anybody in the parish could have had an axe to grind with the late deputy. It couldn't have been him; why, he'd been home all day.

Carl put his truck in reverse then looked up to see his father pulling in behind him, blocking his exit. He stayed put. If the old man had something to say, let him get out and do the walking.

At his son's truck door, Donald narrowed his eyes. "And just where do you think you're going?"

"To meet some friends," Carl said with a frown. "If it's any of your business."

"Don't stay out too late. I'm gonna need your help in the morning."

"But tomorrow's Sunday."

"I don't care what day it is. My sick horse needs tending to."

A sick horse? Please don't let it be Leo.

"Leo's down," Donald said, "and I don't know what's wrong with him. The vet says he can't come until tomorrow morning, and I'll need your help." Donald shook a crooked finger in his face. "And if you know what's good for you, you'll be there bright and early."

Well, wasn't that just lovely? All his planning and preparation had gone straight down the toilet. Oh, well. Leo being sick might postpone the inevitable for a couple of days, but in the end, it really wouldn't matter. *Anything worth having's worth waiting for.*

CHAPTER THIRTY-ONE

*C*arl opened his left eye slowly but only wide enough to see the hands on the alarm clock next to his bed. Straight up nine. Most days, by then he would have been up two, maybe three hours. But this was Sunday. The one day of the week he could do anything he wanted. Other days, his old man would most likely have some backbreaking chore lined up for him. But not on Sunday. Some fools set the day aside for the Lord. Carl Walker set it aside strictly for himself.

Soon, Carl's thoughts shifted to Becky Rayburn. Or Craft. Whatever name she happened to be going by these days. What would she be doing on such a gorgeous morning as this? No doubt wasting time with all the other Holy Rollers in her Sunday school class. Or some other useless activity down at the church. If she had any sense, she would be there with him. But what about the kid? The kid would always be a problem. Every time he saw the little snotty-nosed brat, he'd be reminded of its low-life daddy. And what about when he got older? No way. The kid had to go. Period. After Hank Goodman, of course.

When his bedroom door suddenly swung open and slammed

hard up against the wall, Carl sat straight up in his bed. "How did you get in here?" he shouted. "And what do you want?"

Donald Walker took two steps toward the bed then stopped abruptly. "You left the front door unlocked, junior. Now I'll ask the questions. How come you're not up yet?"

Carl shook his hungover head, feeling it weighed at least a ton. "Better check your calendar, Pops," he said with a smirk. "In case you haven't noticed, it's Sunday."

Donald cleared his throat loudly. "I know full well what day it is. I told you I needed your help this morning. What did you do? Get yourself so liquored up you don't even remember?"

Carl had indeed forgotten. Now it was coming back to him rather quickly. His father had stopped by the evening before and given him specific instructions to be at the main corral the next morning to help with a horse. "Bright and early," the old man had said. Matter of fact, it was the reason he had to cancel his plans for taking out Goodman.

"Oh yeah, the horse thing. Now I remember. No big deal, right? Just a horse."

His face turning a bright shade of red, his eyes bulging, Donald took another step toward the bed. "I'll make you think it's no big deal. Now get up."

Carl grunted long and loud, stretching his arms slowly upward. "I'm getting up," he said. "Just give me a minute."

"I mean now!" With one quick motion, the elder Walker jerked the sheet completely off the bed and slung it haphazardly across the room. In seconds, he had a firm grip on his son's ankle.

"I am sick—and tired—of your reckless—irre—sponsi —bility!"

When Donald dragged him from the bed, Carl's head bounced off the hard, metal mattress railing. "Let go of me!" Carl cried out.

Donald released his vise-like grip, and Carl scrambled to his feet. But before he could utter a single word, his father's large, open hand delivered a stinging blow squarely across his face. "What is wrong with you, boy? I've given you everything! And this is the thanks I get?"

"Don't you hit me again!" Carl shouted, jabbing an angry finger in his father's direction. "Don't you ever hit me again!"

"Or what?" Donald's eyes narrowed to a cold, steely stare. "You gonna kill me, like you did the Craft boy?"

The blood rushed from Carl's face, and a chill shot up his spine. How could the old man even know about that?

"You think I'm stupid, don't you? Well, the sheriff may be, but I'm not!"

"I never said..."

"And do you honestly believe I think Rita just up and ran off? You probably killed her, too!"

"You don't know what you're talking about," Carl said, spewing his bitter response. "I never killed anybody!"

"You've been nothing but an embarrassment to me your entire life! I wish you'd never been born!" The scathing words barely out of his mouth, Donald stepped forward and swung at his son a second time.

Carl easily sidestepped the attempt then reached for the blue and white plate he'd left on his bedside table the night before. The plate still holding his fork and greasy steak knife.

Grabbing the knife, Carl drove the five-inch blade deep into his father's chest, grunting loudly as he gave it a sharp, angry twist. Donald's eyes widened, and he fell to the floor, clutching hopelessly at the wooden handle now protruding from his chest.

"You old fool!" Carl screamed at his dying father while pinning him to the floor with his foot. "See what you made me do! I didn't want to do that!"

~

HANK DIDN'T LIKE HAVING TO WORK ON SUNDAY. NEVER HAD. THE

day held no particular significance for him; it just happened to be the day when most working people got to rest. But, it came with the territory, and he'd just have to learn to accept it. Such was the life of policemen. Of nurses and firefighters. Plenty of others, too, he supposed. Being back on the day shift, and the only unit on patrol, Hank hoped it would be a lazy day and would go by quickly without any hiccups.

With not a single thing happening in the first five and a half hours, Jack suggested they stop by the Tasty Cream and grab a quick bite. Just in case. Miss Wanda Jane's being the only eatery open on Sunday, she'd managed to corner the market on Sabbath Day burgers and fries.

After a rather short discussion, Jack agreed to get out and place the order. Wanda Jane seemed to have quite an affinity for his partner, but the few times Hank dealt with her, she'd eyed him with a certain amount of suspicion. Suspicion of what, he wasn't quite sure.

Jack had barely opened the car's door when the excited dispatcher's voice broke the airwaves. Airwaves that had been silent the entire morning. "Headquarters, SO Four."

Hank picked up the mike and answered. "SO Four. Go ahead."

"Four, we have a disturbance of some sort at Carl Walker's residence."

If they were going to get a call to disrupt their so-far quiet day, no real surprise it would involve their arch nemesis.

"Any particulars?" Hank asked, never taking his eyes off his partner.

"His mama called it in, but she was pretty shook up and not making a whole lot of sense. She did ask us to hurry though."

"Ten-four. We're en-route."

Hank hung up the microphone then blew out a long puff of air. "What do you think he's up to now?"

Jack shrugged as he slid the car into reverse. "I don't have a clue," he said in a calm, even voice. "But I guess we'd better get on over there and find out."

Hank responded with a simple nod. Whatever it was, they'd find out soon enough.

The entire trip, neither one of them spoke. Jack kept his eyes glued to the road while Hank stared out the side window at the barely recognizable shapes flying by. Funny, he thought, how speed distorted the simplest of things.

When the house came into view, Hank was a little surprised to see two vehicles parked out front, and neither one Carl's.

"The black Lincoln is his mother's," Jack said. "The pickup belongs to her husband."

Jack brought the big cruiser to a stop directly in front of the house and shoved it into park. The car hadn't stopped rocking when Mary Jane Walker appeared at Hank's door, feverishly jerking at the handle. "Help me! Please! You've got to help me! Please, hurry!"

With her refusing to back up or release the door handle, Hank had no choice but to open it and steadily push her back. In the time it took to squeeze through the narrow opening, Jack had already made his way around to the passenger side. He grabbed the frantic woman by the shoulders and spun her around. "What is it, Mrs. Walker? What's happened?"

Her eyes were red and swollen. Long, dark lines of mascara streaked down both cheeks like tiny, tire tracks. "It's Donald," she managed, pointing back toward the house. "He's in there."

Hank's eyes met Jack's for confirmation and then he bolted toward the front door. But when his foot hit the top step, he came to a sudden stop. *Slow down,* he told himself. *Take your time.* Carl could easily have parked his truck behind the house and be waiting just inside with a gun. Taking out an intruder—even one wearing a police uniform—would be mighty convenient. He could easily explain to a jury how the mistake had been made. If it ever even made it to one.

Drawing his revolver, Hank continued on with caution. He pushed the unlocked door open and took another small step forward. Just inside the entryway, he noted a large living room off to his right. To his left, the door to a bedroom was standing wide open. It crossed his mind to clear the living room first, but then he noticed the bed's linens lying in a crumpled heap on the floor. He took a deep breath and went inside.

Hank moved slowly and carefully, scanning left to right, then right to left, sweeping his gun from side to side. Once fully inside, he was struck by the absolute silence but couldn't ignore the strange, pungent odor nearly taking his breath.

A scuffle of some sort had indeed taken place. Not only had the covers been ripped from the bed, the nightstand on the opposite side had been slammed up against the wall. What Hank saw next, however, took him completely by surprise. On the floor and jutting out past the foot of the bed was the source of the terrible smell. A pair of work boots covered in manure. Work boots with someone still occupying them.

Hank moved quickly past the end of the bed and couldn't believe the gruesome sight before him. Donald Walker lay on his back, a distorted look of anguish on his face and a steak knife firmly embedded in his chest. Blood, dark and thick—some still wet, some beginning to dry—saturated the cream-colored shag carpet beneath him. Hank was no doctor by any stretch of the imagination, but during his time in war-torn Vietnam, he'd become quite familiar with death and dying. Best he could tell, the old man had been dead for at least two hours. Possibly longer.

Leaving everything just as he'd found it, Hank cleared the rest of the house. No sign of Carl whatsoever. From somewhere up front, Hank heard Jack call his name. His partner soon joined him in the kitchen.

"Where's Mrs. Walker?" Hank said.

Jack raked the back of his hand across his forehead, clearing the beads of sweat. "Out front with her sister, who lives just down the road. I guess the office called her. Sure am glad she's here."

"Yeah, me, too."

"I got her calmed down enough to tell me what was happening, then I called for an ambulance. Clyde and the sheriff are on their way now."

"You saw the body?"

Jack only nodded.

"Pretty rough, huh? You think Carl did it?"

"Happened at his house and he's nowhere to be found?" Jack sighed loudly. "Kind of speaks for itself, I guess."

Hank tried to imagine what would possess someone to kill their own father. Then he remembered the angry slaps to the face Carl had endured the night they arrested him. Something like that could have triggered it, but who could say for sure? Maybe the guy was just crazy after all.

"What do we do now?" Hank said.

"We'll have to wait for the others. Clyde'll be here shortly, and he'll want to take pictures before we move anything. You know the knife will have Carl's fingerprints all over it."

Hank's head bobbed up and down. No doubt about it.

Jack rubbed at his pulsing forehead. "The big question now is where's Carl? If he's gone off the deep end, there's no telling what he might do next."

What Jack said hit Hank harder than any blow to the midsection. If Carl had killed his own flesh and blood, he had nothing to lose. He knew exactly what the guy would do next. He'd go after Becky.

❧

"ARE THE KEYS IN THE CAR?" HANK SAID ANXIOUSLY.

"Yeah, but..." Jack grabbed his partner's forearm. "Hank wait."

"I've got to find Becky and make sure she's okay. You'd do the same thing and you know it."

Jack nodded. "Be careful. I'm sure he'd like to see you dead too."

Hank drove as fast as he thought he could without killing himself or anyone else. Dying in a car crash certainly wouldn't help the woman he loved. The church she attended usually ended its worship service somewhere around eleven-thirty, quarter to twelve. It being past noon already, she would have had plenty of time to make it home.

Even exceeding the speed limit, the trip seemed to take forever. Hank breathed a huge sigh of relief when Becky's house finally came into view and he saw her pickup sitting out front in its usual spot. He slid the big cruiser in behind her truck and shoved it into park. He'd leave the engine running just in case.

First, he'd make sure Becky and Little Ernie were okay. Then, he'd follow her over to Homer's and ask her to stay there until she heard from him again. Once he satisfied himself they would be all right, he'd head back over to Carl's and see how everything over there was progressing.

Hank jumped out and raced up the steps to the front door. He knocked twice and then hesitated. No response. He knocked again with more urgency. Still nothing. He held his breath and then twisted the doorknob, which should have been locked. It wasn't.

Pushing the door inward, Hank called out Becky's name. Again, no response. The house was unusually quiet. Most days, the television or radio would be going in the background. Becky thought it would help Little Ernie get used to noise. Hank called out her name again and then waited just a beat. Not a peep. He ran down the hall still calling out her name but then suddenly, he stopped. Becky wasn't home and all the yelling and wishing and hoping in the world wasn't going to make it so.

Hank's anxious heart continued to beat faster, but he needed to calm himself. He had to think. Her truck was home, and she wasn't. Might not mean anything. Could mean everything. Maybe Homer had swung by after church and picked the two of them up for lunch. If so, they could still be at his house.

Pulling into Homer Craft's driveway, Hank quickly bailed out of the car. Homer walked out onto the porch to greet him. "Hey there, Hank. Come on in."

Hank stayed close to the car and called back, "I just stopped by to see if Becky and Little Ernie are here."

Homer walked to the edge of the porch shaking his head. "No, they're not. Saw them at church earlier though." He pointed toward Becky's house. "Looks like her truck's home now if you want to check there."

"Just came from there," Hank said. "No one's home."

Descending the steps, Homer said, "Surely nothing's wrong."

Hank was hesitant to tell Mr. Craft what had happened. But if Becky and his grandson were in danger, the man certainly had a right to know. He took a deep breath and blew it out quickly. "We just found Donald Walker dead. Looks like Carl killed him."

Homer's face suddenly lost all its color. "Somebody flew by here a little while ago. Don't know if it was a car or a truck. I was inside at the time and didn't think too much about it."

"How long ago?" Hank said, his eyes narrowing.

"Not too long, I guess. Thirty minutes, maybe."

Hank bit down hard on his bottom lip. Thirty minutes. A lot of damage could be done in thirty minutes. Irreparable damage.

CHAPTER THIRTY-TWO

"You had this coming, and you know it," Carl said through gritted teeth. He cinched the rough piece of rope on Becky's wrists even tighter. "All I ever wanted was for us to be together."

After forcing Becky into a straight-backed wooden chair and removing the bandanna covering her eyes, Carl tied her wrists together then repeated the procedure with her ankles. Then he wound the remainder of the rope around her upper body, firmly securing her to the chair. Unless she could somehow free herself, any attempt at escape meant she'd have to take the chair with her.

No one had to tell Becky she was in a pretty tough spot. She'd been in her bedroom putting Little Ernie down for his nap when Carl charged into her house, grabbed her, and put a knife to her throat. She had forgotten to lock the door. He forced her into his pickup, threatening to go back inside and use the knife on her son if she resisted.

At first, Carl told her they were leaving Little Ernie behind. After much begging and pleading from a mother frightened out of her mind, he finally agreed to bring the child along. With her truck still parked in front of her house, everyone would assume they were at home. If her son had been left, no one would have ever known he was there by himself. Becky shuddered to think what would have happened. But when it was all said and done, bringing him along might not have been such a good idea.

"Carl, you're hurting me," Becky said, tears stinging her eyes.

"I'm hurting you?" Carl spat on the cabin floor. "What do you think you've been doing to me all this time? Now stop your whining before I stuff a rag in your mouth."

Though she'd been blindfolded the entire trip, Becky knew exactly where Carl had taken her. The Walkers owned a hunting camp in a secluded area just a few miles north of Crosscut. He'd brought her here when they were still in high school, just to "show her around." When she'd adamantly resisted his fondling, he'd cursed like a sailor and promptly took her home. But that was then.

Used as intended, the Walkers' cabin was actually pretty nice. It featured a large living room, a fully functioning kitchen, an ample bathroom with a tub and shower, and one enormous bedroom. With four sets of bunk beds, it could comfortably sleep up to eight people. Carl told her Little Ernie had fallen asleep just before they got there and that he'd laid him on one of the bottom bunks.

Carl hurried toward the cabin door.

"Where are you going?" Becky said through a whimper.

He stopped mid-stride. "Gotta get things ready for when your boyfriend gets here."

"Please don't hurt him."

Carl strode back over to Becky and knelt down in front of her. He roughly grabbed her cheek between his thumb and forefinger. "How about pretty please with sugar on it? Huh? That too much for you?"

Becky dropped her head when he released his grip.

Back at the door, Carl said, "The quicker you die, the less it hurts. So I've heard, anyway. Tell you what. Since the guy's a friend of yours, I'll try to make it quick."

Carl stormed out, slamming the door so hard behind him that the entire building shook. When Little Ernie cried out, Becky pulled against the ropes with all her might.

"Mama's in here, baby. Mama's in here."

~

HANK COULD FEEL HIS BLOOD PRESSURE CLIMBING TO AN ALL-TIME high. In Vietnam, he'd experienced more than his fair share of tense moments. None more so than the day Steve McMillan had died in his arms. But if anything happened to Becky and Little Ernie, he simply didn't know if he could take it.

Homer told him the Walkers owned a hunting camp just a few miles north of town and it would be the logical first place to look. Off the main highway, it sat at the end of a narrow, dead-end road all the locals called Buckhorn Bend. He'd also cautioned Hank to drive carefully and watch out for the road's numerous twists and hairpin turns.

Just to be on the safe side, Hank had asked Mr. Craft to keep an eye on Becky's house. There was always a chance he could be wrong. A friend could have picked them up for a Sunday after-noon drive. Oh, for that to be the case.

Hank knew he should follow proper departmental protocol. Radio the sheriff and fill him in on the situation. But what if Mayes ordered him to wait for backup? By then, whatever Carl planned on doing, he would have already done. For Hank, there would be no waiting or turning back. He'd feel better with a little help, but under the circumstances, he had no choice. He would have to go it alone.

~

By the time Carl made it back inside, Little Ernie had quieted. Becky had kept talking to her son, her soothing, familiar voice apparently coaxing him back to sleep. And for that, she couldn't be more thankful. A crying child might just push Carl to find a way—some drastic way—to make it stop. And as much as she'd been wishing Ernie could already walk, now she was grateful he had yet to take his first steps.

Carl walked over to the table, grabbed a straight-backed chair —just like the one he'd put Becky in—and dragged it over in front of her. As he sat down, a certain darkness settled on his face. In his right hand, he held a large butcher knife with a worn wooden handle. In his left, a dark gray rectangular whetstone.

"It doesn't have to be like this," Becky said.

"I'm afraid it does." Carl slid the knife's blade slowly across the smooth surface of the sharpening tool. "It's too late for anything else."

"It's never too late."

Carl jumped up from his chair, turning it over in the process. "I killed my old man this morning," he said, his unshaven face only inches from Becky's. "What do you think they're gonna do? Pin a medal on me?"

Becky suddenly felt light headed, and her face began to burn. If he was telling the truth, she and Little Ernie didn't stand a chance. He'd have nothing to lose by killing them as well.

"That come as a shock to you?" Carl righted his chair and sat back down. "I was sick and tired of the way he treated me. Bossing me around. Slapping me. Well, he won't do it anymore. I made sure of that."

Working her hands back and forth, Becky tried her best to loosen the rope. To no avail. But if Carl went outside again, she would do everything she could to get to her son. She'd turn the chair over. She'd scoot. She'd roll. Whatever she had to do.

The odds of her and the chair making through the narrow doorway were minimal at best. But if she could find a way—close the door behind her and lock it—she'd buy herself and her son at least a little more time. Carl was right about one thing. Hank would come looking for them. If he even knew they were missing.

~

BRINGING CARL IN FOR THE MURDER OF HIS FATHER WAS NOT A priority for Hank. Finding the woman he loved more than life itself and her son. But if he had things right, finding Carl meant finding them as well. He just hoped he wouldn't be too late.

Hank would have to be careful driving up to the camp. Carl could be hiding around any corner just waiting to ambush him. No stranger to such things, he certainly didn't want to relive any of his wartime experiences. Steve McMillan's anguished face flashed before his eyes.

From everything Homer had told him, Hank knew he must be getting close. He brought the big cruiser to an abrupt stop on the side of the narrow road and climbed out. He would travel the rest of the way on foot. To avoid giving himself away, he'd have to move off the road and stay strictly with the tree line.

With his pistol already drawn, Hank continued his steady advance. Just around the next curve, the cabin came into view. And as expected, Carl's black pickup was parked right out front. Hank stopped and took a long, deep breath.

Hank moved stealthily from tree to tree, using his natural surroundings for cover. He knew full well Carl could be crouched behind a window watching his every move through a rifle scope. Hank's objective, then, would be to keep his head out of the crosshairs.

When he believed he was close enough, Hank called out from behind a large oak. "Carl Walker! Come on out! We need to talk!"

Nearly a minute passed with no response. He tried again. "Carl! We need to talk! I know you've got Becky!"

Without warning, the front door suddenly swung inward. Carl didn't show himself but yelled back to Hank from the inside. "What could we possibly have to talk about, Goodman?"

"You can still get out of this thing alive!" Hank swallowed hard. "Just let Becky and Ernie go!"

There was an extended pause, and then Carl shouted back, "I have a better idea! Let's go ahead and get this little party started!"

Carl dragged Becky's chair into the open doorway, a bright red shop rag stuffed in her mouth. Waving a large, shiny butcher knife, making certain Hank could see it, he said, "How do you like these apples, lover boy?"

"You don't want to hurt her!" Hank shouted. "Let her go!"

"You're right! I don't want to hurt her! But if I can't have her, neither can you! Oh, and just so you know, I've already taken care of the stupid brat! Looks like you won't get to be his daddy after all!"

Hank's heart sank into his stomach. As gut wrenching as the revelation was, he still had to do something to save Becky. He scanned the area around him. Nothing but trees and thick, impassable underbrush. If he could create some sort of distraction, maybe he could rush the cabin. But the cabin had a porch, and the porch had steps. Carl could easily cut Becky's throat before Hank ever made it to her. Whatever he was going to do, he had to do it now. Hank took a long, deep breath and then—for the first time in his life—he prayed to God for strength.

Stepping out from behind the tree, Hank aimed his pistol directly at Carl's forehead. He'd earned his marksmanship badges with a rifle and had practiced with the revolver only twice. If he took the shot, he might miss and hit Becky. If he didn't, she would soon be dead anyway.

"Better drop the gun, Goodman!" Carl demanded. "Or you're

about to see more blood than you've ever seen! Oh, wait! You're one of our decorated baby killers!"

As he exhaled the breath, still praying with everything he had, Hank began to slowly squeeze the trigger.

∾

CARL DROPPED THE KNIFE—THE IMPACT DRIVING HIM BACK INSIDE the cabin and completely out of sight. The round had hit its mark.

Hank rushed to Becky, making sure she wasn't hurt. Satisfied the blood on her face belonged to Carl, he worked frantically to remove the rag from her mouth.

"Are you okay?"

"Yes."

"Where's Little Ernie?"

"In the bedroom," she said, coughing. "Hurry!"

Hank stepped over Carl's lifeless body on his way to the bedroom. And there, sitting up on one of the bottom bunks with a confused look on his face and his arms outstretched, was the little blond-haired boy he loved as his own. And not a scratch on him.

"He's okay!" Hank called out, tears flowing down both his cheeks. "Becky, he's okay!"

Hank scooped the child up and held him tightly. He'd never felt such an overwhelming sense of relief. Once they put all this behind them—and if Becky would have him—Ernie would be his son after all.

∾

IN LESS THAN AN HOUR'S TIME, THE SECLUDED SPOT IN THE WOODS was crawling with people. Sheriff Mayes, Jack, Clyde, and Chief

Hall all were there, as well as the coroner, an ambulance, Bill and Susan Rayburn, and a much-relieved Homer Craft.

Still visibly shaking, Becky kissed Hank on the cheek and told him she and Little Ernie were going home with her parents. He told her he understood and would do his best to catch up with her later.

Hank went over the sequence of events with the sheriff. Becky would corroborate his story. Under the law, Mayes said what Hank had done was entirely justifiable. A complete investigation would still have to be conducted. The information would be passed on to the district attorney, but even Carl's uncle wouldn't be able to find fault.

Homer Craft walked over and put his arm around Hank. "You did what you had to, son. Thank you for saving Becky and my little grandson." A tear rolled from his eye. "From the bottom of my heart."

Hank took a deep breath and blew it out slowly. He had something he needed to tell Homer. Something he probably should have told him much sooner. "I never told you this, Mr. Craft, but some of us believe Carl killed Ernie."

"Think nothing of it, son. I could have told you the exact, same thing."

"You mean you suspected it, too?"

"I did, but I knew I could never prove it. So I just kept my mouth shut. Guess we'll never know now."

"I know one thing," Hank said confidently. "If it was Carl, he'll never hurt anyone else."

Homer nodded and clamped down on Hank's shoulder. "Let's all go home."

*H*elga Streeter's off the cuff comment ended up being right on the money. The day after Carl died, Rita Hastings's body was found buried in a shallow grave not fifty yards behind Carl's house in a little stand of pine trees. An autopsy would later reveal the cause of death to be blunt force trauma to the head. No real surprise there. She'd no doubt suffered mightily at the hands of the madman the entire three years she spent with him. Why hadn't he just let her go back to her family? No one would ever know for sure. Some speculated if she knew he'd killed Ernie, getting rid of Rita permanently had been the only foolproof way of keeping her quiet. But knowing Carl Walker, it could have been just downright meanness.

Mary Jane opted to hold the funerals of her husband and son separately but on consecutive days. Many wondered how she'd been able to cope with such a thing. As bad as it must have been to lose both a husband and a son, knowing Donald lost his life at the hands of his own flesh and blood surely only added to her pain. A pain she would no doubt take to her own grave.

Donald's funeral was first. Well attended, it featured friends and associates sharing many kind and thoughtful words about the life of the elder Walker. Though he'd gone out of his way to protect his troublemaking son, as a dedicated philanthropist and area businessman, he was still held in high regard by most in the community.

Carl's service was the exact opposite. Held the next day, it drew a few relatives, mostly aunts and uncles, and only a handful of curious onlookers. His "so-called friends," as his father once called them, in life had only associated with him out of fear and intimidation. In death, they simply chose to stay home.

~

HANK GRADUATED THE POLICE ACADEMY WITH HONORS AND IN THE top five of his class. Still, it had been the longest, most difficult six weeks of his life. Leaving Crosscut every Sunday evening had been the hardest part. Especially so soon after everything had happened. Knowing Carl Walker couldn't hurt the ones he loved had made things a whole lot easier. During his time in Baton Rouge, Hank had probably set a new world record for hours spent on a pay telephone. While he was away, not a night went by he didn't talk to his sweetheart at least once.

Becky and Little Ernie both attended Hank's graduation ceremony, as did Ada, Harvey, and the Crafts. He was more than a little surprised to see Bill, Susan, Lester, and Rosalie Rayburn all enter the auditorium together.

At the close of the ceremony, Bill and Lester walked over to Hank with rather somber looks on their faces. They all shook hands then Bill took a deep breath and blew it back out slowly. "I know what you did to save Becky and Little Ernie. And there's no way I can ever repay you. What I can do is say thank you, Hank. Thank you from the bottom of my heart. Mr. Taylor would have been proud."

Hank was about to respond when Lester spoke up. "Son, now that your grandpa's gone, I can't tell him how sorry I am. But I can tell you. I've carried bitterness and resentment around with me pretty much all my life. And it's time to let it go. We all make mistakes, and that's all Jake did." Lester pointed to his son. "Me and Bill here have talked it over and, well, if it's okay with you, we'd like to put all the nonsense behind us."

Before Lester could wipe it away, Hank spotted the single tear sliding down the old man's face. His apology was indeed sincere. Hank couldn't help believing Jacob would have been touched by it as well.

"As far as I'm concerned, Mr. Rayburn, it's all water under the bridge. I love Becky and Little Ernie. And to me, nothing else matters."

Bill and Lester looked at each other and nodded. No further words were necessary.

～

FOUR MONTHS LATER, HANK AND BECKY WERE UNITED IN HOLY matrimony. Though Becky had been a member of the Crosscut Baptist Church pretty much all her life, she and Hank opted to hold the ceremony at Ada's tiny Shiloh Baptist Church. What surprised everyone in attendance most of all was it being a completely unannounced double wedding.

Ada and Harvey were just as excited as two young lovers making their way to the altar for the first time. After all those years, they would finally be man and wife. Hank knew his grandfather would have wanted Ada to be happy—to have someone to look after her and keep her company for the remainder of her life. With him moving out, Hank felt good knowing his grandmother would have a constant companion. And he couldn't have asked for anyone better than Harvey. After all, the old fellow was already family.

Becky and Ada both wore long white dresses while the men sported dark suits with starched white shirts. Harvey confided to

Hank he hadn't worn a coat and tie in forty years and couldn't wait to get out of that one.

"I won't wear another one until they put me in the ground," Harvey said to Hank.

"I sure wish Mama could have been here to see all this," Ada told Becky.

The little country church had been filled to overflowing. And while many a tear was shed when Hank and Becky said, "I do," there wasn't a dry eye in the house when Ada and Harvey exchanged their vows. At the reception afterwards, Bill Rayburn stood up to tell everyone how happy and proud he was to officially welcome Hank Goodman into his family. Those in attendance responded by raising their punch cups high in the air and cheering loudly.

~

HANK SOON BECAME A REGULAR AT CROSSCUT BAPTIST CHURCH. At the end of one particularly moving sermon, he managed to let go of the pew in front of him and make the long walk down the aisle. To the delight of everyone in attendance, he'd accepted Jesus Christ as his personal savior. Hank had finally found the piece of the puzzle he'd been missing all his life. The following Sunday morning, he was baptized into the faith.

The night of his baptism, Hank's dreaded dream returned. There he was, back in the jungles of Vietnam, reliving the death of Steve McMillan. This time, however, the dream took quite an unexpected turn. Instead of looking down into Steve's tortured face, Hank found himself staring at his own. But instead of pain or fear, he saw peace and contentment. The dream quickly faded, and he slept soundly throughout the remainder of the night. Not once did he cry out or wake up in a cold sweat wondering what more he could have done to save his best friend.

Hank greeted the morning with a stretch, followed by a

knowing smile. To him, the meaning couldn't have been any clearer. He had died to his old ways, and from now on, he'd be a brand new man. He and Steve had been closer than brothers, but the time had come to let go of the guilt. And his friend. Steve had been a Christian, and now that he was too, Hank knew he would see his buddy again. Would the dream ever return in its earlier form? He hoped not. But if it did, he'd be much better equipped to deal with it.

~

HANK, BECKY, ADA, AND HARVEY WERE ALL AT THE CEMETERY THE day the stonemason delivered Jake's tombstone. After much thought, Hank decided not to put up "the grandest monument of them all" as he had earlier planned. An honest, down-to-earth, working man, his grandfather would have wanted only a simple, proper marker.

What Hank settled on, with the help of his grandmother of course, was a double stone with Jake's name on the left and hers on the right. Harvey agreed it would be only fitting the two of them rest next to each other for all of eternity. When his time came, he wanted to be buried beside Evelyn. With the stone in place, Hank said a brief but heartfelt prayer.

Back at Ada's, the four of them sat on the porch, eating her delicious "big as your head" tea cakes, drinking coffee, and swapping humorous stories. When he heard a faint popping sound somewhere off in the distance, Hank sat up a little straighter, craning his neck just a bit. As each minute passed, the sound grew louder and louder.

Finally, Becky said, "What in the world is that?"

Hank swallowed hard, trying his best to maintain his composure. "It's Grandpa's old John Deere," he managed. "Coming back home where it belongs."

ABOUT THE AUTHOR

 Growing up in the colorful, multicultural, state of Louisiana, **Bruce A. Stewart** was reared with an appreciation for diversity and a love for small town life. After high school and a couple of years of college, he began his twenty-eight year career as a Louisiana State Police trooper, retiring as a sergeant in 2009. During that time, he witnessed the humorous, the sad, the tragic, and even the unimaginable. These life experiences give him tremendous credibility when writing about the many aspects of the human condition. Having been deployed to New Orleans in the aftermath of Hurricane Katrina and Lake Charles after Hurricane Rita, he has seen firsthand the determination and courage of ordinary people thrust into extraordinary circumstances. Bruce writes Southern Fiction with a touch of humor, romance, suspense, and inspiration.

f 𝕐

www.cleanreads.com